THE LAST KISS

Sally Malcolm

So he will never come but in delight,
And, as it was in life, his name shall be
Wonder awaking in a summer dawn,
And youth, that dying, touched my lips to song.

The Last Meeting — Siegfried Sassoon, 1918

CHAPTER ONE

12th October 1917, Flanders, Belgium

Ash's fingers had grown stiff and cold around the pen. He'd lost track of how long he'd been sitting there, staring at the blank sheet of paper before him, watching it waver in the flinching candlelight. Above him, the guns thundered on, spitting their full-throated hatred at the enemy.

There were, perhaps, two hours until dawn.

Dislodged by the bombardment, dirt sifted down onto his makeshift desk — something West had cobbled together to allow him to take a stab at writing the letter before the next push. If only the words would come.

The gas curtain across the doorway stirred and Ash looked up as footsteps clumped down the wooden stairs. They weren't very deep here; firing line dugouts never were. He was lucky to have this modicum of privacy and didn't object to the intrusion. Welcomed it, in fact, because he recognised that steady tread and the broad figure that accompanied it: Private West, his batman. And friend, though propriety kept them from admitting as much.

"Thought you'd be sleeping, Captain."

Ash smiled. "You thought no such thing."

"Hoped then." West had to stoop beneath the corrugated iron

ceiling; he was a fine figure of a man, taller and broader than Ash. He set a mug of tea on the desk. "Made you a cuppa, sir."

"I won't ask by what miracle you managed that." Laying down his pen, Ash wrapped his cold fingers around the enamel mug and inhaled the steam. Not much like the tea his mother would serve at Highcliffe House, but a bloody luxury in the firing line. He lifted it to his lips and took a sip. "I hope you made one for yourself, West."

An equivocal wave of one hand — no, then. "Did you get any sleep, sir?"

"With this racket going on?"

"You need your rest. Busy morning ahead."

Yes, busy was one word for it. Ash's guts went watery in anticipation of what was to come. "I have to write this blasted letter to Tilney's mother first. She deserves —" He put down his mug with a thump, sloshing the tea, embarrassed that his hand had started shaking. Again.

Thing was, he couldn't stop thinking about Jimmy Tilney.

The lad had bought it a week ago, during a night time reconnaissance patrol. Under fire, Tilney had fallen into a flooded shell hole and, despite their frantic efforts to reach him, he'd drowned in the mud. Over the years, Ash had grown numb to death, but that desperate drowning haunted him day and night. Tilney had been barely more than a boy and one of Ash's men. He should have been able to save him.

West squeezed his shoulder, making Ash jump. He hadn't noticed West move around behind the desk, and that wasn't the first time he'd lost track of things in the last few days. Thoughts of Tilney kept intruding and distracting him. "We did what we could for him, sir," West said. "Nothing more we could have done. Not with those sodding machine guns at work."

The weight of his hand was a warm comfort and Ash leaned into his touch. He needed to write this bloody letter and put an end to the matter. "I don't know where to start, is the thing. I've got no comfort to offer his poor mother."

"Then tell her the truth."

"The truth?" Startled, he looked up into West's grim face. His eyes, a warm hazel in daylight, gleamed darkly in the guttering candlelight and his sunny blond curls were dulled to tarnished gold. But for all that, he was a beautiful man. Beautiful to Ash, at any rate.

"Tell her Jimmy was a fine lad. Tell her he made his friends laugh and the local girls swoon, and that we enjoyed listening to him playing that sodding penny whistle. Tell her he served his king and country with honour and that he died bravely."

"He died crying for his mother."

West squeezed his shoulder again. "Spare her that, sir. But the rest is true — or, true enough."

"True *enough*. Perhaps, if the people at home knew the real truth, they'd find a way to end this...this bloody farrago of a war."

"She's his mother, sir."

"I know. But it feels like lying. I don't want to lie anymore, West. Bad enough that I'm the one who...who..." Suddenly, he could taste the metallic tang of the whistle in his mouth. Hear its sharp screech in his ears.

Over we go boys. Good luck!

"Drink your tea, sir. And write your letter — you won't rest till it's done. Then maybe we could read for a spell, until... Until it's time. We left Watson at a dramatic moment yesterday."

Despite everything, Ash found a smile. West had the astonishing ability to cheer him even in the bleakest of circumstances. "Yes. Let's do that."

He picked up his pen and began to write, plucking out as much truth as he could find and offering what small comfort was possible. God knew it wasn't much. After all this time, it should have become easier and yet each letter was harder than the last. They all felt like lies.

When the job was done, he took his tea over to the narrow pallet on which he'd failed to find any rest. West joined him there and they sat shoulder-to-shoulder, backs against the sandbags, with the candle set on an overturned crate at West's side. From his breast pocket, West pulled out Ash's copy of *The Hound of the Baskervilles* and opened it to the right page. Ash sipped his tea and then offered the mug to West. "Go on," he said when West declined, "I know you've had none yourself. We'll share it. I'll read first, then we'll swap."

And so he began. "Chapter Twelve: Death on the Moor. '*For a moment or two I sat breathless, hardly able to believe my ears. Then my senses and my voice came back to me, while a crushing weight of responsibility seemed in an instant to be lifted from my soul. That cold, incisive, ironical voice could belong to but one man in all the world... 'Holmes!' I cried — 'Holmes!'*'"

He read on until West nudged the mug against his hand and they swapped again, Harry reading while Ash finished the tea. Overhead the guns continued to smash the German lines — such was the plan, at least — and despite the noise, with West's warm body next to him, Ash's exhaustion finally began to overwhelm him. Setting the empty mug aside, he let his head sink onto West's shoulder and closed his eyes. He didn't move when he felt West's cheek come to rest against the top of his head, but smiled as he listened to him read until the words blurred and slurred...

"Captain Dalton." He was woken by West's hand on his arm, a gentle shake. "Sorry, sir, but it's time."

West sat next to him still, but the book was put away and Ash could see first light creeping around the edges of the gas curtain. His stomach clenched, his heart racing sharply. Morning had arrived, cold and cruel.

West's hand tightened on his arm. "We'll have to finish that chapter later, sir."

Later. It felt as longed for and unreachable as home.

"I'm afraid I dropped off. We might have to repeat some of it." Their gazes tangled and locked, too raw for bravado now. Ash's faux bonhomie fell away. "Good luck today, West."

West's throat moved as he swallowed. "You too, Captain."

Above them, the barrage continued unrelenting, their guns firing five miles west, towards the village they were attempting to take. Had been attempting to take since July. What the hell could be left of it now?

"It's six-thirty, sir."

Less than an hour to go. It was past time he was outside with the men. Ash rose and West helped him on with his trench coat, buttoning it like a London valet before handing him his tin hat. Another pause followed. Then Ash said, "I don't want to…to let the men down today."

"You, Captain? Not a chance." West squeezed his shoulder. "We'll get through it, don't you worry. We'll get through it together."

How to explain that it wasn't for himself that he worried, that there was something he feared more than his own death? Impossible, of course. The best he could do was grip West's forearm. "Together."

There was no more to be said. Ash led the way out into the miserable morning where his men watched him from drawn, frightened faces. None of them had slept, counting down the hours until the attack, and he felt guiltily grateful for his short reprieve with West.

"Taff," he greeted the dark-eyed Welshman sitting smoking on the fire step.

Taff's fingers shook as he lifted the gasper to his lips. "Captain Dalton." His guarded gaze moved to the dugout and back, aware as all the men were — as Ash was — of the unearned privileges his rank enjoyed. "Get some kip?"

"Hardly, with this racket." Ash forced levity into his voice. "I dare say there'll be post waiting when we get back to the relief trench. It feels like an age since you've had a letter. All of two days, I should think."

Taff gave a reluctant smile. "My missus does like to write, sir."

"And we all want to know what happened about…what was his name? Your neighbour's story about the vicar and the missing pig."

A flash of teeth. "Mrs. Evans. Terrible gossip, she is, sir. I don't believe half of what she says."

And so it went on, the excruciating duty of finding a word here and there for each of the men while they endured these last dreadful minutes of waiting, a grotesque *noblesse oblige* that Ash probably resented as much as his sullen, frightened men. His rank gave him no special insight when staring death in the eye and nobody knew that better than himself. But Little Bill looked rough, scared almost out of his wits, and Ash spared him a firm hand on the shoulder as he passed. "You'll have a story to tell your sweetheart when you're home, eh?" The boy nodded, eyes wide and glassy. Ash resisted the urge to hug him. Instead he had the rum passed around and let Little Bill drink liberally.

He checked his watch. Six forty-five. Half an hour to go.

His head felt woolly, blood pounding in his ears. Fear did that, he'd learned. Scattered your wits, broke your nerve. He looked up into the sky, fading remorselessly to grey, and made out the tangle of wire above them. A scrap of uniform fluttered there, dank in the dank morning. Some poor sod, dead. Him, maybe, in a matter of minutes.

Terror closed his throat, accelerated his racing heartbeat. He felt clammy and sick. God, he hoped he didn't lose his nerve, not in front of the men. Men? Boys, some of them. Beautiful and full of life when they were laughing together behind the lines, kicking about a football or telling off-colour jokes. Grey-faced now, they looked even younger than their too-few years.

An odd thought struck him: at least Tilney had been spared this dreadful bloody wait. His drowning had been sudden, unanticipated. The thought almost made him laugh, but he swallowed the terrifying bubble of hysteria. Dangerous, that. Rum lingered in the back of his throat and his watery guts squirmed. If he survived this damned war, he'd never touch the stuff again.

Carefully, he set one foot on the ladder that would take him over. How far would he make it before he was cut down? Ten yards, a hundred? Would it be a shell or machine gun fire that did for him? If he made it to the German lines, maybe a bayonet to the belly. Or would he get stuck on the wire? His fingers, of their own accord, drummed out a tune on the ladder as if playing a mute piano.

If you want to find the private, I know where he is,
I know where he is, I know where he is.
If you want to find the private, I know where he is,
He's hanging on the old barbed wire…

He felt for his whistle, secure on its leather lanyard. His mouth was dry. From along the line came a rumpus, someone shouting and quickly stifled. It took men like that sometimes, the long wait. It broke their nerve. And who could blame them? This was tortuous.

He checked his watch. Six fifty-nine.

Time was crawling, he'd never known it to move so slowly. And yet too fast. Their lives were measured in moments now. He cleared his throat. "Fifteen-minutes," he told the men.

Behind him, feet shuffled as the men moved about, making whatever peace they could, bracing themselves to meet their fate. It would be easier to be one of them. The weight of giving the order, of leading men to their ends, felt heavy as iron.

A shoulder brushed his, solid and steady. He glanced sideways and found West watching him. In the growing daylight, he could see the warm hazel of his eyes and the curl of his golden hair beneath his tin hat. West's friendship was everything to him here. He'd made the last three years bearable, even pleasurable at times. It wasn't right, of course, for a man like Captain Ashleigh Arthur Dalton, son of Sir Arthur, to be friends with plain old Private Harry West. But friends they were, closer than brothers. How many nights had they spent in conversation or in reading aloud to each other, playing cards with the men or in Ash's quarters? How many nights had they hunkered down side-by-side in the support trench, sharing warmth and the comfort of each other's presence?

And if anything happened to West today, Ash didn't know how he'd bear it.

Well, he couldn't bear it. Simple as that.

He'd rather die himself than lose Harry West.

"I've still got your book in my bloody pocket," West said quietly, smiling ruefully as he tapped his hip pocket. "Hope it doesn't get too wet."

Ash had to clear his throat before he said, "Sherlock Holmes?"

"Aye, sir. Should have left it in the dugout with the rest of your kit. Sorry."

"Well." Ash huffed an approximation of a laugh. "If we're pinned down for any length of time, perhaps we'll read the next chapter?"

West laughed at that. He had a deep, contagious chuckle. "Imagine that, sir. Fritz stumbling over us sitting there, reading a book, happy as can be."

Ash snorted, his tension easing for a moment. And then rushing back in as a dozen horrible images unfolded in his mind, each more likely than the absurd one they'd painted. He checked his watch. "Ten minutes."

West nudged his shoulder again. Not so much nudged as pressed their arms together. Ash returned the pressure, taking comfort from it. He hoped West did, too. "Mother said they've had a terrific crop of apples this year. I hope — " He glanced at West. "When this is all over, I hope you'll visit me at Highcliffe House. Our cook makes a marvellous apple crumble."

A smile tugged West's lips. "I'd like to see your stables, sir. And perhaps take a ride in that forest of yours."

"The New Forest? Yes, it's beautiful. Especially at this time of year — with the turning leaves, you know. The colours…" His throat tightened with a terrible yearning for the trees and heathland of his boyhood. "Christ, this was woodland once, West. And there's not a single damn leaf to see for miles."

"There will be again. One day."

There was some comfort in that, he supposed. He flexed his fingers on the ladder, tapping out that little tune again.

If you want to find the private, I know where he is…

Time ticked on. "Five minutes, boys."

"Captain Dalton?" West sounded different, low and urgent. He reached out and covered Ash's hand where it rested on the ladder. "I want…" Their gaze locked and for a moment Ash saw in West's eyes everything he couldn't say, all the words neither of them could speak.

Ash turned his hand beneath West's and wove their fingers together, squeezing hard. "Another chapter of Holmes later." He made it a promise. "And a shot of whiskey at Toc H, if we're lucky."

After a lingering moment, West pulled his hand free. "Yes, sir."

Ash checked the time. "Three minutes, boys." His stomach pitched. "Affix bayonets."

He managed his own, ruthlessly suppressing the tremors in his hands. Just as it clicked into place, the barrage stopped. The morning rang with sudden silence, Ash's ears buzzing in the absence of noise. This was it then. "Two minutes," he said quietly, heart pounding like a terrified rabbit's. He had to swallow twice before he said, "First rank to the fire step."

Behind him and at his side, his men lined up. Looking down the line, he could hardly bear to see their ashen faces, some fixed as granite, others mobile with fear, lips moving in silent prayer or other incantation. Ordinary men, ordinary boys staring death in the eye. God, but he ached with the pity of it all.

"One minute." Thank God his voice didn't shake. Eyes fixed on his watch, he lifted the whistle to his lips. It tasted chill and metallic, worse than the rum.

The minute hand ticked to 07:15.

From down the line came the first shrill blast, slicing through the deathly silence. Ash blew his own piercing whistle and began to climb. "Off we go, boys. Good luck!"

Hard on his heels, West growled, "And God help us all."

Then no man's land stretched out before them, a pockmarked hellscape of blasted trees and mud and death. Low cloud crouched above them, as heavy and bleak as the cratered ground beneath their feet. Ash's mind turned sluggish with fear, focus narrowing only to the few yards around him, heart hammering loud in his ears. He knew only that he must advance and keep his men with him. "Stay in line!" he shouted, conscious of West's steady presence at his left as they ran forward in a half-crouch, slip-sliding in the treacherous, drowning mud. Gunfire sounded to their right, but nothing close to them yet. Perhaps they'd be lucky. Perhaps this time the bombardment really had taken out the German guns. He kept going, leading his men on, deeper into the wasteland.

They'd covered almost a hundred yards before machineguns opened fire, raking across their line. Someone dragged Ash down into the mud: West, his hand fisted in Ash's uniform.

"Find cover!" Ash yelled as his men fell and scattered.

And then the shells began, screaming overhead so close Ash could feel their scorching heat across his back. One hit behind them — almost in their trench — and the ground convulsed, raining mud and debris down over them. Laying prone, heart pounding hard against the earth, Ash prayed they wouldn't be buried alive. Christ, any end but that.

Then West was tugging on his arm again, yelling something Ash couldn't hear. Was he deaf? He scrambled to his feet. Smoke blew everywhere and he couldn't see his men, but he sounded the whistle anyway to help them find their way to him as he staggered forward. Still advancing, as ordered.

They were under heavy fire now. So much for the bombardment knocking out the German guns. Another shell hit to their right, the concussion knocking Ash back to his knees and he went half-sliding over the lip of a flooded shell hole. Machine gun fire kept him down, arms over his head as bullets peppered the ground behind and before him.

West wasn't holding his arm anymore. He couldn't see him. Fuck.

"West?" He turned, squirming in the mud, and saw West on his hands and knees several yards back, shaking his head as if dazed.

Ash's heart seized. "West!" He couldn't hear his own shout; the noise of the bombardment was ear-splitting. "West!"

He slithered backward, trying to find his feet. Through the blowing smoke, West kept appearing and then disappearing like a mirage. Or a ghost.

No. No, no, no. Not that. He wouldn't lose him. He couldn't.

Another smoky plume blew over them and away. West had struggled to his feet, still shaking his head. And in a single moment of clarity, as if the mists had parted, West lifted his head and their eyes met across the field of slaughter. Such a look! Relief, terror, desperation.

Love.

But then West's eyes widened in horror. He flung his arm out, reaching for him, as the earth erupted beneath Ash's feet.

For a second, he was airborne and the world fell silent. Then it rushed up to meet him, smashing the air from his lungs. Searing pain engulfed him. He couldn't breathe, couldn't see, couldn't move. Oblivion.

When he came back to himself, he was sprawled on his back, cradled in West's arms, looking up at his dear face. His first thought was relief. West was alive. He looked unhurt as he held Ash up out of the sucking mud, a filthy hand stroking the hair from his face. But his eyes were red-rimmed, his mud-splattered face ashen. "It's alright, Captain. I've got you. Everything's alright."

It wasn't. Something was very wrong.

Ash felt paper thin, cold and fading. It was an effort to keep his eyes open. He couldn't feel his legs and didn't dare look, gazed only into West's desolate eyes. All he needed to know was written plainly there. He tried to lift a hand to touch West's face, but even that was too much. His lips formed a word — West's name — but no sound came.

He felt no pain, only grief to be leaving him.

All around them the shrieking riot of war continued, but between them fell a terrible silence. "Oh God." West's voice broke and he clutched Ash against the sodden kaki of his jacket. "God, *please.*"

Ash was sinking, grey crowding the edges of his vision, but he tried again to speak. He had to. "Harry…" The name whispered past his lips, just loud enough to make West look at him. Ash tried to smile, to convey in these last moments how West had been everything to him in this nightmare — his solace, his succour, his burgeoning joy.

"Captain." Pale tracks cut through the dirt on West's face, tears gathering at the corner of his mouth. "Ashleigh…." He leaned down and kissed his brow like a mother might kiss her child, a last kiss offered to the dying.

Then he shifted and Ash felt the unfamiliar pressure of lips against his own, tasted mud and blood and salt tears. A lover's kiss at last, its sweet promise unfulfilled.

When Ash woke again it was in a clearing station and to raging agony.

But Harry West was gone, sent back up the line to hell.

CHAPTER TWO

One month later — 18ᵗʰ November 1917, Passchendaele, Belgium

Hollowed out, exhausted, Harry West hunched against the remains of a building that must once have been a home and dragged on a fag before passing it down to Tyler, slumped on the ground near his feet. The lad took it with a shaking hand and drew in a couple of lungfuls, passing it along to Little Bill.

It had been a bloody few days, this final push into the village. And now here they were, after months of fighting, five sodding miles from where they'd started. The brass hats were calling it a victory, but they could bend over and fuck themselves as far as Harry was concerned. Victory? It was a sodding disaster, that's what it was.

He spat out the sour taste and squinted at the grey sky, watching a couple of reconnaissance planes fly north. There'd been a time, not so long ago, when he'd wondered what it would be like to fly above it all and look down on the battlefield. He and the captain had mused on it, trying to sketch out a future where men might fly from town to town instead of taking the train. Fanciful stuff, but the captain had always loved to dream.

Imagine if… I wonder whether… What do you suppose…?

No point in wondering now. The captain was gone and the world was a darker place for it. Harry's world was, at any rate. Dark and hopeless.

Christ, he wished they were *doing* something. All this sitting about waiting gave him too much bloody time to think — and thinking took him close to the edge. He'd been hovering there since he'd carried the captain to the dressing station and watched, helpless, as they'd stretchered him away, his face death-white and one arm swinging lifeless over the edge of the stretcher.

That first evening he'd sat in the miserable rain and stared at the captain's blood beneath his fingernails, waiting for dark to fall so he could climb onto the fire step, light a fag, and let a sniper end it for him. What had stopped him were the men around him, turning to him in their grief, looking to him for hope he didn't bloody have.

The captain will make it, sir, won't he? I've seen men survive worse.

He'd held on for them that night but hoped in his heart that he'd click it in the next push. He hadn't. And now, over a month later, he just felt empty. For the best part of three years he'd lived and breathed death, yet he still couldn't make himself believe the captain was gone. Not him, not Captain Dalton.

Not Ashleigh.

He closed his eyes against the memory of the single time he'd used the captain's name, of the wrenching tenderness of that moment, held now in the hollows of his heart. Love, yes, but not like anything he'd known before. Nothing like the furtive desire he'd felt for other men. What he'd felt for the captain had been pure, a connection of the soul not the body. And without him, Harry was lost.

A kerfuffle further down the street roused him. Taff, returning from the Field Post Office. All the men stirred. Thanks to the fighting and the advance, they hadn't had mail in days.

Little Bill scrambled to his feet and Harry took the fag from his fingers. The lad had a sweetheart back home and her letters did more than anything to bring a smile to his pinched face. Harry watched as Taff handed out letters and postcards — he had quite a stash — and something like a smile touched his lips to see Bill's glee when he was handed two letters. At least someone was happy.

Harry wasn't expecting anything. His sister was working and didn't have much time between that and keeping the children fed and clothed. Mum wrote twice a month, and it wasn't her time. So he was surprised when Taff called out to him, waving an envelope. "Something for you, Harry." His face was carefully set. "It's from Calais."

With a frown — barely daring to think what this might mean — Harry shoved himself away from the wall and clambered over the rubble. "Thanks." He glanced at the address but didn't recognise the firm hand. His heart, what was left of it, tightened. "Anything for you?"

Taff patted his pocket. "From the wife." But he wasn't smiling, his attention fixed on Harry's letter. They all knew the nearest Base Hospital was in Calais. If the captain had made it that far, this could be news.

Harry gave Taff a nod and, expecting the worst, walked away from the others. If it was notice of the captain's death, he couldn't let them see him weep. And he knew he would. As much as Harry's heart believed the captain was gone, this final proof would crush him.

With the letter in hand, he slunk into the shadows of Passchendaele's shattered church and squatted with his back against the remains of a wall, hands shaking as he stared at the envelope. The air was sharp with brick dust and he rubbed at his nose. Procrastinating.

Fuck it. Taking a deep breath, he tore the letter open.

My dear West, I wanted to write sooner but I've had rather a time of it...

An ugly sob of pure, impossible relief ripped out of his chest, so violent it felt like pain. He could barely read the faint, shaky words through his tears, could barely suck in a lungful of gritty air. He was half-laughing, half-choking as he tried to devour the whole letter in one go, scrubbing his eyes, skipping over words in his haste to understand.

…and am only now capable of putting pencil to paper. I won't trouble you with the details. Suffice to say that I'm alive, thank God, and, if not yet well, on the way to being so. I don't remember much, but enough to know that I owe you my life — among every other debt I've accrued at your expense.

Please write as soon as possible. I'm to be sent home once I'm fit to travel and you may imagine how I fear for you, and for all the men. I'm starved of news and depend on you for information.

I can't express everything — it's too much — but I trust you understand and know that I remain your most loyal and grateful friend,

Capt. A.A. Dalton

Harry sat for a long time staring at the words, reading them again and again. He hadn't dared hope and now his heart was rioting, relief chased along by a desperate, impossible need to get to Calais. To see for himself, to be with his friend. To hold him.

"Harry?" Taff kept a careful distance. "We wondered whether you'd had news. About the captain."

Harry looked up, swiping at his eyes. He felt raw, as if Taff could see the bare truth of him. But Taff just watched him steadily and Harry remembered that all the men loved the captain. Not like he did, but well enough.

He pushed to his feet. "Aye, I have." He held out the letter so that Taff could read it himself. "Sounds like he'll make it."

Taff's smile split his grubby face. "Praise God." He skimmed the letter, then handed it back. "He don't say whether they saved his leg."

Harry shook his head and folded the precious letter, holding it close. "There was nothing left to save, Taff. It's a bloody miracle they saved his life."

They shared a look and neither added *For now.*

"I'll tell the others." Taff waited for Harry to nod before he scrambled back over the rubble of the church toward where the rest of the company were sprawled, reading their mail.

Harry couldn't join them yet, he needed a little longer to get his ill-disciplined feelings under control. Leaning back into the shadows, hidden from the world for a moment, he allowed himself the risky joy of pressing his lips to the letter, to the places where the captain had touched the paper.

"Thank you, God."

It was the first prayer of gratitude he'd offered in years.

Chapter Three

Five months later — April 26th 1918, Hampshire, England

"Ashleigh, darling, do be careful."

His mother's voice chased him across the lawn to the edge of the stream where he watched the water flow past in an endless spill and dance. It glittered in the fresh spring light, untouched and unchanged by the passing of the years. As boys, he and his brother Dodge had played here, the usual things boys did, he supposed: racing paper boats, catching tadpoles in jars, splashing around until they were soaked to the skin.

Dodge worked for the War Office now. Mother and Father were terribly proud of their eldest son. He'd had a good war and the peace, when it came, promised to be even better; his election as a Member of Parliament was all but guaranteed. To that end, Dodge had married the Honourable Emily Medhurst four months ago and there was already a baby on the way.

Ash found himself praying it was a girl. He couldn't bear the thought of bringing another boy into the world, of teaching him to laugh and play on the banks of an English stream only to send him to flounder and drown in the filthy mud of Flanders.

"Darling!" His mother startled him, her hand touching his elbow. "Don't stand so close to the edge. What if you topple in?"

He gritted his teeth against her kindness, adjusted his grip on his cane, and turned to say, "I w-won't topple in. But if I d-d-did, I'd get w-wet. That's all."

She tutted and tugged him back a step. "For me, Ashleigh. Think of your poor mama."

His poor mama in her elegant summer dress of palest yellow, dark hair barely tarnished by a scattering of grey, and her narrow face shadowed beneath a wide-brimmed hat. Her hand on his arm was part comfort and part tether, holding him there in the garden, in his parents' house, in the unreal, unchanged world. Not that he had anywhere else to go. He'd only been on his feet — foot — again for three months, and that with difficulty. The thought of returning to his position at the bank made him breathless, made him cling to the illusory securities of his childhood home.

Made him want Harry West at his side again, with his bright grin and warm hazel eyes, lighting Ash's world even at the darkest of times. But West was still at the front. He may be dead. Ash didn't know because he hadn't had a letter in two weeks.

Mother pressed his arm. "Come along, we'll have some tea and cake. You're still too thin, you know. Oh, and I've invited the Allens to tea. You remember Miss Allen? Olive Allen?"

"Of c-course." He turned, unable to swallow a grunt of pain when the stump of his leg, lost just below the knee, rubbed against his newly fitted prosthetic.

His mother's grimace was half pity and half embarrassment. She hid it quickly, adopting a bright smile as she looped her arm through his. "Olive was supposed to marry Percy Cross, poor thing."

Percy Cross, who'd copped a packet in the first year of the war. A laughing, handsome boy, Ash remembered. Like so many other boys who'd never come home, whose bodies were left to rot in the mire. Boys like Jimmy Tilney, with his penny whistle and insolent grin, who'd drowned in the mud because Ash couldn't save him.

"But she turned him down — much to her mama's

displeasure — and then the war came and… Well, she can't be so fussy now."

Ash blinked, the green grass suddenly too vivid and the sky a dizzying blue. He couldn't catch the meaning of his mother's words. "Too fussy about w-what?"

She gestured with one hand, as if shooing away a fly. "You're still a handsome boy, darling. Despite everything."

He stopped walking, leaning on his cane to take the weight off his sore leg. "Mother — "

"Now!" She held up a staying hand. "Your war is over, Ashleigh. It's time to think about the future. And Olive Allen is such a capable young woman. She's a VAD, you know, at the auxiliary hospital they've set up at Chewton Lodge. She could look after you and — "

"I d-d-don't — I d-don't need looking after. I'm n-not a…a…*c-c-cripple*."

But he was in her eyes, and in the world's. He wasn't the man who'd marched to war a lifetime ago. He was someone else now, someone who limped along with a cane and couldn't face taking the train to London. Someone who woke shouting in the night, sweat-soaked and shaking, who couldn't quite believe that this world of spring gardens and tea parties existed while his men were still fighting at the front.

While Harry West was still fighting.

"You're getting distressed again," his mother scolded, lips pursing. "You really must make an effort, darling. We all have to carry on."

As if getting out of bed every day wasn't an *effort*. But he did as she asked and sat in the garden drinking tea and eating the seed cake he remembered from his childhood, making polite conversation with Miss Allen and her mother.

Olive, it transpired, was a painfully awkward young woman. Too tall to be elegant and possessing features more likely to be called strong than pretty, she seemed to fold in on herself as if attempting to hide in plain sight. Ash felt a distant pity for her, chafing as she clearly was beneath her formidable mother's rule, but beyond that he had no real interest. He had no real interest in anything, these days.

The only spark he saw in the girl was when the subject of the vote arose. Mrs Allen sniffed and pronounced, "Well, *I* certainly shan't be voting. I'm quite content for Mr Allen to represent *my* interests."

At that, her daughter's expression darkened with irritation, but still she held her tongue; it looked rather more like tactical retreat than surrender.

"I think," Ash ventured, "it's a shame the v-vote is s-still so restricted. Surely a w-w-woman of one and twenty is as sensible as a m-man of that age?" He smiled encouragingly at Olive. "M-more so, some might say."

Not quite meeting his eye, and in a voice rather too loud, she said, "Given the advantage of the same education, Mr. Ashleigh, I believe there would be no difference in intellect whatsoever between the sexes."

Ash smiled because he'd talked of such things with West. It had been easy to imagine a world where the barriers of sex, class and race were torn down when he was living and dying shoulder-to-shoulder with men from all walks of life and from all corners of the Empire.

Death did not discriminate.

For all its horrors, the war had opened his eyes to many things. And to West, most of all. Harry West was the sort of man Ash would never have come to know in the ordinary way of things, the sort of man who might have served in the stables at Highcliffe House. Before the war, West had been an ostler at an inn in Bethnal Green, living in a small back-to-back house with his parents and, more recently, his widowed sister and her two girls. But in West, Ash had found his soul's partner. A kind, thoughtful man with a passion for justice (and horses), blessed with an easy, honest affection that Ash had never found among his own set. Certainly not within his family.

There was more to it than that, of course. Ash's peculiar affection for his own sex meant that what he felt for West went deeper than ordinary friendship, for his part at least. Whether West felt the same, Ash didn't know and had dared not ask. Sometimes he'd thought… But there were too many eyes at the front and he'd refused to risk exposing West to the danger of court martial. Besides, their friendship was too important to endanger simply to satisfy Ash's romantic curiosity.

And yet he'd never been closer to another man in his life, would never be again. He felt with absolute certainty that their profound bond, forged in the hellish crucible of war, was inimitable. Never to be repeated and never to be forgotten.

Christ, but he missed Harry West more than he missed his damned leg.

His mother clucked her tongue against her teeth and changed the subject. "Ashleigh was always quite the horseman, you know. I think you like to ride, Olive?"

"Not really, Lady Dalton. I prefer to motor…"

Ash didn't hear the rest of Olive's reply. He shifted in his seat and gazed out across the tidy lawn to the stream, and beyond that to the fringes of the New Forest in spring leaf. He tried not to see shattered trees, like dead men's fingers clawing up from the ruin of the world. He tried not to dwell on all that, he tried to make an effort. To look forward.

If only there was something worth seeing on the broad, bleak horizon.

CHAPTER FOUR

Nine months later — January 17th, 1919, London, England

Harry West reached England two months after the armistice, demobbed at the dispersal station in Crystal Palace, and made his way home through a city stricken by the influenza.

His own parents had perished last summer, before the war ended, but fate had spared Kitty and the girls and for that he was thankful. They greeted him with a flurry of emotion when he opened the door to number six Bethnal Road. Kitty wrapped her thin arms around him in a hard embrace while Dot and little May danced around them, half-shy and half-excited to see their Uncle Harry. There wasn't much food, but they made the most of what they had and, as he told his sister, he'd eat anything that wasn't a tin of Maconochie.

That night he made up a bed for himself next to the kitchen stove, lay there staring at the ceiling and didn't sleep. It wasn't the homecoming he'd dreamed of night after night at the front. He didn't feel elated, he didn't feel relieved. He didn't even feel like he was home.

Perhaps it was because Mum and Dad were gone. Perhaps it was because he wasn't the same man who'd left four years ago. But mostly it was because — He rolled over and sat up, digging into his holdall for the captain's letters. It was too dark to read, but he didn't need to see them to know what they said. He'd read them so often that holding them was enough.

Unfolding the first letter, pressed flat from where he kept it between the leaves of *The Hound of the Baskervilles*, he ran his fingers over the paper. There were several letters in all, held safe in Captain Dalton's book. Two from Calais, two from a hospital in Southampton, and the rest from the captain's home. Well, his parents' home: Highcliffe House, Hinton, Hampshire. The last one had arrived shortly before Harry left the rest camp in Dieppe and if there were more they hadn't reached him. Probably wouldn't, now that he'd been demobbed.

He knew he should write to the captain and tell him he was back in England, give him his address, but something made him hesitate. It wasn't like they could be friends, not in this old unchanged world where he'd have to doff his cap to Mr Ashleigh Arthur Dalton. And yet the thought of letting their friendship end hurt like the devil. He wanted to see the captain at least once more, to see him hale and healthy, so his last memory of the man wasn't tourniqueting the bloody remains of his leg or holding him up out of the drowning mud and watching his eyes roll back in his ashen face. He'd like to remember those soft brown eyes better, he'd like to see them smiling and warm. He'd like to see the captain happy.

He'd like to kiss him.

His heart clenched at the forbidden thought, cramping around the empty longing he'd once felt for home. Only this yearning was for something he'd never had and could never have; he was wishing for impossible things.

Harry spent the next two months looking for work, silently resenting his sister for having a job when there was nothing for a man who'd given four sodding years in service to his country. But there were too many men back from the war and nobody was hiring, especially not with the influenza holding the city in its fist.

Harry felt himself increasingly distant from the world. He spent hours walking the banks of the leaden Thames, staring at laughing girls and handsome boys as if through glass. He could see them, hear them, but couldn't reach out to touch them. The war — He couldn't talk about the war, not even to Kitty. Not to anyone who hadn't been there. Sometimes he met the eyes of a man on the underground, saw a kind of recognition, a haunted look, and they'd share a nod. Strangers together in a strange land, navigating a world they just didn't fit anymore.

A cold winter bled into a damp spring. The London fogs continued as soupy as ever, made uncanny by the masks people had taken to wearing — some to keep out the influenza, others to hide horrific souvenirs from the fighting. Poor bastards. Better to have lost your legs, Harry reckoned, than your half your bloody face.

As he contemplated one sorry blighter scurrying through the fog, tin nose and fake moustache ill-concealed by the wide brim of his hat, Harry thought, with guilty gratitude, that he was glad the captain's pretty face hadn't been torn up — not that smooth skin, not those expressive lips that curved into a shy smile, not those eyes of softest brown beneath his fall of dark hair. Perhaps the man he was watching could read his mind, because he glanced over through the fog as if knowing he was being observed. No doubt he was used to it. Harry nodded, touched the brim of his cap in an awkward salute, and the man looked away, disappearing into the mist.

Harry shivered. These masked shadows in the fog made him feel like he was living in a weird purgatory of lost souls. He felt lost too, a wraith in the mist, not quite himself. Not quite home. Not quite anywhere.

Not without the captain at his side.

He thought he'd hidden his turmoil from Kitty until one evening when they were sitting by the kitchen stove, him on the rug with his back propped against her chair. "I wish you was happier, Harry," she said. "I wish you could smile sometimes."

It was a cold night in early March, their fire too small to do more than toast them one side at a time — his shins were hot, his arse was freezing. It was luxury compared to the front, but he couldn't help missing the comradely press of the captain's arm against his as they drowsed together beneath their coats, the intimate weight of his head against Harry's shoulder while he read aloud. "What do you mean?" He focused on the fire, following the dance of the flames. "I'm happy to be home."

"Are you?"

"'Course I bloody am." He looked up into her face, into her knowing eyes, and conceded, "I'd be happier if I had work. I hate being idle."

Kitty reached out and ran her fingers over his head, through his hair. "What about that captain bloke?"

Harry's heart stuttered like a faulty automobile. "What about him?"

"Well, don't he have some big house in the country? He might have use for a stable hand."

His flash of relief — she didn't suspect — was chased by a shrinking horror. Ask the captain for work? "Christ, no."

"No what? No he ain't got a big house, or no he won't have use for a good nag-man?"

"No, I can't ask him for work."

Kitty sniffed. "Don't see why not."

"Because — " How to explain? "Because he'd want to help, and I don't want him to feel obligated."

"Thought you said he was your friend."

"He is. Was…"

"Well then, why not? Friends help each other."

He edged closer to the stove, ducking out from beneath her hand and wrapping his arms around his warm shins. *Because we were friends, because he looked at me like an equal, because I couldn't bear him to look at me like a servant.* "Because it wouldn't be right."

A long silence followed, the coals shifting, their heat ebbing.

Kitty got to her feet, ready for bed. "Truth is," she said, "we need the money. You're welcome here, course you are. It's your home. But…"

But his was another mouth to feed and his war pension was a pittance. "I'll find something, Kitty. Soon. And if I don't…" He scrambled to his feet, turned to take her hands in his. "If I ain't got nowhere else to turn, then I'll ask the captain before I see you or the girls go hungry. I swear it."

He'd have to be on his knees to go cap in hand to Captain Dalton, but even so the thought of seeing him again — even in such dire circumstances — lit a fire in Harry's heart.

And that alone should have warned him of the danger.

Chapter Five

On a breezy May afternoon, clouds scudding across a pale sky, Ash gazed through the dining room window and wished he was outside breathing the fresh air instead of Mrs Allen's cloying perfume.

They were eating luncheon together, his father and mother, Mrs Allen and Olive. Over the last months, he and Olive had become cautious companions — much to the delight of their respective mothers. He felt guilty about the deception, because he had no intention of marrying Olive or any other woman, but it suited him that his parents hoped matters would proceed along those lines. It freed him from their interference, allowing him to devote time to his reading and recovery.

The doctor said his nerves were shot and prescribed quiet and rest, perhaps a lifetime of them. But Ash wasn't certain it was his nerves at all. He rather thought his ennui had a deeper cause, one which he barely dared acknowledge to himself and certainly couldn't confess to a doctor.

He missed Harry West.

Ash hadn't heard from him since before Christmas and the loss was jarring. He'd thought their friendship inviolable, but perhaps West didn't feel the same. Perhaps he had no use for the crippled son of Sir Arthur Dalton. Perhaps the future they'd talked about, a future where the divisions of class were no more, would never come to pass. God knew he couldn't see much evidence of an egalitarian future around the dining table that afternoon.

His father, with his Victorian moustache quivering, was enumerating the new Prime Minister's many failings while Culham, the footman, who'd been with the Royal Hampshires at Ypres, stood silently watching them eat as if it were 1819 and not 1919. The wrongness of it struck Ash so hard he could barely cut his cold ham. He had to tamp down a mad desire to leap up and scream.

No, not a mad desire. The madness was sitting there as if nothing had changed.

Across the table, Olive caught his eye with a flashing gaze. As often happened when his father started pontificating on politics, Olive was fuming. Ash smiled apologetically, but in truth he was grateful for the distraction. If he let his dark thoughts take hold, God only knew what he might do.

A moment later, Olive's fork clattered loudly onto her plate. "Really, Sir Arthur," she blurted, interrupting him mid-flow, "I must protest. The establishment of a Ministry of Health will benefit us all — the whole of society is advantaged when the health of the poorest is improved. Disease is no respecter of rank, sir."

"Olive!" Mrs Allen hissed, darting a wary glance at Sir Arthur.

He stared at Olive, bristling at being so addressed by a young lady, but they'd all become accustomed to Olive's social oddities over the past few months. "Madam," Sir Arthur said stiffly, "the business of government is business, not nannying those who — "

Thankfully, he was cut off by the dining room door opening. "Apologies, Sir Arthur," Grieves said, turning his attention to Ash. "But there's a…person outside asking to see Mr Ashleigh. Rather a rough — "

"What person?" Ash said, before his father could speak. "Who is it?"

"He gave his name as West, sir."

Dear God, impossible. For a moment Ash couldn't move, he just

Sally Malcolm

stared at Grieves' impassive face.

"Would you like me to send him away? I — "

"No!" Leaping to his feet, Ash grabbed his cane, his heart a live thing pounding against his ribs. "My God…" He laughed, dazed by delight. "My God! Where is he?"

"Ashleigh!" His mother exclaimed at his profane language while his father regarded his emotional display with raised eyebrows and a slack mouth.

Ash stumbled back from the table. "Sorry," he said to the ladies. "I'm sorry, I have to — "

Walking as fast as possible — curse his leg; he couldn't run — he left the room and hurried to the front door, which stood ajar. The fresh spring air riffled through the flowers on the hallway table, sunlight dazzling him as he flung the door wide. And there he was: Harry West, silhouetted against the pale gravel driveway, a dark but unmistakable figure.

"West!" Ash called, limping down the steps as fast as he could manage.

West turned, swiped the cap from his head, and broke into a grin. "Captain. I — "

"My God, man!" Ash flung his arms around him with a laugh and such wild joy he couldn't think straight. "My God, West, I can't believe it."

After a hesitation, West returned the embrace, thumping Ash on the back, then quieting and holding him tight for a long, sweet moment. Dear Lord, Ash felt like he was breathing for the first time in forever. He didn't want to let go, wanted to absorb West's presence like balm. "My God, it's good to see you." His voice sounded rough, throat thick with emotion, an unmanning prickling in his eyes.

"Aye, you too."

Ash pulled back far enough that he could really look at West, holding him by the shoulders, his cane discarded, feeling the man's familiar strength beneath his hands. He looked thinner than Ash remembered, his strong jaw and nose sharpened, and there were shadows beneath his bright hazel eyes. But he was smiling, gazing at Ash as if lost for words.

"I can't believe you're here," Ash managed at last. "Good God."

West laughed softly. "No, me neither. I—" His attention shifted over Ash's shoulder and he stiffened. It was only then that Ash realised his father had followed him outside. Ash turned awkwardly, stumbling as his duff foot snagged in the gravel. West caught his elbow, steadying him, and for a moment their eyes met and—Christ, how he'd missed this man.

"Father," Ash said, dragging his gaze away from West. He smiled to see his mother and Olive in the doorway, too. "Everyone, th-this is Private West. The m-man who saved my life."

"Not a soldier no more," West said and nodded to Ash's father. "Sir Arthur."

"Ashleigh has told us a great deal about you, West. I must thank you for what you did for my son."

"No need," West said, pushing a hand self-consciously through his hair. "He'd have done the same for me, or any of the men. He did, for some of the lads. And more."

A silent moment fell between them, shared memories that didn't need to be voiced. Lord, it felt good that West just *knew*. Tears thickened Ash's throat, emotions surging like they hadn't in months. "W-well," he said, trying to control himself, "come in. J-join us for luncheon." He looked around for his cane, but before he could stoop to retrieve it West had picked it up and handed it to him. Ash gave a rueful smile. "Blasted thing."

West shrugged, squinting into the sunshine. "Could've been worse."

They both knew the truth of that.

"Come on." Ash looped his arm through West's to haul him along. "Are you hungry? You m-must—"

But West resisted, his attention darting between Ash and his father. "Probably shouldn't," he said, pulling his arm free.

Ash stared at him, bewildered. "What? Why not?"

West looked embarrassed, frowning down at his boots, and the falling silence seemed to suck all the noise from the world.

Into it sliced his mother's crystal voice. "Perhaps Mr West would be more comfortable downstairs, darling?" She walked, smiling, down the steps. "Grieves, have cook make Mr West a plate."

"Mother!"

"No, she's right," West said. "Truth is I… I came here looking for work. I ain't had much luck in London and I thought you might have need of a stableman."

"Work," Ash said stupidly.

West's jaw tensed, fingers twisting the cap in his hands. "I shouldn't have come. I didn't want to, but — "

"Do you need money? I can help you. I — "

"Ashleigh," his father cautioned.

West's head jerked up, eyes flashing with indignation. "I don't want money. I'm not here to beg."

"Of c-course not. I d-didn't mean — " Mortified, he lowered his voice, gripping West's forearm. "We're *friends*, for God's sake. I owe you my life."

"You don't owe me nothing. I shouldn't have thought to come, only my sister insisted."

"Kitty? H-how is she? And the girls?" West had talked about her all the time. Had something happened?

A small smile. "Well enough, but — See, she's working and I ain't. And I can't let her put food in my mouth and — "

"We have w-work for you. Plenty, if you want it."

But West shook his head. "I can't. You don't owe me."

Ash tightened his grip on West's arm, trying not to pay too much attention to the lithe strength of sinew and bone. "I *do* owe you," he said urgently. "As a brother in arms, if nothing else. My God, West, don't tell me you've forgotten it all."

He looked up, distressed. "No, I ain't forgotten."

Ash let out a breath. "It's not charity," he said in a calmer voice.

"The house has b-been understaffed since Kitchener recruited half the village, and God knows f-f-few enough came home. We can give you work, West, and you'll be doing *us* the f-favour." He turned as he spoke, looking at his father, daring him to object. "West's an excellent stableman, sir. I c-can vouch for him entirely. And you know Boyd n-needs help."

His father gave a small nod. Happier, no doubt, now West was in his proper place and not threatening to take a seat at the dining table. But the iniquity irritated like lice under his shirt and provoked a hot flare of anger. As if the man who'd shared every privation, every joy, every danger at the front, the man who'd carried him to safety on his back, wasn't fit to sit at his table. Incomprehensible, all of it. Maddening. It was —

West touched his arm, a brief but firm pressure. "Thank you." With a look, he added, *Calm down, it's alright.*

For a long time, Ash held that look, then he turned back to his parents and Olive. Damned if he was sending West to the kitchen. "My apologies to your m-mother, Miss Allen, but I think I'll show West the grounds. Grieves, please ask Mrs Pierson to prepare a small picnic for us both. It's a b-b-beautiful day to be outside, eh, West?"

"That it is," West said, clearly torn between relief and embarrassment.

Ash smiled. "Good God, I've missed you."

"Aye." West held his gaze only for a moment before looking away. "I've missed you too."

***

"Those are the stables," the captain said with a careless wave of his hand. "I'll introduce you to Boyd later. He's our head groom."

Harry nodded, at once grateful and mortified that it had come to this. But he needed the work, he needed it for Kitty and for his own pride. Nothing but that could have driven him to this, and yet... Well, he couldn't deny that it was bloody good to see the captain again. Harry's heart had all but burst at the sight of him standing in the doorway, his voice ringing out in greeting. When their eyes met it had felt more like homecoming than anything since reaching England. And then the captain had embraced him and Harry's arms had gone around him and—

That line of thought risked straying onto dangerous ground.

He brought his attention back to the here and now, where they were ambling along a gravel path. Highcliffe House rose up on his left, a substantial country pile of red brick with ivy clinging to its walls and roses drooping elegantly around its large white-framed windows. Something from the last century, Harry supposed, or maybe the one before. The garden they were walking through had an air of genteel neglect, overgrown shrubs tangling in the borders, and he guessed at the fate of the gardeners and groundsmen who'd once worked here. Dalton clearly hadn't been exaggerating when he said the house was understaffed. In the distance, half hidden by the winding border, Harry made out an attractive circular doorway in the garden wall, promising secrets in the forest beyond. Altogether it was painfully bloody charming, a world away from Bethnal Green and its back-to-backs, and exactly the dreamy idyll the captain's wistful descriptions of home had always conjured.

Not that the captain seemed particularly dreamy today. Harry glanced at him as they walked, their slow pace accommodating the captain's pronounced limp, and Harry's heart floated disconcertingly free. Captain Dalton looked so much the same as he used to, yet somehow entirely different. He was in civvies, for starters, dressed in a brown tweed suit with a half-belt jacket and slim trousers—the clothes nicely set off his shoulders, narrow hips and lean legs. His dark hair was mostly hidden beneath his cap, his profile as elegant as ever, but there was a tension about him that Harry had noticed right away. He could see it around his eyes, in the slight tick of the muscle in his jaw, the stiff way he held himself as he walked, shoulders bunched, knuckles white on the head of his cane.

For all that he was home, the captain—Dalton—wasn't happy.

Harry had an urgent, unexpected impulse to reach out and take his hand. He'd done it so often in the firing line, when a whizz-bang fell too close and the captain started out of his skin. Just a reassuring touch, a comfort. *Steady on, I'm here. We're alright.* He looked like that now, Harry thought, possessed by that same nervy tension, as if he was expecting Fritz to pop out from around the corner of the stables. Only he was home now, where he should feel safe.

Dalton caught his eye and Harry looked away, conscious of being caught staring. "Did you…?" Dalton sounded hesitant. "D-did you receive my last letters? I sent them to Dieppe but I suppose once you'd d-demobbed they went astray."

Swiping off his cap, Harry ran a guilty hand through his hair. He was sweating in the sun. "Sorry. I should have given you my address in London."

"Yes, you b-bloody well should."

He smiled at Dalton's tone, looked over to find him smiling back. "I didn't know what to say, if I'm honest. It's different now we're on Civvy Street."

Dalton frowned. "'It' being what?"

"I dunno. Everything, I suppose." He jerked his head at the house. "Your dad's lord of the manor, and mine — " The pain struck out of the blue and he clamped his mouth shut, keeping it in. Mine was a grain lift operator for the PLA, he'd been going to say. Mine *was*…. He swallowed.

"West?" Dalton stopped, leaning on his cane as he turned. "What is it?"

Harry shook his head, a clot of emotion clogging his throat. Christ, what was this? It had been months since he'd had the news and he wasn't the sort to mope. But the way Dalton was watching him touched a raw patch, something unhealed. Harry wanted to turn away from it, hide it from Dalton, but a deeper part of him stretched out blindly seeking comfort. "I, uh. I lost him. And mum. The influenza did for them last summer, while I was still in bloody Flanders. They were buried before I even knew they were gone."

"Oh West." Dalton put a hand on his shoulder, stepped closer and drew him into a one-armed embrace. "Why didn't you tell me?"

His arm was strong around Harry's back, the wool of his suit warm when Harry dropped his forehead onto his shoulder. Dalton smelled faintly woodsy, like rosemary or cedar, clean and comforting. They stood like that for several moments while Harry dragged in long steadying breaths and got himself back under control. "You've got your own troubles," he said eventually. "You don't need mine an' all."

Dalton huffed his disagreement and drew back. "A trouble shared, and all that, West." He squinted toward a gate in the garden wall. "There's a bench through there. Shall we sit and eat? You must be hungry."

He was. He hadn't had breakfast and it was well past noon. But mostly he was grateful for the change of subject and took the chance to wipe his eyes while Dalton walked over to open the gate. Beyond it, everything looked wilder. A stream ran into a large pond, overgrown on all sides by rushes and lily pads, the edge of the forest encroaching on its far shore where a large willow dipped its branches into the water. Dalton led the way to a wooden bench at the water's edge, set to one side at the end of the path, and manoeuvred himself down with obvious relief. His leg must be painful. Of course it bloody well was, and might be for the rest of his life. A permanent memento of his service to a hard country.

"How much did you lose?" Harry said, looking down at the stiffly articulated ankle and trying not to think about the warm slip of his hands in the captain's blood, the way it had pulsed between his fingers as he'd tried to tighten the tourniquet.

Dalton glanced up. "They saved the knee, thank God, but not far below it I'm afraid." He tapped his shin with his cane and it gave a wooden thud. "This thing's not bad, though. Better than the first one I had. Damned torture that was." His expression changed, softening. "West, I've never been able to thank you —"

"Bollocks you haven't. I've got at least three letters' worth of nothing but your thanks."

Dalton gave his shy smile. "Well, not in person."

"You'd have done the same for me."

"Yes."

"Enough said, then." Harry rubbed his hands together, disposing of the subject. "Now, how about some grub?"

Perching on the bench, he watched as Dalton ferreted in the knapsack the cook had given him and fished out two paper-wrapped sandwiches. He sniffed one and smiled. "Ham and pickle sound alright?"

"And how!" It was better than alright, in fact, with lashings of butter on soft white bread, a tangy tomato pickle and tender smoked ham. Harry ate with more relish than he'd felt in a long time. Must be the country air. They ate in silence, enjoying the food and each other's company, watching a couple of birds diving down into the water for their own lunch. Black feathers, with red beaks and foreheads. Harry didn't recognise them, but then again he was mostly familiar with starlings and pigeons. He was about to ask, but Dalton got there first.

"Moorhens," he said, breaking off a piece of bread and throwing it into the water, smiling as the birds sped toward the treat. "Hungry girls. Look at them go!"

"They know a good thing when they see it." Harry glanced at the knapsack. "Did your cook put anything to drink in there?"

"Yes, I think there's tea." Dalton hauled out a black thermos and two Bakelite cups, which he handed to Harry, and poured them each a cup. "No sugar, I'm afraid."

"Ah, I'm used to that."

Harry handed Dalton his tea and smiled when Dalton knocked their cups together. "To absent friends." Between them, nothing more needed saying.

Harry took a moment to breathe in the fragrant steam, beginning to relax. Nothing like a good cuppa to set a bloke right. Next to him, Dalton sighed softly and stretched out his bad leg, flexing the knee. Then he closed his eyes, tipped his face to the sun, and Harry thought how strange it was to be sitting there on the bank of this tranquil pond with the captain at his side in this time of peace. How strange that the sky above was blue, the air clear, the sun warm. How strange that these ordinary things seemed extraordinary, that his world was still calibrated to a crueller cadence.

"Penny for them?" Dalton said, without opening his eyes.

Harry was glad of that because it gave him time to study the man's face. Dalton had taken off his hat and the sun gleamed on his dark hair, a thick lock of which fell, as always, over his left eye. Harry would have liked to push it out of his face so he could see him better. It was a beautiful face, no denying that, with dark lashes and a straight nose, elegant lips. Lips he'd kissed once, though he was sure the captain wouldn't remember. Sensitive features, they'd be called, but Harry knew all too well the steel that ran down the captain's spine. He wasn't soft, for all his tender feelings. But there were lines around his mouth that looked new, a frown between his brows and shadows under his eyes. Harry wanted to ease them, if he could.

"Tuppence for them, then," Dalton said when Harry didn't answer, lips lifting into a smile.

Harry's stomach pinched — damn him for being a fool — and he looked away, back to the pond. "Just thinking, the last time you and I shared a meal was in the support line, that night when Taff was trying to teach us his Welsh song. Remember? How did it go? My hair n' wool..."

Dalton laughed. "*Mae hen wlad fy...* and then something. I don't recall it all."

"Aye, you got it right. Course you did." Quick as a flash was Captain Dalton — spoke French, German and Spanish. Welsh too, apparently. "You and Taff were singing so loud we thought bloody Fritz would come over and tell you to give it a rest."

"Taff has a fine voice," Dalton said. "Have you heard from him?"

"Only that he's got another nipper on the way. Doing his patriotic duty to restock the population, he says."

Dalton smiled, although it was a melancholy expression. "Sounds like Taff. I'm glad he made it. He was so fond of his wife, kept all her letters. Carried them everywhere, remember?"

"Aye." Harry glanced back over the water, thinking of his own letters kept neatly in the captain's book. "Lucky blighter to have her."

Silence fell save the hush of the wind through the leaves, the chirping of moorhens. Dalton shifted his leg and sat up a little straighter. "How about you, West? Do you have someone? A...a girl, I mean."

"Me? Nah." He'd said that too fast. "I mean, I ain't really in a position to go courting."

"But if you were? Is there someone on the horizon?"

Harry daren't look at him, afraid he might see the truth. "Not likely." With the airless dread he'd feel approaching a live shell, he added, "And yourself?"

"Well..." Dalton sighed and Harry felt a ridiculous clench in the pit of his stomach. "My parents would like me to marry Olive Allen — the young lady you saw earlier — but, frankly, it's the last thing I want to do."

Which wasn't, Harry noted, the same as saying it was the last thing he *would* do. He knew what these toffs were like, marrying for money and family connections, and felt a flare of anger. It was that kind of nonsense that had got them into the bloody war in the first place, toffs and their family ties and disastrous alliances. He might have said as much once, and the words were on the tip of his tongue, but then he remembered that Dalton was his employer now and he'd better keep his trap shut. Irritated by the thought, he said, "Perhaps you could show me the stables." It came out sharper than he'd have liked, and Dalton turned a quizzical eye on him. "I mean, if it's convenient. Sir."

"Well you can cut that out, for a start."

"Cut what out?"

"That 'sir' business. I'm not your commanding officer now, West. In case you hadn't noticed."

Harry lifted an eyebrow. "You *are* my employer, though."

"Well, bugger that too." Irritably, Dalton began packing their cups back into his knapsack. "We're friends before anything else."

"Yeah, but — No wait." Dalton was already trying to interject. "You have to admit things are different now we're home. Well, *not* different. That's the point. Things are the same as they were before the war and we can't — "

"No they b-b-bloody well aren't!" Dalton glared at him, dark eyes snapping. "Do you really think so, West? D-do you think anything can ever b-be the same as it was before the war? Because I bloody well don't. I c-c-can't stand all this nonsense. Why can't we be friends? Who says we c-can't be friends, for Christ's sake?"

"Your father and mother. There's two for starters."

Dalton's lips pressed together. "And what d-do they know about anything? What d-do any of them *know*? Christ." His hand, holding the strap of the knapsack, was rigid, white knuckles clenching around the canvas. His whole body had tensed, face white bar a spot of furious pink on each cheek.

"You're right," Harry said evenly, feeling his earlier irritation fade, replaced by a pulse of concern. Dalton had always been on the nervy side, but Harry had never seen him angry. "I mean, *I* think you're right. We who were there, we know, don't we?"

"Yes," Dalton said thinly. "Christ, they were happy enough for us to die together b-but God forbid we *dine* together."

Harry smiled, reached out slowly, as if toward a spitting cat, and took Dalton's hand. His fingers felt cold and stiff. Harry squeezed them. "You're right. We *are* friends. I didn't mean to say we weren't, it's just... I dunno. It's different, back home. People don't understand. It's like we don't fit no more."

Dalton nodded and beneath Harry's hand he turned his own over, threading their fingers together. "We d-don't fit. That's it exactly." He hesitated, then in a lower voice said, "B-but we fit together, you and I."

Harry swallowed. He'd never been quite sure about the captain, never dared push his luck in that direction. It hadn't been worth the risk in the army, but now he saw a question in Dalton's eyes and couldn't look away. "Aye, we do," he said, voice rasping across the edges of things unsaid. "We've seen the world through different lenses. We've seen what men really are, underneath all this, and it's changed us."

Dalton's eyes widened and then he relaxed, his colour improving. "God, I'm glad you're here. It's been b-bloody awful, these last months."

"Funny, isn't it?" Harry squeezed his hand. "Sometimes I feel like coming home's been harder than the sodding war."

"Yes, it's — "

Behind them, the gate gave a startling squeal. Dalton yanked his hand free and Harry spun around to see a sullen lad in shirt-sleeves and waistcoat slouching towards them, all skinny legs and arms. He was maybe seventeen. Harry had seen boys like him taken apart by shellfire, scattered to the wind so there was nothing left to bury. "Mr Ashleigh?" The lad's Hampshire burr rounded his words. "Sir Arthur's asking for you. Says to see him in his study."

Dalton gave a tight nod, not looking up from fussing with his knapsack. "Very well. Thank you, John, p-p-please tell him I'll be along d-directly."

John gave an obedient nod, but Harry didn't miss his watchful expression, nor the insolent tilt of his hips as he stood there staring at them. "You heard Mr Ashleigh," he said, wanting rid of the lad. "Go on with you." Dalton glanced up at that, surprised, and the boy turned to go, giving Harry an unfriendly eye as he left.

Trouble, that one, Harry thought.

But the notion didn't linger. More pressing was the way Dalton had pulled his hand away, the slight flush still tinting his cheeks. It suggested what they'd been doing needed concealing. It suggested it was something more than simple comfort between old comrades.

And that set Harry's heart pounding like a howitzer.

Chapter Six

Ash directed West to the stables, pausing to watch his friend stride away before heading back to the house and his father. West walked with a rolling swagger, the confident gait of a confident man, and Ash remembered pacing beside him, striding out through Rouen in search of a bar, their steps matched and both high on the exhilaration of being away from the guns with forty-eight hours leave. He remembered how their hands had brushed, the sound of West's laughter and the weight of his arm slung around Ash's shoulders. Comrades, friends, brothers-in-arms. Closer than brothers.

He could still hardly believe West was here. Just thinking about it made his heart race, a hot sensation burning behind his breast bone. The idea of West working for the family made him uncomfortable, but it did have the single enormous advantage of bringing them together in a way Ash had never dared dream. He'd see West all the time and the thought of having his friend so close, of having someone near who *knew* without him having to explain, was an enormous relief. He was surprised at how happy it made him, and then he was surprised that he barely remembered the feeling. Had he felt happy once since he'd returned from the war?

Perhaps not, but he was happy now and smiled helplessly as he watched Harry swing his bag over one shoulder, the muscles in his arm bunching beneath his coat. He looked so hale, so strong and whole. Ash's chest squeezed, the physical admiration he'd always felt for West pressing against his ribs, swelling into something rather painful. Compared with his own spare frame, West was everything a man should be: a golden-haired, broad-chested, smiling Adonis. There'd been a time when Ash would have given his right arm to look like Harry West. Or to touch him...

"Mr Ashleigh?" John Pierson slouched in front of the French doors that stood open to the garden room and Ash waved him on, embarrassed to have been caught so blatantly admiring his friend. He should be more circumspect.

John slipped into the house, swallowed by its shadows. He was the housekeeper's son and as frustrated a young man as Ash had ever known. Longing to go to war like his brother, John had yet to recover from the injustice of the armistice having been signed before he was old enough to be blown to bits in service to his country.

Ash made his careful way across the gravel, listening to the uneven crunch of his steps, the alien third tap of his cane. He tried not to long for the days when he and West strode out together, step for step. Tried not to regret their passing, nor to think how he must look to West — broken and disfigured.

After the bright spring sunshine, the darkness of the house felt stifling and he paused to let his eyes adjust. The garden room sat still and empty, the clock on the mantelpiece ticking, a fire unlit in the grate. It might have stood like this for a hundred years. He felt its stillness, the unchanging permanence of the room pressing in on him, and for a moment it was difficult to take a breath. He half turned back to the door, longing to be outside again with West. But from deeper within the house came the sound of his mother's laughter; she and the Allens must be in the front parlour, where the light was better in the afternoon. Ash hesitated, knowing he had to see his father, wanting to run until his lungs burned. But he couldn't run anymore and a pang of sympathy for Olive, stranded with the stifling old matrons, returned him to his duty. He at least owed her an apology for abandoning her in favour of West. Once he'd spoken to his father, he'd rescue Olive. She'd like West, he was sure. Ash would take her to the stables and introduce them.

Fortified by that thought, he turned towards his father's study, passing his makeshift bedroom on the way. It had been the breakfast parlour but Mother converted it to a bedroom when Ash was first discharged from hospital, so he didn't need to bother with the stairs. He still wasn't fond of stairs. He couldn't put enough weight on his injured leg to climb them normally, so it took an age. Coming down was more painful still.

Stopping outside his father's study, Ash knocked and waited for the curt "Come" before entering. He tried not to feel like a boy summoned into his father's presence.

Sir Arthur sat behind his large mahogany desk, a pair of spectacles perched on his nose, mutton chops neatly trimmed and only slightly overflowing his high wing collar. Born and bred a Victorian, Ash's father had not adapted well to the advent of the twentieth century. In point of fact, he hadn't adapted at all — with the possible exception of his love of motor cars.

"Ashleigh," he said, removing his spectacles. "You know why I wished to see you, of course."

He imagined it had something to do with West. "I'm afraid not, sir."

His father gestured for him to sit, an accommodation to his leg that felt like a pointed reminder of his limitations. Perhaps he was over-sensitive to such things. He was over-sensitive to many things these days. Either way, Ash didn't insult him by continuing to stand and lowered himself carefully onto the offered chair. "Thank you."

"This West fellow," Sir Arthur said. "What do you make of him turning up here asking for work?"

Ash set his jaw. "Sir, you must understand, Harry West is my friend — "

"Nonsense." Sir Arthur's moustache bristled. "I understand what it's like among fighting men, Ashleigh, the comradeship etcetera — very much like school days — and no doubt you feel a certain responsibility toward one of your men. But I don't like the way that fellow came here, sniffing about for money."

"He didn't!" Ash flushed angrily. "Sir, West is the b-best man I ever knew. He didn't come here looking for money or —"

"Podsnappery, Ashleigh! The only reason I didn't turn him out on his ear was because of" — he gestured awkwardly at Ash's leg — "the service you say he rendered." He folded his hands on the desk. "But to greet him as you did..."

"I greeted him as a f-friend."

"Quite. And in front of the staff. For a fellow officer I could forgive your... your *sentimentality*. But you simply can't go about *embracing* the lower orders. It won't do. Look at all the trouble it's caused in Russia."

Ash stared, at a loss, a desperate bubble of laughter expanding in his chest. He tamped it down hard. "D-do you mean —? Are you referring to the B-Bolsheviks, sir?"

"If that's what they call themselves. Started with too much fraternisation between the ranks, a disruption of the social order."

Different lenses, West had called it, the way they'd seen mankind stripped bare, down to its bloody bones. Private or general, illiterate or scholar, honest British tommy or young Indian *jawan* — they'd all lived and died the same in the end, equally possessed of brutality and compassion, of love and hate. Of pity. Of blood. Just men clinging to their humanity and finding joy in each other, in scarlet bursts of friendship as bright and unexpected as the poppies that bloomed among the dead.

He had no way to explain any of this to his father. He was looking at Sir Arthur across time, across a chasm of experience, looking back into his own lost past. He might have thought as his father did, once. Thank God his eyes had been opened, their lids torn away so he had no choice but to see the truth.

Sir Arthur huffed awkwardly; Ash had been staring too long.

"Well, don't let it happen again, Ashleigh. I won't have the staff unsettled. We get along here very well, just as we always have. No need for anything to change."

Ash opened his mouth to say *Everything* has *changed, don't you see?* But no words came out. He wetted his lips, looked down at the foot that wasn't his own. "Harry West is my friend, sir. I won't deny that."

"Don't confuse a natural sense of *noblesse oblige* with friendship, Ashleigh. Granted, the man rendered you a service—"

"He carried me on his back from the firing line to the Forward Dressing Station, wading thigh deep in mud the whole way." His voice thickened with emotion. "Three miles, at least, and under heavy bombardment." He remembered none of it, yet the images his mind had painted haunted his dreams. He'd slogged through those same trenches himself to reach the front line, knew what West must have endured with the deadweight of a man on his back. The thought caught at his breath like wire.

"Yes, well, very brave I'm sure." His father's jaw ticked, uncomfortable with Ash's unmanly display of emotion. "But rank must be observed. You're the son of a baronet. West is—at your request—a servant in our stables."

He looked up. "He's my friend."

"No, he is not." Sir Arthur's eyes narrowed to dark slits. "We have standards to uphold, Ashleigh, for the good of the household. For the good of the country. Heavens, would you bring socialism here?"

Ash balanced precariously between laughter and rage. "I hardly think sharing a d-drink with Harry West will ferment revolu—"

Bang! His father slapped his palm on the table. Ash jumped half out of his chair. Blood roared through his ears, drowning out whatever his father might be saying, his words slurring into the low drone of distant guns. He fought a ridiculous urge to duck, fixed his gaze on the polished wood of the floor—*floorboards, not duckboards. Look, you idiot!*—and breathed in through his nose, out through his mouth, willing his heart to stop galloping, willing himself to breathe past the tightening of his chest. *You're alright. You're safe. You're home.* Slowly, slowly panic loosened its grip and the room came back to him, or he came back to the room. His father's drone resolved itself into words, words that began to take on shape and meaning.

"…to the dignity of the family. Do I have your word, Ashleigh?"

He blinked several times at his father, aware of cold sweat running down his spine and a churning in the pit of his stomach. "Y-y-yes, sir." He didn't care what he was saying, didn't care that the stammer was worse; he needed to get outside, into the air.

Sir Arthur released a breath of relief. "Very well. We'll say no more about it."

Heart hammering, it was difficult to sit still. He felt airless. "If y-you'll excuse m-m-me, sir." He pushed heavily to his feet, the growling ache in his leg howling into a roar of pain. "I should return to M-Mother and the-the-the — "

"Good Lord, boy, spit it out!"

" — the Allens."

"Yes, very good." His father gave him a closed look. "And don't be too long about that business, Ashleigh. Valuable catch like Miss Allen won't wait forever."

Christ, he couldn't deal with that too. He just nodded and turned toward the door, grimacing at the snarl of pain when the prosthetic settled into place. Sweat beaded on his top lip and his shirt clung damply to his back, making him shiver. The world tunnelled as he stepped into the corridor beyond, collapsing around him, and he barely made it back to his room, barely managed to fling wide the window and suck in a heaving gasp of air, almost choking on the cloying fragrance of early summer roses. *Home,* he told himself. *You're home.* But his leg hurt like the devil and when he stared across the garden his mind's eye painted a hellscape, bodies writhing in mud, white like maggots beneath blue rotting skin. *You're home and Harry West is here.* He fixed on that thought, clung to it. *Harry West is here and you're home.* Slowly, slowly his heartbeat settled. His muscles uncoiled, his chest relaxed and his vision cleared. In the garden, the dead receded and he saw forget-me-nots and foxgloves, lilac and lavender — the English garden reasserting itself once more.

When his hands had stopped shaking enough that he could manage the buttons, he changed his shirt, pasted on a bland smile, and went in search of Olive Allen.

***

Harry had always loved horses. As a nipper, he'd started work at the Angel Inn under the stern eye of the old ostler, George Hawkins, who'd remembered the days when the Angel had been a real coaching inn and still bemoaned the advent of the accursed railway.

The stables at the Angel had been full of noise, bustle and horseshit and it had been Harry's favourite place in the world. Although its eight stalls were always in use, business had started tailing off even before the war wrought its changes. Now, Harry could imagine a time when inns would need to stable motor cars instead of horses. He'd seen the future, after all, and it was lousy with machines.

So it was with a sense of enormous nostalgia that he stepped into the stables at Highcliffe House. Sunshine flooded through a circular window at the apex of the gabled roof, setting a million motes of light dancing. The air smelled of hay and leather and Harry's nose itched pleasantly. Four stalls stood empty, but a pretty mare poked her head out at the end of the row and next to her a larger animal snorted a feisty welcome. Harry cast an eye across the tack and noticed a layer of dust settled over everything. Didn't look like anyone had been riding for quite some time. The floor was solid beneath his feet, but in need of a good sweep, and cobwebs hung in wispy swags from the rafters above the hayloft. Like everything else at Highcliffe, the stables felt gently neglected.

"You're West then, are you?"

The rumbling voice came from behind him and Harry turned to see a wiry old man standing in the doorway, squinting at him from a weathered face, small eyes glittering beneath his battered cap.

"Yes sir," Harry said, setting his bag down on the floor. "Are you Mr. Boyd?"

"Just Boyd." He held out his hand. "I'm glad to see you, lad. I take you as a good sign."

Harry lifted an eyebrow as they shook, the old man's grip very light. "A sign of what?"

Boyd gestured around them, swollen arthritic knots gnarling his finger joints. "Sir Arthur's keen on motoring."

"Ah. Well, I suppose it's the future."

"So folks say." Boyd sniffed. "If it were up to me, I know where I'd send those infernal contraptions. And it's some place the sun don't shine. Come on, let me introduce you to the girls."

Harry grinned, deciding he liked this weathered old man, and followed him further into the stable.

"This is Bella," Boyd said, clucking at the pretty chestnut mare, his swollen fingers stroking her nose. "And that fine creature next door, that's Sable — a little high in the instep, mind, but a beauty to ride once she'll let you."

"Let you?" Harry offered his hand to be sniffed.

"Oh, she's fussy about her riders, that one."

"I bet you're just discerning, aren't you, girl?"

Boyd snorted. "Discerning, aye." He watched as Sable huffed and snuffled and eventually permitted Harry's touch. "She was Mr Ashleigh's horse — well, still is, but he don't ride no more."

Harry kept his attention on the horse, on the white patch on her neck, and moderated the level of interest in his voice. "How come?"

"Because of his leg, I suppose. Ain't ridden since he come back from the war. Shame, because Mr Ashleigh was a good horseman. Sir Arthur and Lady Dalton, they never much cared for riding. Neither did Mr Roger."

Harry would have liked to see Dalton ride, could imagine his lean frame moving with the animal, thighs flexing as he rose and fell. He cleared his throat, face flushed. "Don't see why his leg should stop him riding."

"Nor do I, but he won't be persuaded. Least ways, not by me." Harry felt the man's gaze on him and, after a pause, Boyd added, "I hear you served together."

"We did. No better officer than Captain Dalton, let me tell you. All the men loved him."

Boyd gave a grunt of approval. "Always a good lad, was Mr Ashleigh. I was sorry my Eddie weren't with him at the front."

Harry closed his eyes. There was a protocol, he'd discovered, to this uneasy dance. You didn't ask, you just waited to be told: Ypres, Verdun, Loos, Gallipoli, Passchendaele. The Somme.

Boyd sighed heavily. "He's in Southampton now. Drives a bloomin' motor car, of all things. A 'chauffeur' he calls himself."

Harry laughed in relief. "Bet that didn't go down well."

"That's a safe bet, son. Bloody 'chauffeur'!" His expression changed and he looked away. "Course, we're grateful he come home in one piece, body and soul. I thank God for that every day."

Into the silence that fell, Harry found himself saying, "I bet we can get the captain — that is, Mr Ashleigh — back on his horse. It'd be good for him to ride again if he enjoys it, chase away some of them blue devils."

"Good for the stables too." Boyd flashed a grin, showing the gaps between his teeth. "And our jobs, eh?"

"Yeah." Harry turned back to Sable so Boyd couldn't see his expression; he couldn't help smiling at the idea of doing something to lift those lines of tension from around Dalton's eyes. And if that brought them together more often, then who was he to argue?

Boyd spent the next hour or so showing Harry the rest of the stables and outlining his duties. It quickly became clear that the old man hadn't been managing for a long time, not with those arthritic hands, and it didn't look like his feet and back were in much better shape.

"I get young John in to help, sometimes," Boyd said, once Harry had stripped off his coat and tie and grabbed a broom to start sweeping out the unused stalls. "But he's not got a feel for horses, too interested in aeroplanes and tanks and guns."

Harry grunted. "He's welcome to them. I've seen enough to last a lifetime."

"I bet you have. Ah, bloody stupid business, if you ask me." Harry looked up and Boyd lifted a placating hand. "No disrespect to the boys who perished, mind. God rest their souls."

"You'll get no argument from me." Harry returned to his work, relishing being useful. He was looking forward to getting the place ship-shape again, of using his days to build something up, to make something better. "Don't often hear that kind of talk from those who weren't there, though."

Boyd grunted, shuffled his feet where he leaned against the stable wall. "My son was there. When you're a father, lad, you'll know that's worse than being there yourself."

Maybe it was true, but Harry would never be a father. He had no intention of marrying, had decided years ago that he wouldn't live that lie. But he remembered how Dalton had cared for his men with a kind, paternal zeal and thought that, perhaps, it wasn't only parents who felt that depth of love. "I reckon —"

"Ah, h-here he is!"

Harry looked up, surprised to see Dalton himself in the doorway, a young lady in tow. Boyd scrambled away from the wall. "Mr Ashleigh," he said, touching his cap. "Miss Allen."

"Boyd." Dalton looked sallow, his smile strained. "Miss Allen, m-may I present my good friend W-West? West, this is M-Miss Olive Allen."

Miss Allen studied him. She was a well-built woman with carelessly pinned dark hair and an uncomfortably direct gaze. "Hello, West. Ashleigh talks about you all the time." And then, to his surprise, she offered her hand to shake.

"I —" He glanced at Dalton, who gave a slight shrug, before

wiping his hand on his trousers and shaking Miss Allen's hand. "Nice to meet you, Miss." This, he thought, as she gave his hand a firm shake, was the woman Dalton's parents wanted him to marry. It was ridiculous that he should envy her. And yet...

"You should persuade him to try riding again," Olive said — her opinions apparently as direct as her gaze. "He won't listen to me, but it would be good exercise for his leg."

"Yes, it would." He glanced at Dalton. "Don't see why you can't, sir."

"W-well, you wouldn't. You st-still have t-t-two legs." Dalton looked away as soon as he'd spoken, as if ashamed of the outburst, fingers flexing on the head of his cane. He was leaning on it bloody hard and Harry hadn't missed the worsening of his stammer, either.

"Oh, that's no excuse," Olive said, either ignoring or oblivious to the awkward tension. But Harry caught the concerned look she darted at Dalton and liked her better for it. "There's plenty of men in your position, and worse, who can ride and bicycle and all sorts of things. I'm a VAD at the auxiliary hospital at Chewton Lodge," she explained to Harry. "It's where they send officers to convalesce. We've one poor chap who's lost both legs and one arm."

Dalton flinched. "B-b-basket case," he said, laughing and looking at Harry with desperate eyes. "That's w-what we used to call them, remember? Poor chaps, evacuated from the front in a b-basket. Can you imagine?"

Into the awkward silence, Harry said, "Don't have to." Then he turned to Miss Allen. "Perhaps you'd like to see the horses, Miss? I expect Boyd can show you."

Olive stared blankly at him for a moment, then caught on. "Oh. Yes, well, I don't know much about horses, more of a motorist myself, but we do have a couple of beasts for the men at Chewton..."

Boyd led her away with only a quick glance over his shoulder at Dalton, who stood rooted to the spot. Harry took him by the elbow and felt the iron tension in his muscles. "Come on, let's take a little walk."

Dalton didn't move, staring after Olive. "Christ, I n-n-need a gasper. D-do you have one?"

"Aye, but you ain't smoking it in here. Come on, outside."

Harry half guided and half pushed Dalton out into the afternoon sunshine, then reached into his pocket for his cigarettes. Dalton's hand shook so hard Harry was surprised he got the fag to his lips, but he did and leaned in as Harry struck a Lucifer. Dalton took a long, deep drag and then another, eyes closed. He didn't seem to want to talk, so Harry just stood with him and watched the way his shaking fingers held the cigarette. Musician's fingers, he'd always thought, slender and elegant like the rest of him. He knew Dalton played the piano, or had done. He'd heard him once at Toc H, hammering out *Hanging on the Old Barbed Wire* to raucous applause from the men and pinch-faced disapproval from his fellow officers. Not that Dalton had ever much cared what the other officers thought.

"Hell," he said eventually, opening his eyes, "w-was I just t-t-terribly offensive?"

"Aye."

He took another drag, eyes fluttering closed again. His lashes were very long for a man, cheekbones sharply defined. Harry wasn't sure whether he'd noticed that before, or, if he had, whether he'd just tried not to pay too much attention. "It's my b-bloody father," Dalton confessed at last. "Sets me off. D-d-doesn't mean to, just—I feel like I c-c-can't b-breathe around him."

"Reminds me a bit of General Lowe, your old man. Remember him?"

"W-with that infernal sword? Yes, hard t-to forget. Poor b-bastard. I hope they buried him with it." Flashing Harry an over-bright smile, he looked like he was held together by spit and grit. "Olive means w-well. I shouldn't have said that about the b-b-basket cases."

"She doesn't strike me as easily shocked."

"God, no. She's an oddity. Tough as old b-boots. That's why

Mother think's she'll be g-good for me. Able to n-n-nurse me, you see." His smile wobbled. "Christ, w-what a thought."

Harry snorted, half in derision and half to mask the sharp contraction in his gut. "You don't need nursing."

"D-don't I?" Another drag on the cigarette. "Not m-my leg. That's a b-bloody nuisance, of course, b-but…" He blew out a long, smoky breath. "You know, I c-can't even get on a train. C-c-can't even bear the station. It's not the crowds. That's what p-people think, but it's not. I'm n-not afraid of being jostled, falling over or b-bashing my leg." He gave another brittle smile, knocked the ash off the end of his fag, and said no more.

It had started to cloud over, the stiff breeze ushering in a grey bank of cloud from the west. The vanguard was just creeping over the sun, filtering the colour out of the day. Harry took a guess. "It's the whistles."

Dalton's gaze snapped to his, dark and despairing. "Yes."

"Takes me that way too, sometimes. Gets me thinking about things I'd rather forget."

"W-w-what —" His voice rasped through the stammer. "What do you do?"

"Think of something else." Harry cut off Dalton's budding protest with a hand on his wrist, the bones delicate and strong beneath his fingers. "It's different for me. I never had to blow the thing. I never had to give the bloody signal." Dalton's pulse raced under his fingertips where they pressed into the soft flesh beneath the cuff of his shirt. It made Harry's own heartbeat accelerate, his thumb moving in a slow sweep across the inside of Dalton's wrist.

His eyes widened, dark pits in his ashy face. "I c-can't bear it sometimes," he whispered. "Remembering their f-faces before we went over. I can't *bear* it."

Harry tightened his hold on him. "Yeah, you can. You are."

"B-barely."

"Barely's all you need. We've got through worse together."

His lips parted as if on a silent word, then he said, "Together."

Harry's mind erupted with a wild wish to pull Dalton into his arms, to feel his body, hard and lean beneath the warm wool of his jacket. His heart cramped in sudden, formless longing.

"Sometimes," Dalton said with a laugh like thin ice, "I'm certain I'm going stark raving m-mad. If you knew the things running through m-my head, West!"

Would they be the same things running through mine?

He dropped his hand from Dalton's wrist to take a step back, still feeling the heat of the man's skin against his palm and curling his fingers into the fading warmth. "I, uh, meant what I said before." His mouth moved clumsily around the words. "I reckon you could ride again. Reckon it would be good for you, an' all. Good exercise."

Dalton dragged on the end of his fag and dropped it into the gravel, using the tip of his cane to stub it out. "W-would you help me?" His gaze fixed on something distant in the garden. Or beyond it, perhaps, in a darker place.

"Course I would. Maybe we could ride out together?"

A flicker of a smile, warmer than before. "I'd like that. I'd like t-to ride in the forest again."

"Then we will," Harry promised and turned at the crunch of approaching footsteps. It was Olive leaving the stables with what sounded like deliberately heavy footsteps. She smiled awkwardly when she caught his eye and he retreated another step from Dalton, giving a formal tug of his cap. Dalton's expression tightened in displeasure, but how else was Harry supposed to behave in front of people? "Come and find me anytime you're ready to try." He nodded to Olive and again to Dalton. "Miss Allen. Mr Ashleigh."

And then he retreated to the stables, Dalton's eyes on his back the whole way.

CHAPTER SEVEN

It should probably have felt unmanning to let himself be driven by a woman, but Olive was so confident behind the wheel — she drove ambulances, too — that Ash didn't give it much thought as they swung out through the gate and onto the narrow lane beyond. No doubt his father would have an opinion on the matter.

West watched from the paddock where he was exercising Bella and turned as they passed, his rolled-up sleeves and the open neck of his shirt catching Ash's eye. When Ash lifted his hand to wave, West nodded and turned to watch the car leave. For the past few days, Ash had avoided him, partly in response to that wretched interview with his father but mostly because he hadn't liked West seeing him rattled and stammering. Bad enough about his leg without having his other infirmities on display. He'd prefer West saw him as the officer he'd once been, not the man he'd become.

"I'm glad you agreed to see Major Edwards," Olive said as they left the house behind. "He's a good doctor. I'm sure he can help with the pain."

Ash wasn't convinced, but Olive had been nagging him for weeks and he didn't have any better ideas. "The d-doctor in Calais said it's because they used a guillotine at the clearing station. Damages the n-nerves, apparently. Well" — he laughed — "d-damages them more, I suppose. But b-better than gangrene."

"Yes." From the corner of his eye he saw her lips pinch. "I think it's worth you seeing him anyway. He's always reading about the latest research." She glanced at him, taking her eyes completely off the road for a moment. "About all sorts of things."

There was a look in her eye as she said it that put Ash on edge. Olive was entirely too direct. He rather liked that about her, even though his mother thought it gauche. For now, he decided to change the subject. "It's nice to g-get out of the house," he said, relishing the rush of air as they drove, the green fragrance of the hedge whipping close to the car. Olive was a good driver; he appreciated her competence and felt safe in her hands. Unlike when he was with his father, who drove with complete disregard for either the rules of the road or of nature. His mother point blank refused to get into a motor car with him, which Ash suspected was rather his father's objective.

It wasn't far to Chewton Lodge and they arrived shortly before ten o'clock. Ash had known the house his whole life, but he approached it now with a sense of trepidation. There were fewer men here than during the war, but those who remained were the worst cases — multiple amputees and those with faces so disfigured they might prefer to hide away behind the whispering trees that shielded the house.

He felt uneasy as they drew up in front of the lodge, as if once he set foot within the hospital he might never leave. Christ knew he'd seen enough hospitals for one lifetime. Olive, on the other hand, was radiant as she jumped out of the car and called cheery greetings to the men sitting on the lawn in their bath chairs. In this place, she came alive in a way Ash had never seen before and he watched her, astonished.

She flashed him a grin. "What?"

"Nothing." He found himself smiling too. "You look d-different, is all."

Her expression turned self-conscious, awkward as she often was in his mother's parlour. "I have a purpose here," she said as she walked around the car to help him out. "I can use my mind and I'm respected for it and — Oh, Ashleigh, you can't possibly imagine how that feels when you've never felt anything like it in your life."

He scanned her face, feeling a painful clash of emotions. This damned awful war had liberated her. The slaughter and maiming of a million men had carved out a bloody space for women like Olive to fill, women trapped by social conventions that had propped up the world forever. The same stupid bloody rules that forbade his friendship with West. They should all be torn down and he was glad to see their foundations shaking, but the idea of finding anything good in the carnage turned his stomach. It felt like disrespecting the dead. And the living dead, he thought, looking around at the haunted men staring at him from the lawn. Was Olive's newfound freedom worth their suffering? Was his affection for West — vital though it had become to him — worth the piteous death of any mother's son? How could he bear to consider it a *good* thing?

"Come on," Olive said, taking his elbow to help him up the steps. "In we go."

The house didn't look like a hospital, more like a down-at-heel hotel. A light scent of carbolic soap fragranced the air, not the cloying hospital smell he remembered from his time at the base hospital in Calais or in the General Hospital in Southampton. This was a place for convalescence, after all, not surgery. The butchery had already been done. There were men on crutches, with sticks, or in wheelchairs in various rooms. Some laughing and playing at billiards, other's just watching through vacant eyes. And there were others with disfigurements it was difficult to witness, although Ash stood his ground as a man approached with a raw knot of scar where his nose and one eye should have been.

"Good morning, Captain Albright," Olive said, fixing him with that unflinching gaze of hers. "I'll be along to see you shortly."

The captain made a noise that might have been agreement, but it was hard to understand through the mess that was his mouth, and

Ash just nodded at him as his one remaining eye took him in. The man had all his limbs, but Ash thought that was probably envy he saw in his ruined face. God help him, but Ash felt grateful he'd got off so lightly.

"It's not easy to see, is it?" Olive said quietly as she led Ash along a narrow corridor toward a number of offices. "Poor man's stupid wife can't stand it, hardly comes here to see him. So much for love."

Ash found himself thinking of West and couldn't imagine abandoning him under any circumstances. "Don't suppose there was m-much love there in the first place."

Olive snorted inelegantly. "No, I dare say you're right. Youth, good looks and a pot of money is what passes for love in our circles isn't it?"

Ash laughed. "Good heavens, Olive!"

"What? I know you agree."

"Well I d-do." He lifted a teasing eyebrow. "Only I think you're b-being rather generous. The youth and g-good looks go out the window so long as the money pot is big enough."

"Or there's a title in the case."

They looked at each other and smiled; it felt as though they were reaching an understanding. "Our p-poor mothers. If they could hear us now."

Olive's smile faded. "Our mothers live in a different world."

"I rather think they do. F-Fathers too."

After a silent moment, Olive said, "Well, come along. Major Edwards is in here and he can see you before morning rounds."

The doctor was younger than Ash had been expecting, a thin harried-looking man with wispy blond hair and a kind face. He came out from behind his desk as Olive introduced him, hand out to shake.

"Pleasure to meet you, Mr Dalton."

"Major," Ash said, reminding himself that he didn't need to salute.

Edwards gave a bland smile, then looked past him to Olive.

"Would you look in on Rawlings, Miss Allen? He had a rather bad night and I'd appreciate your assessment."

"Of course." Olive nodded at Ash. "I'll come and find you later."

When the door closed, Edwards said, "Well, shall we take a look?"

Ash had to steel himself to this; he hated it. Sitting in the chair opposite the desk, he began the task of rolling up his trouser leg and unstrapping the prosthetic. Edwards crouched on the floor in front of him to look and Ash turned his head to gaze out of the window. It looked over the lawn that ran down to the gate and the road beyond. There were pine trees all around, murmuring together, and a breath of scented air pushed in through the partly open window to riffle his hair.

"Not bad," Edwards pronounced, his fingers lightly exploring the wound. "Any infection after the surgery?"

"Yes, some."

"But not for a while now? The scar feels solid, no granulation of the tissue."

"Hmmm," Ash said through his teeth.

"Some chafing, though. I think we can do better on the prosthetic. They're doing excellent work at St. Mary's. Do you bicycle or ride at all?"

Ash glanced at him. "N-no."

"Neither?"

"No."

"Swim?"

"I was t-t-told not to — in c-case of infection."

"No, you should be fine to swim so long as there's no skin abrasion." He pressed the withered muscle, then further up above the knee. "Some exercise would be beneficial. And I can show you a better technique for padding the stump. We have a lot of experience here. Of course, Olive — that is, Miss Allen — could show you too, if you allowed it. She's an excellent nurse. Especially gifted with our non-verbal cases." Edwards pushed to his feet with a grunt of effort and went to a cupboard, pulling out a box of bandages. Then he dragged over another chair and sat. "Would you mind lifting your leg?" He gave a rueful smile. "My back…"

Eyes once more fixed on the window, Ash did as he was asked.

Edwards got to work in silence, then after a moment he stopped. "You'll need to watch, you know, to learn the technique."

"Yes, of c-c-course." He turned his head, made himself look as Edwards carried on, explaining what he was doing as he went. It was a hard sensation, looking at this thing on the end of his leg that didn't feel like part of him. He hated it, hated having to deal with it every day, hated the pain. And felt guilty for all of that because he could have had half his face shot off, he could have lost all his limbs. He could be dead. What right did he have to feel sorry for himself?

"How does that feel?" Edwards said once the prosthetic was back in place. "A little better?"

Ash rolled down his trouser leg and put weight on it. The pain was less sharp, he thought. "Yes, b-better."

"Good. I do think we can get something lighter for you, though, if you're interested? We'd need to take measurements, but it shouldn't be too long. I think you'd find it a lot more comfortable." He moved to sit behind his desk, that same bland smile on his face, and said, "Do you think about it much?"

Ash blinked. "It?"

"Losing your leg."

"Well, it's rather hard to f-forget it's n-not there."

"I mean *when* you lost it — the way you lost it."

"I d-d-don't remember that." Edwards didn't reply, just let the silence expand. Ash knew his lie was obvious. "Wh-why does it matter?"

"Have you always stammered?"

"I d-don't. Always." He clamped his jaw shut, hating the ways he was betraying himself. "Only when I'm d-d-distressed."

Edwards spread his hands on his desk. "The interesting thing about the human mind is the way it gets around things — if you try, say, to shut something in it'll always find another way out. Do you have nightmares? Intrusive thoughts?"

Ash turned his gaze back to the window. "I thought I w-was here about my leg."

"You are. But sometimes wounds go deeper than the flesh, Mr Dalton."

He felt his lips part in something like a smile. "Shot nerves, you m-mean?"

"It's got nothing to do with nerve. It's an injury, like any other." Ash considered him carefully, looking for a trap in his words, but Edwards only smiled. "A great deal of work's been done on the subject of war neurosis, you know. Generally speaking, it seems that men who are able to talk about their war experience are less likely to be plagued by difficult memories."

"T-talk to who? N-n-nobody wants t-to hear about it."

"No, they don't do they? I don't think it much matters who you talk to as long as the person's willing to listen. A friend. A doctor, if that's easier. It usually is. I could refer you to someone, if you like."

Which might have been alright if he hadn't had secrets to hide – a memory that haunted him as much as the horror. The press of West's lips against his own felt like a fever dream, an unnatural desire any doctor would feel obliged to treat. Or report. "I'll c-c-consider it. Thank you."

Edwards had one of the orderlies drive Ash home since Olive was busy working. He glimpsed her in her VAD uniform before he left, bright and in her element as she consulted with Edwards, and thought it was a tragedy that her parents would rather have her overseeing dinner parties. What right did the old have now, he thought bitterly, to determine how the young should live? What respect was due to those who'd sacrificed a generation to their complacent folly?

He was still angry when he got home and couldn't bear to go into the house for lunch. Even the thought of it was suffocating. After dithering in the driveway, watching the hospital car drive away, he walked slowly to the stables. The new dressing was helping and the pain felt duller, which only gave him more space to consider what to say to West.

He'd reached no conclusion when he stepped through the stable doors and found West hard at work cleaning the tack. He looked rather glorious in his shirtsleeves, blond head bent over the saddle he was working with saddle soap, the muscles of his forearm bunching with the movement. The air smelled like lanolin and beeswax, horse and home. Ash took a deep breath to clear the hospital stink from his lungs.

West glanced up. "Oh," he said, hand poised over the saddle. "Morning."

"Hello," Ash said stupidly. "Um, settling in alright?"

A dry smile caught at the corner of West's mouth. "Aye. Boyd seems like a good bloke and the room's comfortable enough. Smells a bit of horse, but I don't mind."

"If there's anything you need b-by way of furniture or-or-or anything…" He trailed off helplessly. West looked at him but didn't speak, swallowing as if the answer was stuck in his throat. As if it couldn't be spoken. And Ash felt another surge of frustrated anger. "Oh sod this," he snapped. "Sod all of it. And all of them."

"Sir—"

"D-Don't call me that."

Setting the saddle aside, West climbed to his feet. "Mr Ashleigh—"

"Ash! For Christ's sake, my friends call me Ash. And you're-you're-you're the best friend I ever had." He swiped at the stable door with his cane, blinking hard, and swallowed the roughness in his throat. "I hate this. How d-dare they tell us w-w-we can't be friends?"

West let out a long breath, clearly at a loss. What could he say? *It's not his place to offer an opinion.* Ashamed of making such a fuss—Captain Albright's ruined face sprung to mind—Ash looked away, searching for an apology. Before he could find one, West said, "How about we go for a ride?"

Ash stilled. "A ride?"

"Don't have to go far, just to give you the feel of it again. Maybe to the pub in the village for a pint?"

He hadn't ridden since he got back. At first it was because he couldn't stand the idea of riding about the countryside while his company — while West — was fighting at the front. And then, after the armistice, he'd simply not had any incentive to endure the inevitable pain and humiliation of being less capable than he'd once been. But now? "Yes. God, yes, let's."

West smiled. No, it wasn't a smile it was a grin that lit his eyes from within. "Alright," he said, rubbing his hands. "Perhaps you should ride Bella the first time? I'll take Sable."

"If she'll let you."

"Oh, we're becoming friends." He reached for the saddle he was cleaning and nodded toward the door, eyebrow cocked. "Well, go on then, you can't ride in your fancy suit. Go and get changed."

Ash felt a surge of something vital, like electricity, racing through his body. He laughed. "I'll be right b-back."

When he was halfway out the door, West called after him. "Uh… Ash?" His heart tripped over itself at the sound of his Christian name in West's gruff voice and he stumbled as he turned, grabbing the door to keep his balance. West looked serious, tension in his face. "We done our duty. God knows, we gave our all for King and Country — *you* certainly did. So I reckon we get this in return. They bloody *owe* us."

Ash tightened his fingers on the door, heart thrashing inside the cage of his ribs. "Yes. Yes, they b-bloody well do."

***

Harry had both horses saddled by the time Dalton got back, wearing jodhpurs and boots under his half-belt jacket. It looked so much like his old uniform that for a moment Harry froze. Dalton glanced down at himself with a rueful expression.

"Yes," he said. "I know."

They shared a look and said nothing more. "Come on then." Harry offered Bella's reins and waited for Dalton to come and take them.

"Well, old g-girl." He stroked the horse's nose, leaned in and nuzzled against her. "You'll be good to me t-today, hmm?"

Harry had to look away, a band tightening around his chest. He remembered that gentle tone, the way the captain had adopted it with the men sometimes. He remembered one night, when they were sleeping in the relief trench under a crystal sky, cold falling like blades, watching the captain tucking his own greatcoat over Little Bill, who was dozing, shivering and fevered. *There you go, old chap, that'll help.* He remembered how his own heart had swollen with emotions that were easier to allow in the trenches, easier to call camaraderie or fellowship, as he took off his own coat — *Come on, sir, we'd best share* — and they'd huddled together beneath it, their scant warmth mingling and the captain's head growing heavy on his shoulder. But here, those feelings had nowhere safe to go and the bands around his chest felt like prison bars.

Dalton led the way out of the stable, Bella following compliantly. Harry took Sable, already frisky with the prospect of exercise. She'd want to race, of course, and would need a firm hand. He doubted Dalton would want to even trot today.

There was nobody in the stable yard, which was good because Harry knew Dalton wouldn't want an audience. Although he thought mounting wouldn't be a problem, he could envisage the dismount being more difficult. He hitched Sable to a post and came to take Bella's reins. "Up you go then," he said, watching Dalton's wary expression.

"It feels — It's like going back in t-t-time, getting on a horse again."

"You're allowed," Harry said. "You're allowed to go back to your old life."

Dalton caught his eye. "I'm n-not sure I can, is the thing. It feels like we should b-be going forward if any of it's to have m-meant anything."

Harry smiled, helplessly fond. He admired how deeply Dalton thought about the world, but sometimes his tendency to brood was his own worst enemy. "It's just a horse," he said.

A huff of breath, a chuckle. "Yes, alright, I'm thinking too much. P-Point taken." He grabbed the pommel, half lifted his left leg to the stirrup, then frowned because of course that was the bad one. "Other side," he decided and moved around behind Harry, a hand on his shoulder for balance in passing, his touch, his weight, a nostalgic comfort. "Not used to mounting from this side," Dalton explained, oblivious to Harry's flush of feeling. He seemed to manage well enough, however, as he swung up into the saddle. The only problem was getting his other foot into the stirrup. Harry moved around to help him. The prosthetic felt strange, hard and unforgiving in his hand as he slipped the boot into the stirrup. Dalton looked down at him with tight-lipped embarrassment. "Thank you."

"You're welcome," Harry said and patted his leg. Only it wasn't his leg, so he moved his hand up until he felt the soft give of flesh beneath Dalton's knee and, past that, the muscle of his thigh. He told himself it was a casual touch, but Dalton's eyes went very dark, lips parting, and Harry's hand wanted to linger. "Alright?" he said. "Stirrups the right length and…and everything?"

A swallow, a slight nod. "Yes, very good." Dalton looked abruptly away, toward a scuff of footsteps from the gate: Boyd, with John Pierson slouching along behind, coming into the yard.

"Boyd," Dalton said, clipped and jolly once more. "West here has persuaded me to ride. We're going to try for the Oak."

Boyd gave a gappy grin. "Good to see it, Mr Ashleigh. Very good to see it." John lingered by the gate and Boyd told him to hold it open, which he did with his usual sullen-eyed expression. Harry found himself wondering what the boy saw, not that there was anything to see, but John's mouth twisted in an insolent smirk as he pulled open the gate and it raised Harry's hackles.

With no choice but to ignore the lad, he unhitched Sable and swung up into the saddle, bringing her around next to Dalton's horse. "Ready, sir?" he said, self-conscious under the boy's gaze.

Dalton's expression flickered but he didn't protest the 'sir', just said, "Shall I lead the way?"

With a nod, Harry watched Dalton urge Bella out through the gate. John touched his cap as he passed, Dalton gave a patrician's nod in return, and Harry followed. He didn't look at the boy, just listened for the gate scraping across the path as it closed behind them.

Deciding to put the insolent beggar out of his mind, Harry fixed his attention on Dalton. He had what the gents would call a 'good seat'. That was, he sat nice and straight with a good feel for the horse's movement, although he was clearly putting more weight on the right than the left stirrup and it was throwing him somewhat askew. Harry tried to imagine how much downward pressure he'd be able to exert through the prosthetic, but without having seen how it fitted it was difficult to judge. "A little to your left, if you can," he called out as they walked the horses down the drive toward the lane.

Dalton glanced over as Harry drew parallel, so they were riding abreast. "Can't easily," he sighed. "Rather p-painful."

"Ah well, it's good enough then." Harry smiled at him. "How's it feel otherwise, to be back in the saddle?"

A pause. "Strange, I suppose. Nostalgic." He nodded at Harry. "You ride well. Sable's n-never normally so pliant."

"I love horses, me. And they know it."

"I remember." Dalton smiled, a soft expression that was mostly in his eyes. "You were half in love with those old cart horses in Poperinge."

Harry laughed at the idea. "They were nice old girls. Let me talk to them about all sorts of things I couldn't tell no one else."

"Not even me?" Dalton seemed genuinely surprised. Maybe even hurt.

Harry turned away from that look, fixing his smile so it didn't vanish. *Especially not you.* "Ah, you know how it was. Some things you had to keep inside your head."

"Except when you were talking to horses."

"Yeah, well, they didn't understand." Harry threw him a more genuine smile. "French, see? Didn't speak a word of bloody English."

Dalton laughed, a sound as bright and wonderful as the day.

When they turned out of the gate, Dalton led them to the right and up along an impossibly leafy lane. The banks sloped shallowly upward, trees leaning in to form a canopy of translucent green, shimmering as the breeze stirred the leaves. Bracken covered the forest floor, its earthy tang filling the air, and there was no noise but the horses' hooves and the twitter of birdsong. Harry thought he saw Dalton's point; this was a million miles away from the modern world. He could imagine how easy it would be to hide here, to turn your back on the brutalities they'd seen. He wondered whether Dalton was tempted to do just that — and whether he was afraid he'd give in to temptation.

"Funny thing, you talking to horses. Chap I saw at Chewton Lodge this morning said I should t-t-talk about my leg and w-what happened." His lips turned up into a rueful smile. "Says it would help with the n-nightmares and the st-st-st-st…" He gave a frustrated wave of his hand and gave up.

Harry watched him, chewing on one lip. "Do you remember it, then? When you were hit?" *When I kissed you.* "I hoped you wouldn't."

Dalton looked straight ahead. "Some of it. I remember flying up and b-back. I remember hoping I w-wouldn't land in a shell hole. I d-d-didn't w-w-want to drown." The green wash of the leaves gave his skin a deathly pallor, or perhaps that was just Harry's own memories surfacing. "I remember you p-pulling me up, out of the mud, and-and-and…"

And kissing you. Oh Christ.

"…and not much after that. I d-don't remember it hurting until

I got to the clearing station and then..." He looked down at his hands, which were white on the reins. "Well. I'm n-not sure Major Edwards is right about the t-talking."

Harry wasn't either — he wasn't one for dwelling — but he had noticed one thing. "The stammer's worse when you're upset, isn't it? Like when you'd had a set-to with your father, or when you're thinking back on things. So, I dunno, maybe the captain is on to something?"

A smile twitched the corner of Dalton's lips. "Maybe t-talking to the horses saved you from this?"

Harry fell silent, thinking. How much to say? "It, uh, it's not like I don't have bad memories."

"Of course." Dalton reached out to touch his arm. "I d-didn't mean that. You h-h-have stronger nerves than me, that's all."

"Bollocks. I didn't have my bloody leg blown off, did I?" He knew his smile was forced because, if truth be told, he wasn't sure losing a leg could have been much worse than that horrific slog down the line to the dressing station with Dalton a deadweight on his back, terrified that he'd be a corpse before Harry got him help — and terrified he couldn't survive losing him.

Dalton didn't say anything more and for a while they rode on in silence, slowing as a few of the forest's wild ponies ambled across the lane in search of juicier foraging on the other side. Harry watched them with a smile. "Must have been nice, growing up here."

"Idyllic, yes. School was rather a shock, as you c-can imagine."

"I'll bet, if it was anything like my school." He grinned at Dalton's awkward smile. "It's alright. At least I got to go home at night. I'd have bloody hated boarding school."

"Yes well, I did hate it, with a passion. Still, I suppose it prepared me somewhat for the privations of war." He gave a dry smile. "At least the food was better at the front."

"Waterloo was won on the playing fields of Eton, eh?"

Dalton grunted. "Maybe, but bloody Ypres wasn't."

"Don't suppose you're allowed machine guns at Eton." He

adopted an approximation of Dalton's accent, "Would rather spoil a jolly good game of rugger, old bean."

For a moment, Dalton looked horrified, then he laughed with such a brittle bark that Sable startled and Harry had to soothe her. "Dear God, I hope I don't sound like that — old bean."

"Only a little." Harry grinned at him. "It gets worse when you've had a drink, to be honest."

"And my mother complains at the course language I've picked up." His smile was as brittle as his laugh. "As if that's the w-worst thing I brought back from Flanders."

"The worst thing," Harry said, seriously, "would be the bloody lice. I hope you ain't given them to your mother."

"Ha! She'd disown me." He gave a shivery wiggle. "I'm itching just thinking about the blighters."

The Oak, when it emerged from the trees, was a quaint old thatched pub. White-painted plaster and black-framed windows peered past flowering window boxes toward a pretty village green where a few wild ponies grazed. Harry could hear the trickle of a stream and saw a flash of water on the green — the village pond, complete with ducks no doubt. "Blimey," he murmured, "you really did grow up in a fairy-tale."

Dalton smiled, but the tension was back as he glanced around. "That's what it seems like now, doesn't it? A fairy-tale. D-doesn't feel real anymore."

"But what does?" Sometimes, Harry doubted anything would feel real after the intensity of the war. What joy or pain could ever compare?

He walked Sable toward the stables at the back of the pub, where a young lad shuffled out to meet them. Harry dismounted and handed him Sable's reins, then turned to watch Dalton bringing Bella to a halt. He glanced around the small stable yard and hesitated, shifting his weight from left to right and back again, clearly considering his dismount. Whichever way he did it, there'd be a lot of weight on his bad leg.

"Probably best to lead with your left," Harry suggested. "I'll help — take your weight on the way down."

A sigh, more of frustration than anything else. "Yes, alright." Dalton patted Bella's neck — "Sorry about this, old girl" — and swung his bad leg over and down. Harry caught him at the waist, taking his weight as he descended so he didn't land with a jolt. It was as close as they'd been since that embrace when Harry first arrived. He could smell Dalton's woodsy fragrance, could feel the edge of his ribs, the flex of his waist and the jut of his hips as Harry's hands shifted lower to steady him. Harry held him there, balancing him while he extricated his right leg from the stirrup, the vulnerable nape of his neck bent forward, so close Harry could feel the warmth of his skin.

Hell, but suddenly he wanted it — everything he'd denied for the last four years. Wanted to pull Dalton back against his chest, wanted to slip his arms around him and hold him, wanted to put his lips to that exposed skin and —

Dalton listed back. Just slightly, but a definite pressure, a transfer of weight as if he'd deliberately leaned into Harry for the space between two thoughts. And then he was upright and stroking Bella's neck and Harry was stepping back, heart hammering and mind leaping as he dropped his arms. What was that? What *was* that?

"Damn it," Dalton said unsteadily. "I left my cane in the stables."

It took a moment for Harry to marshal his thoughts well enough to answer. "Uh, do you need it? The pub's right here."

Dalton turned, a flush of pink tinting his pale cheekbones. "Might I borrow your shoulder?" He flashed that devastating shy smile of his. "We can sit at the bench there, outside, if that's alright?"

With a nod, Harry turned so Dalton could put a hand on his shoulder as they crossed the yard to the front of the pub. His fingers gripped tight, digging into the muscle of Harry's shoulder, and he had to resist the urge to slip an arm around Dalton's waist to take more of his weight. He could feel how Dalton limped, the weight he didn't put on his injured leg, and felt a hot pulse of frustration that he couldn't be of more help. "Thank you," Dalton said when they reached the bench, sitting with a sigh of relief.

In the direct sunlight, the tired circles under his eyes were more pronounced and Harry couldn't help reaching out to touch his shoulder. "Guinness?"

"Yes." Dalton smiled. "Just the thing." He ferreted in his pocket in search of change, but Harry waved him off.

"My shout."

When he emerged from the pub a few minutes later, two halves of Guinness in hand, he found Dalton gazing out over the sleepy green. Or perhaps he was elsewhere because his focus was distant and he started when Harry's shadow fell over him. "There you go," Harry said, handing over his stout and joining him on the bench, sitting shoulder-to-shoulder. For a while, they were silent. The ponies grazed, heads down and peaceful, and the handful of houses that surround the green looked pretty as a postcard in the spring sunshine.

"Sometimes I think this is what it might have looked like in the salient — before," Dalton said. "And I imagine — What if it had been here, the fighting, you know?"

"Would never have been here."

"Yes, but it was *here* to the people of Ypres, wasn't it? Their here. They — I think they understand war better on the continent than people do here, don't you? They must do."

Harry took a sip of his Guinness, smooth and bitter in his throat. "You suppose that's a good thing, do you, that women and children know war like we do?"

"Maybe."

Harry turned to look at him, eyebrows raised. "How d'you work that out, then?"

"Because then they wouldn't think that this is what it was all about — 'this blessed plot, this earth, this realm, this b-b-bloody England.'"

Harry sighed, leaning back on the bench to better see Dalton's profile: pale, tense, unhappy. His heart pinched at the sight. "You've got a bad case of the blue devils, ain't you?"

"It all just feels so bloody p-pointless sometimes."

"The war?"

"All of it. What was it for, if everything goes on the same?"

Harry stretched out his legs, let his arm uncurl along the back of the bench behind Dalton who had hunched forward, elbows on knees. "Some might say this is what we were fighting for."

"Yes, exactly. That's what my f-father thinks. But y-you weren't fighting for village greens and sodding p-p-ponies, were you?"

"Nah, I was fighting for seven and six a day." More money than he'd ever earned.

"And the men," Dalton said after a pause. "That's who-who-who we were fighting for in the end, wasn't it? The other men."

He looked so dejected sitting there, shoulders hunched, as if he'd been transplanted straight from the line to this pretty English hamlet. Or as if he'd brought the bloody front line with him; Harry could practically see the Verey flares arcing over his head. And he couldn't help himself, he let his hand drift away from the bench to touch Dalton's back, knuckles grazing his shoulder blade. Dalton stilled. "We were," Harry said softly. "That doesn't make it futile, though, does it? We fought for our company and for each other — we fought to bloody survive. What does it matter what the old men at home think?"

With a sigh, Dalton leaned into the scant pressure of his touch. It made Harry's chest squeeze tight. "Because they think it was glorious. 'Our Glorious Dead.' It m-makes me sick. If they'd seen — " He didn't go on; there was no need. Harry flattened his palm against Dalton's back, rubbed up and down. "And n-nothing has changed. Nothing."

"That ain't quite true. I can vote now, for one thing, and so can the women."

"Some women."

"That's progress, though, isn't it?"

"Hardly a land fit for heroes." Dalton gave him a sallow smile. "D-don't tell me you think it's enough."

Harry smiled too, couldn't help it. Dalton's intensity had always made him feel so bloody affectionate. "I'm saying it's a start. And you know that's a load of old tosh, anyway. We ain't heroes."

"*You* are," Dalton said with a flicker of that reserved smile. "To me, anyway."

Christ alive, he wasn't making this easy. Or — a heart-thumping notion — maybe he wasn't trying to make it easy. Maybe he was trying to make it something else. Harry's arm twitched as if to pull Dalton closer, but the familiarities of the trenches were absent here and anything else would be impossible. They couldn't risk it, even if Dalton wanted to. Could they? And what if Harry was wrong? What if Dalton was just battered and lost and all he wanted from Harry was companionship? He pulled his hand away, sick at the thought of damaging a friendship that meant the world to him.

Dalton stayed quiet and still for a while, then he pulled out his pocket watch and glanced at it. "Better get back, I suppose. I'm in for it already for missing luncheon. But thank you" — a brief glance — "for-for-for getting me back in the saddle."

"We'll do it again. Maybe go further next time, see how you get on with a trot or a gallop."

"Yes, I'd like that. W-we could make a day of it if you have time."

"You're the boss," Harry said, but the joke fell flat and Dalton's smile faltered. He turned away, put his hands on the bench and pushed himself to his feet, standing for a moment staring out across the green. Harry stood too, with a swift flare of anger at the bloody injustice of it all. "Sorry, didn't mean to — "

"To t-tell the truth?" Dalton shook his head, shoved his hands into his pockets. "It's alright."

Harry touched his elbow. "That ain't the only truth."

Their eyes met and held, and held and held, but Harry couldn't interpret the expression in Dalton's searching gaze. "It's not," Dalton said at last, "but it rather overshadows the rest."

That felt like a blow, all the sharper for hitting a tender spot. "Look, I never wanted to ask you for work, and if you want me to go —"

"Christ, no. I want you here. I w-want —" He turned his head, frustrated. "I don't c-care about any of that, only that w-we c-c-c-can't — We c-c-c —" He flung his arms up. "Oh for God's sake!"

Harry took him by the shoulders, turning him around. "We *can*. We can be friends, alright? I won't be taking tea with your mum, but we *are* friends. And, as your friend, I'm telling you to stop picking at the whats and whys of the whole bloody world and just…just live your life. You bloody well earned it." Dalton blinked at him, eyes wide in his pale face, and Harry was suddenly very aware of his shoulders under his palms, of how close they were standing. But he decided to take his own advice and not give a fig. "You could start," he finished quietly, "by calling me Harry, when it's just us. If you'd like to."

A smile, that sweet smile that turned him inside out. Jesus, but it was going kill him one day. "Harry," Dalton said, testing the word, shoulders relaxing and his weight swaying forward. "Yes, alright. Harry it is. That's — Thank you, Harry."

"You're welcome — Ash."

And God help them both.

CHAPTER EIGHT

A sh slept with the window open and the curtains wide enough to let in the moonlight. He couldn't bear to wake in the suffocating dark, unable to see who and what was around him. And he woke a lot, his nights disturbed by troubled dreams and circling thoughts. Sometimes he still shouted out, found himself sweaty and bolt upright in bed with the dreamscape vivid around him. No one came anymore. He'd told them not to because his mother's white, harried face in the dark, the need to reassure her, just made it more difficult to cope. She couldn't offer comfort and he was in no shape to comfort her.

As he'd done tonight, he'd rather strip off his damp pyjama top, light a gasper, and sit at the window staring at the black silhouettes of the trees. Back when he was first home, when the war was still on, he'd sometimes heard the distant thunder of guns when the wind blew from the south. To hear them, to know what the men were suffering without him, had been a worse torture than his healing leg and almost enough to make him lose his mind.

But there was no such noise tonight, thank God. The guns had fallen silent almost half a year ago and the only sound that night was the patter of rain in the trees and the slowing beat of his heart.

He'd got used to the lack of sleep, had rather come to enjoy the night's quiet hours before dawn slipped in and brought the world along in its wake. In the dark, he could think. He knocked ash off the end of his cigarette, watched the tip glow red as he took a long drag. There was plenty to think about tonight and, for a change, it wasn't the past that preoccupied him but the present. Or, more specifically, West.

"Harry."

He liked the way the name felt on his lips, liked the emotion it conjured — something like excitement, something like hope. Alien feelings, these last few years, where the horizon had been so unremittingly bleak. Realistically, he knew nothing could come of his feelings for Harry, but in the privacy of the dark he allowed himself to remember — the first kiss to his brow, the second to his lips, Harry's voice breaking over his name as he'd held him to his chest, the strength of his embrace and the heat of his sorrow. And the knowledge that he'd mattered. He'd mattered to Harry West.

He dropped the remains of his cigarette out the window and lit another, the flare of the match dazzling. His mind wandered into imaginings, into dreams of being held by Harry again, of a different kiss, of what it might feel like to press his lips to Harry's, to lay him down in the grass, to touch his chest, his hair, his shoulders. To make physical the affection forged in the fires of war.

Christ, what a thought.

Yet it wasn't new. It had pulsed beneath the surface of his affection for as long as he could remember. But so what? His fate had been fixed from birth: a career in the city like his father, married to a suitable girl like his brother.

Suffocating.

Maybe he could have stomached it before the war, but everything was different now. He'd lived at the very boundaries of life, met death and diced with her himself, and discovered what it was to love. To really love. Not the pallid domestic duty that sloshed about his family home, but a fierce protective red raw love for the men he'd fought beside.

The thought of squeezing back into his stifling pre-war life stopped his breath in panic. In truth, the only time he breathed easily was with Harry, whom he loved with that same red raw ferocity — and whom he'd love with passion given the chance.

But he wouldn't get that chance. The world forbade it.

"Fuck the world!" he shouted, and then laughed because it was ridiculous.

Thousands — hundreds of thousands of men dead, far more maimed — and none of it was enough to change a damned thing. What use was his own defiance next to that? He took an angry drag on his gasper, tapped his fingers against the windowsill because he couldn't pace, and wondered whether the Bolsheviks didn't have the right idea after all. Overthrow it all and start again.

His hands shook and he closed his eyes, took in another lungful of smoke and tried to calm down. Harry would tell him he was thinking too much.

Christ, he wished Harry was with him tonight.

With a stifled growl, he pushed away from the window, knocking into the table beside his bed and sending the lamp crashing to the floor. He froze, sucked in a breath, felt it ragged in his lungs, and prayed that no one came. He couldn't bear their concern. Standing, one hand braced on the windowsill for balance, the only sound in the room was his harsh breathing and the rage beating like wings in his ears.

Outside, a breeze rustled the trees, catching the curtains and billowing them into the room, rittling Ash's hair and cooling his bare skin with a brief patter of wind-blown rain. There was no other noise, no sound of footsteps in the corridor outside his room or on the creaky staircase. If anyone heard, they weren't coming. At least they'd learned to stay away.

Then, a crunch of gravel outside. He turned and saw a face, pale in the light creeping over the horizon. It was John, the housekeeper's son. Christ knew what Ash must look like, standing shirtless at the window. Half crazed, probably.

After a pause, the lad touched his forehead and Ash gave a stiff nod, unmoving until John walked away. Then he sat back down with a jolt, lit another cigarette, and waited for the dawn.

***

Morning arrived, dank and uninspiring. A low mist hung over everything, pierced only by the distant drone of the Southampton foghorn.

"You hear Mr Ashleigh last night?" John said as he slouched around the stables with the broom.

Harry stopped in the middle of mucking out, leaning on his spade. "What do you mean?"

"Shouting and making a racket. Like he used to when he first come back." John's lip curled, though he kept his eyes on the floor as he gave it a desultory sweep. "Nightmares, mum said. Like a baby."

A flare of concern, then anger, tightened Harry's hand into a throttle hold around the neck of his spade. "Be glad you can't imagine his nightmares, lad."

John snorted. "My brother, Pete, he never had no nightmares. And he saw a man's head blown clear off his shoulders. Went rolling like a football, he said."

Then Pete's a bloody liar, Harry thought sourly. What he said out loud was, "So what? We're all different."

John shrugged and didn't answer, carried on his half-hearted sweeping. Boyd had pressed him into the task and the boy was making his discontent plain in the utterly shit job he was doing. Ignoring him, Harry got back to his own work, although he was distracted now. He wasn't surprised that Ash suffered from nightmares. He'd always had several layers of skin fewer than the rest of them, always thought too much, always felt too much. And he wasn't happy, that was for sure, plagued as he was by this new bristling anger he directed at the unchanging world. Harry shoved his spade into the muck, scraped it along the flagstones with a rasp of metal, feeling irritable and helpless. He'd give a lot to be able to comfort Ash through his nightmares.

"He was half bloody naked, too," John said with a smirk. "Just standing there at the window, bold as brass."

The spade jolted against stone, jarring Harry's arms. "What the fuck are you talking about?" The boy's eyes flared at the curse, but Harry didn't care. "Well? I asked you a question."

"I ain't lying," John said sullenly. "I was on my way back from the bog and heard all this crashing about. He threw something, I reckon. I heard it smash. Frightened the bloody skin off me at any rate. And when I looked, there he was, standing at the window all white like a ghost. Half *fucking* naked."

Harry's mind shied away from the image, stomach contracting anxiously. Christ, poor Ash. "The man can't help his dreams. You should mind your own bloody business."

"I *was*. 'Till he started yelling like a looney."

"Then keep it to yourself. Ain't you got no respect for a man's privacy?"

"If he wanted privacy, he shouldn't be standing there with his curtains wide open, should he? What if a girl had seen?"

"I — You know what? Shut up. It ain't none of your business."

A shrug. "Thought it was funny, is all. Him an officer and crying like a baby. But Pete said all the officers were a bunch of la-de-dah pansies, afraid to get their feet wet, while the real men like him was — "

"Then *Pete* doesn't know what he's fucking talking about!" The noise of the spade hitting the floor ricocheted through the stable. Harry didn't even remember throwing it down, his mind pounding with a thick, angry dread.

John had gone white. "Don't you speak about my broth — "

"Out," Harry snarled, teeth gritted to keep himself from grabbing the insolent little shit and thrashing him into the ground. "Get. Out. I ain't listening to any more of the shite coming out of your mouth. Go on, run back to your mother. You ain't fit to work like a man until you can behave like one."

The boy shook, but with anger rather than fear. He threw down his broom with a clatter. "Alright, keep your hair on." A sly know-ing look crossed his face. "Oh, I forgot. You and Mr Ashleigh were bosom chums, weren't you?"

The hair on the back of Harry's neck stood on end. "You don't know what you're talking about."

"No?" That wretched insolent smirk tugged at his lips. "Maybe I do."

"You think so?" Harry lurched forward, using all his height and bulk to intimidate. "What do you reckon you know?"

Fright in his eyes now, John glanced away. "Nothing."

"What was that?"

"Nothing."

"That's right. You ain't never been to war and you know sod all about men who have. So keep your mouth shut. If I ever hear you disrespecting Ash" — *shitting hell* — "Mr Ashleigh again, you'll feel the back of my hand. Understand?"

John squirmed, embarrassed and angry, and Harry felt his pulse quicken because there was danger here. He recognised the vindic-tiveness in the lad's half-grown face, the malicious mind flicker-ing behind his evasive eyes. Harry always found it best to smooth things over with gits like John Pierson, buy a bloke a drink, make a friend of an enemy. But he didn't seem to be thinking straight when it came to protecting Ash, and maybe that was the biggest danger of all. He'd opened his mouth to speak, to try and defuse the row, when a shadow fell over them both.

"Oi, now, what's going on here?" Boyd stood in the doorway, drizzle beading on his coat, and he didn't look pleased.

"Nothing. John's got work to do in the kitchen, is all."

Boyd stepped further into the stables and jerked his head toward the door. "Go on then, boy. Do as you're bid."

John hesitated and Harry's heart skipped. Fuck, now he was afraid of the little shit. But in the end John just said, "Alright then" and slid a cold glance at Harry as he slipped past Boyd, disappear-ing into the mist.

And that ain't the end of that, Harry thought with clenching unease.

"Well?" Boyd said when they were alone.

"He was — " He picked his words with care. "Seems Mr Ashleigh was, uh, bothered by bad dreams last night and the boy thought it was his business to laugh about it. Repeated some nonsense his brother told him about officers, too, and — " Hell, just the thought of Ash alone and upset tied him in knots. Thinking of that little bastard watching, sniggering and making sly insinuations choked him. Not that rounding on the lad would have helped, most likely he'd just made it worse. "Ah, I'm sorry. I shouldn't have lost my rag."

Boyd pulled off his cap and ran a hand over his thinning hair. "Too much like his father, that's John's problem. You did right, chastising him, if he was disrespectful about Mr Ashleigh."

"Will his father want words, do you think?"

"Doubt it. He's six feet under and has been these last ten years. Got drunk, wandered into a mire, and did us all a bloody favour. Bert Pierson was a nasty piece of work. And, not to speak ill of the dead, but so was young Pete. God rest his soul. I'm afraid John's going the same way."

Harry stilled. "Pete's dead? John's brother?"

"Aye, at the Somme."

"Bloody hell. I didn't know." Harry rubbed a weary hand through his hair. "I wouldn't have said — Bollocks. The boy's grieving a father and a brother, then. Not surprised he's a little shit."

"Bert died a long time ago, but the lad looked up to Pete, right enough. Though maybe he shouldn't have." Boyd's gaze dipped to the floor and after a hesitation he said, "Be careful of John, Harry. The Pierson's have a vindictive streak a mile wide, the whole bloody lot of 'em."

"Careful?" He tried for a laugh, but it came out flat. "I think I could hold my own if it came to a fight."

"Aye, so you could, but he won't fight fair. He'll go for your weak spot, lad, if you show it. That's what he's been taught."

And Christ knew Ash was his weak spot. Ash and what Harry felt for him — maybe, what they felt for each other. He gave a stiff nod. "I'll keep that in mind."

But he couldn't help thinking it was too late; he'd already shown his hand and John Pierson had seen it clear as day.

***

The mist lifted by noon, resolving into a sporadic drizzle. Nevertheless, the horses had to be exercised and Harry wasn't letting Boyd do it in all this damp, not with his arthritis.

After arguing the point, he grabbed a lunge line and took Bella down to the paddock, squelching his way through the mud. He walked her for a few minutes, paying out the line, then had her trot and eventually canter. She was kicking up clots of mud and he could feel his socks getting wet as water seeped into his boots. He tried not to let it remind him of anything else, chose to keep his thoughts in the present. It wasn't like he could avoid mud and rain for the rest of his life and he'd rather not be put in mind of anything he'd sooner forget every time the heavens opened.

As he was slowing Bella to a walk, he sensed a presence behind him. Turning with the horse, he saw Ash leaning on the fence, watching. He lifted a hand to wave and Harry's chest somehow contracted and expanded all at once. Despite a lurking sense of danger, he couldn't help smiling and, after a couple more circuits, decided Bella had had enough exercise, called her to a halt and unhitched the lunge line. "Good girl," he said, stroking her neck, then let her nose at the grass while he squelched across the paddock toward Ash.

He looked pale today, even his lips were colourless, making his dark eyes and hair stark by comparison. But he smiled when Harry approached, the drizzle clinging like tiny jewels to his tweed jacket and the tips of his lashes. He looked… He looked lovely, and that wasn't something Harry had thought before, not in so many words. Their friendship at the front had been intense, but it had been about comfort and companionship and the scraping out of joy from the very worst of circumstances. Here, with the pressure of war gone, those same powerful feelings were overflowing into new channels, like a river bursting its banks.

"You're good at that." Ash nodded toward Bella. "She was listening to every word."

"Aye, well, she's a good girl. Stick around and you'll see something different with Sable — she likes to buck and jump all over the shop." Ash gave a drawn smile and Harry took a breath, plunging in. "Heard you had a bad night."

Ash stiffened, his fingers clenching on the fence until his knuckles went white. "W-what?"

"John said he'd heard something about it. Gave him what for, mind you, for gossiping, but still…" More gently, he said, "You alright? You look peaky."

Ash turned his head away, jaw tense. "Feel like such a fool, after all this t-t-time. I should b-be over it."

"All this time? War's only been over five months."

"M-mine's been over longer."

"Has it?" One eye open for anyone watching, he covered Ash's hand where he was gripping the fence. His fingers felt cold and damp from the rain. "I ain't sure yours is over at all. God knows, you're living with the consequences every day."

"And I'm hardly alone in that." He turned back with a brittle smile. "C-can we talk about something else?"

Subdued, Harry took his hand away. "Alright." An awkward pause followed, punctuated only by the occasional snuffle and nicker from Bella as Harry racked his brain for something else to say. Then inspiration struck. "You want to try lunging Sable? She might respond to your commands better than mine."

"Oh, I'm n-not sure I could —" Ash glanced down at his leg, paused a moment, then looked up with a determined set to his jaw. "You know what? To hell with it, why not t-try?"

It took half an hour to get Bella back to the stables and to fetch Sable, leaving Boyd to rub Bella down while they headed back out to the paddock. At least the sky had brightened, although Harry wasn't sure the watery light flashing through the clouds and lancing up from the puddles to blind him was any better. Somehow, the harsh spring sunshine felt bleaker than winter. But he did his best to ignore it, concentrating instead on getting Ash settled with the lunging line and whip in the correct hands.

"Tell her to walk," Harry said, stepping behind Ash so as not to get in his way, "and use the whip behind her to make a space, like a section of pie, so she knows to move forward. No need to touch her, just hold the space. And keep yourself behind her as you turn — that's right — let her know you want her to keep moving."

Ash did as he was told, payed the line out slowly so Sable walked in wider and wider circles. She snorted and tossed her head, but otherwise behaved herself, even when Ash brought her to a trot. Harry divided his attention between the horse and her master, thrilled at the sight of Ash's smile, the way he bit at his lower lip in concentration, the flush of satisfaction driving the pallor from his cheeks. He looked good like this: purposeful, calm and in control. Not haunted and angry. Harry found himself smiling.

And then Ash stumbled, his bad leg sliding in the mud. Harry grabbed him, hauling him up so hard they staggered into each other, forcing Harry to throw his arms around Ash to keep them both on their feet. And then they were just standing there, breathing into the warm space between them. Harry was intensely aware of his hands resting on Ash's lean back, of the rise and fall of his breathing. "Alright?"

Ash nodded, looking up with such an expression it fixed Harry to the spot. He couldn't move, lost in those soulful brown eyes. Ash's lips parted — pinker now than before — and Harry swallowed hard, rocked by a fierce flush of arousal tingling across his skin.

Then Sable was pulling on the line, forcing Ash to turn with her, to pull away from Harry, and the moment was lost. But there was no hiding from what it meant, no evasion. What he'd long felt for Ash — for the captain — had emerged like a butterfly from its mud-caked chrysalis, transformed into something beautiful and fragile and exposing. It had always been love, he'd always called it love, but now he knew it was more. Now, in that moment, he knew that he was *in love* and helpless to stop. He was lost, entirely lost, and it was terrifying and wonderful and completely impossible.

Ash laughed when he brought Sable to a canter, oblivious to Harry's confusion, gleeful in a way he hadn't seen since Rouen. Harry laughed too, eyes filling, heart bursting. Christ, what must he look like? Glancing around, afraid of seeing John's sly gaze, he wiped his eyes and tried to pull himself together before Ash noticed.

Bringing Sable back to a trot, then a walk, Ash turned, beaming. "Thank you, Harry. This is just what I needed. I spend entirely too much time inside my own head."

"Aye, that you do," Harry said, afraid his heart might be beating in his eyes, afraid Ash could see that it beat only for him. "And Sable listens to you better than me, that's for sure."

"She was always my girl."

"Still is. You should try riding her again."

"I will. I want to feel confident on Bella first." A hesitant look. "Talking of which, I was hoping we could ride out tomorrow if the weather clears up. I could ask cook to pack us some grub. Will you have time, do you think?"

All the time in the world. My whole life if I could share it with you. "I should think so. About eleven, suit?"

Ash nodded "We could try and reach Rowbarrow Pond. It's so peaceful out there in the spring, lots of wild birds. It's pretty and" — he glanced away, pale cheeks pinking — "and-and secluded."

"It sounds nice." Nice? Sweet Jesus. It sounded like an invitation. It sounded like trouble. It sounded bloody irresistible.

Ash gave him a cautious — hopeful? — look. "Let's make a day of it, then, shall we?"

CHAPTER NINE

Olive called in later that afternoon. She strode across the lawn to where Ash was listening to his mother complain about the state of the herbaceous border and the lack of any competent gardeners these days. His thoughts were happily elsewhere, back with Harry in the paddock, in that moment when time had seemed to stop and he'd felt caught in a liminal space between the old world and the new, the old Ashleigh and the new.

He'd never kissed a man, although he'd thought about it a great deal in the abstract. At school and at Cambridge he'd harboured passions for other boys, but they'd been Platonic in the most cerebral sense. At the front, things had been different. He'd become more intimate with men there than he'd ever been before — all the men had been intimate, sleeping, cooking, and eating together for weeks on end, burning lice from each other's clothes, dressing minor wounds, nursing each other through colds and chills and the long anxious nights. At home, all of that would have been called women's work, but at the front they'd had no choice but to care for each other and there his tender feelings for Harry had thrived. Now, back in society's straitjacket, those feelings were seeking new expression and his body was coming alive in ways he'd not had time for at the front. Standing with Harry in the paddock, practically in his arms, had felt like standing on the cusp of something irrevocable. In that moment, he'd wanted to kiss him almost more than he'd wanted to breathe. Everything would have changed if he'd done it, he'd have stepped into a world where he was a new person: Ashleigh Dalton, a man who kissed other men, who desired other men, who loved other men.

The question that preoccupied him while his mother rambled on about the rhododendrons was whether Harry wanted to take that step with him. Ash thought he did — he hoped he did — but to make an error in such a situation would be calamitous.

Such were his thoughts as Olive came striding across the lawn towards them, her skirts flapping out behind her. Rather shorter skirts, Ash suspected, than her mother would approve, far above Olive's ankle boots. She was smiling as she walked, but Ash saw something else in her face that made him frown — tension gathering around her eyes and at the corners of her mouth.

"Olive, how lovely to see you," his mother gushed. "Just in time for tea."

"Oh, I've not come for *that*, Mrs Allen." Olive's gaze flicked to Ash, oblivious to her bad manners. "I'm here on orders from Major Edwards, in fact. He's visiting a colleague in London tomorrow, Ashleigh, and asked me to take measurements for the new prosthetic he discussed with you."

His mother's fingers tensed on his arm. "I see." Her tone implied that such things should not be discussed in polite company. Olive, of course, didn't care a whit for polite company.

It was enough to provoke Ash into agreeing, even though the last thing he wanted was Olive, or anyone else, prodding and poking his leg. "Splendid idea," he said, with rather more gusto than he felt. "Thank you for taking the trouble, Olive. I could have come to Chewton Lodge and seen you there."

Olive shrugged, the tension not leaving her face. "Quite all right, I was passing anyway. Shall we go to your room?"

"Of course." The fact that his mother didn't object was testament to the extent to which his bedroom, cobbled together on the ground floor, was nothing but a sickroom. And Olive, the woman she'd see him marry, was nothing but his nurse. In both their eyes, he had become sexless — a patient. It made him even more grateful for the heat in Harry's gaze. Harry, who saw him as a man, not an invalid. And, if Ash was right, a man to be desired.

That thought provoked a smile as they turned back to the house. It amused him that he harboured a secret passion that neither woman could possibly imagine. He wondered what they'd think if they knew how his blood burned for Harry West, how he, above all, was the one Ash would have liked to take to his bedroom.

They left his mother at the door to the garden room and, while she rang for tea, Ash led Olive to his bedroom. The maid had been in to make the bed — the lamp he'd smashed had been swept up and replaced by another — and fresh flowers sat in a vase on the mantle. The fire had been set, but not lit, and with the window wide open the room felt rather chilly.

"Well," Olive said as he went to sit on the bed. "I hope you don't mind this?"

He shrugged. "It's not my favourite thing, but Major Edwards thinks this new prosthetic will be better. I'm in no position to object."

"I meant me doing this." She turned and closed the door. "I know you feel self-conscious about your injury."

"If I do, that's my silliness, not yours."

She turned, shaking her head. "Lots of men feel the same way, you know. Even the ones who brazen it out in public have a little cry at night. I hope — That is, I'd like you to be honest with me." Her gaze moved away from him. "I hope we're friends enough for that."

He got the distinct impression that they were discussing more than his leg. "I hope so too," he said, and in the spirit of honesty added, "You're right, I don't like looking at it and I don't like — I don't want people to think of *that* when they see me. Stupid, really, when I see what other men have to face."

"Just because other men are having a bad time of it doesn't mean you can't feel what you feel, Ashleigh. We're all different." She pulled the chair from the window and set it in front of the bed, sitting down with her bag on her lap while she rummaged and pulled out a tape measure and note book. "Come along, then. Let's have a look."

Gritting his teeth, he rolled up his trouser leg and unstrapped the prosthetic, setting it aside. Olive had draped a square of muslin over her lap and he lifted his leg onto it, turning to look out of the window as her cool hands came to rest just below his knee. "It's healed well," she said, with a clinical curiosity that made him smile. "I've seen much worse. The wound itself healed *very* cleanly. You're lucky, Ashleigh." A pause. "Not lucky. I mean — "

"I know what you mean, and you're right. I *am* lucky." He turned from the window to look at her face, that strain he'd noticed earlier tightening around mouth. "Tell me how you are." Olive's hands stilled in the act of sliding the tape measure around his knee. "You seem rather tense. Are you alright?"

She gave him a stiff smile and carried on working. "You pay too much attention."

"I try to. Will you tell me what's troubling you?"

"Oh, it's nothing really, simply that… Well." She took a measurement, noted it down with a pencil in the notebook. "It's just that my father is rather heaping on the pressure on the marriage front."

"What kind of pressure? Has someone made you an offer?" He smiled. "Or does he expect *you* to propose?"

She gave a short laugh. "I think he'd prefer to do that himself. At least" — she glanced up, her gaze falling just shy of his — "I'm rather afraid he's spoken to Sir Arthur. You know, regarding your intentions."

"Oh." His face heated, but Olive didn't see because she was concentrating on measuring from his knee to the truncated end of his leg.

Would it be so bad, he thought, it if was Olive? They could

probably be friends and God knew he'd make no demands on her in the bedroom. It would certainly be convenient to have a wife, a veil to draw over his friendship with Harry. And perhaps it would give Olive more freedom, too? He cleared his throat. "Um, Father's not mentioned anything to me, but — That is w-would you l-like me t-to offer — ?"

"Good God no!" She jolted back, aghast, and it took a moment for her to compose herself enough to add, stiffly, "Nothing personal, Ashleigh. I just couldn't abide anyone…" She closed her eyes and gave an involuntary shudder. "I don't want to marry, that's the crux of it. I don't want to…to become a man's possession. And that's what marriage means, you know, when it comes down to basics. A married woman has few rights, even over her own body."

Mortified, Ash simply nodded. What had he been thinking even considering the idea? He may not have any intentions on Olive's person, but she couldn't know that and he could hardly explain. Besides, wouldn't it be just as wrong to use her as a…a screen? As if she had no desire for personal happiness and intimacy, no dreams for her own future beyond marrying. He felt thoroughly ashamed of himself. "P-please don't trouble yourself. I d-don't have any immediate plans to marry." He wanted to assure her that her robust refusal hadn't offended him. "M-my father is keen on it, that's all."

Olive watched him with that assessing gaze of hers, as if she were trying to lift his skin and see how he worked beneath. Eventually she said, "He'll be disappointed, then. Your mother too. Good Lord, and *my* mother!"

"Ha!" Ash gave a rueful smile, relieved that the tension was broken. "They'll be furious with *me*, for not asking you. I see your tactics, Miss Allen. Very shrewd."

"I promise to do all in my power to deflect any blame. Perhaps…" A sigh. "Perhaps I shouldn't call so often? But I rather enjoy your company, Ashleigh. I can't bear the endless parade of afternoon teas and dinner parties Mother drags me to in search of a suitable beau. I feel like a prize heifer at the market."

"Then call here anyway. We can be friends, can't we, without the world expecting us to marry?"

"I find the world to be extremely intrusive in general." She cocked her head. "Not too keen on your friendship with Mr West, is it?"

His heart kicked; her penetrating gaze was rather unnerving. "Harry saved my life," he said blandly. "My friendship with him is not negotiable."

"I'm glad to hear it. Boyd tells me West got you back on a horse."

"He did." The thought of that ride made him smile and he had to bite the inside of his cheek to keep from grinning like a loon. "We're riding out again tomorrow, in fact."

"Splendid." Olive smiled, but it was a wistful expression. And then all in a rush she blurted, "Oh, don't you wish you could just escape?"

He laughed. "From Hampshire?"

"From Hampshire, from society. From everything! I wish we could just do what we pleased without anyone telling us we shouldn't."

Ash identified with that wish in ways Olive couldn't imagine. Clearing his throat, he said, "What is it *you* want to do, Olive, if you could?"

For a moment she didn't answer, but he suspected she was considering whether to confess rather than what to confess. She lifted her chin and said, "I'd be a doctor at the Elizabeth Garrett Anderson hospital in London."

"Heavens! That's quite an ambition."

"For a woman, you mean?"

"For anyone. But, yes, surely more difficult for a woman. Do they even…?" He felt gauche asking whether any medical schools admitted women. "That is, where would you train?"

"At the Royal Free Hospital School of Medicine for Women, in London. But — Well. Major Edwards thinks I have potential, but without Father's support how could I ever afford it?" Her shoulders sank, her hands coming to rest on Ash's leg. "I won't inherit anything until I marry, and since I refuse to do that…" She forced a smile, over-bright with frustration. "As it is, Father already thinks it's high time I stopped volunteering at Chewton — now the war's over."

Ash snorted. "Has he forgotten all those men who still need nursing, who'll need it for the rest of their lives?" His anger flared just thinking of those poor souls at Chewton Lodge, hidden away from the world behind swaying pine trees. Not so glorious as the dead, were they, those maimed and disfigured men? "The war's not over for everyone."

Olive squeezed his knee, a gesture of solidarity. "My father — our fathers, I suppose — want things to go back to the way they were. But we can't let them, can we? No matter how much the old men huff and puff, we can't let things go back."

"We?"

"Our generation. The war shook us up, Ashleigh, and we simply can't land back where we started. I shan't, at any rate."

Her defiance made him smile despite the anger knotting his chest. "Then what will you do?"

"I haven't decided yet."

"But you'll tell me when you have? I'd like to help, if I can."

"Would you?" She looked at him, her gaze scrutinising as the pause lengthened. Outside, someone crunched along the gravel path and Ash glanced out to see John strolling along with a basket of laundry to be hung out. When Ash turned back to Olive, she was slipping her notebook into her bag. "All done," she said briskly. "Now I must dash and get these measurements to Major Edwards before he leaves for the evening."

Ash watched her while he strapped on his prosthetic, noting the determined way she avoided catching his eye. Whatever she might have said, it was clear she'd decided to keep it to herself. He felt rather disappointed not to have earned her trust but understood her circumspection. He'd never dare confess his feelings for Harry to anyone, and her hopes might be equally scandalous in their way—her position, as a woman entirely dependent on her father's favour, was infinitely more precarious. He pulled his trouser leg back down and used the bedstead to lever himself to his feet. "Thank you for doing this," he said and moved to open the door for her. "And Olive? If there's ever any service I can render you in return, as a friend, I hope you'll ask."

She picked up her bag and met his gaze squarely. "Perhaps, one day, we'll be able to help each other, Ashleigh. As friends." Then she reached out her hand to shake. He took it with a smile, realising that, for all her oddities, he'd come to think rather highly of Olive Allen. "Enjoy your ride tomorrow. Please give West my regards."

With that, she strode out of his room, her heels clacking against the parquet floor all the way along the hallway.

CHAPTER TEN

For the first time in a long while, Ash woke up with a sense of anticipation the next morning. He even found himself humming while he shaved, imagining the possibilities of the day ahead. The man in the mirror smiled back at him like a fool and Ash turned away with a shake of his head. He had to be careful.

His good humour remained undimmed until he stepped into the dining room where his father was waiting, the newspaper folded beside his plate, moustache twitching. Mother looked up with a bland smile. "Good morning, darling, did you sleep well?"

No. I never do, as you well know. "Very well, thank you."

"The bacon's rather overdone this morning. I must speak with Pierson."

"I rather prefer it crispy," Ash said, and took an extra helping. "Please pass her my compliments while you're at it."

His father made a noise, an impatient harrumph, as he took a mouthful of his own breakfast, from which Ash deduced he was in for one of his father's talks. He gritted his teeth and carried his plate from the sideboard to the table, nodding his thanks to Culham who poured his tea.

"Out riding today, I hear," Sir Arthur said.

"That's right. Thought we might go as far as Rowbarrow Pond."

"Good to see you getting your nerve back," his father said, with approval. "Taking West with you, eh?"

"It-It-It —" Damnation. He wanted to say *It's not about 'nerve'* but, of course, his father didn't understand. And his mention of Harry had thrown him off.

"Spit it out," his father said, glancing up at him.

Ash closed his eyes, took a breath. "W-West helps me m-mount and dismount, sir. It's rather d-difficult w-with my leg."

Another grunt, whether of agreement or not Ash couldn't tell. "Well, mind what I told you about being over-friendly with the staff, Ashleigh."

"Did you invite Olive, darling?" His mother's sharp look belied her artless smile. "I'm sure she likes to ride."

"Olive is working today," he said smoothly, pleased that his excuse was at least truthful.

His mother's lips pursed but his father said, "I've made an appointment for you with Pollock next Tuesday, Ashleigh. He won't hold your position at the bank indefinitely and it's time you got back into *that* saddle, too."

Cold, clamping panic gripped him. Pollock and his father were both Clare College men — that's how Ash had been given his position in the first place — and a meeting meant returning to Pollock's offices in London. It meant returning to that stifling old world that had hardly fitted before the war and now felt intolerable. It meant taking the train.

"I can't." The words slipped out before he could stop them and he cursed himself for speaking them aloud. His face flushed, heart pounding. He reached for his tea to wet his dry mouth, but his hand shook when he tried to pick it up and tea sloshed into the saucer. Damn it to hell. Damn it all to hell.

"Nonsense." His father's moustache twitched but he didn't look up. "You've been coddled here long enough, boy. If you can ride a horse, you can sit on a train. Besides, how can you marry if you don't have an occupation, eh? I didn't raise you to be idle."

Appetite gone, Ash gave a curt nod. "Yes, sir." He could do

nothing but agree. His father was right, in a way; he couldn't be idle for the rest of his life. It was just that the thought of sitting in Pollock's offices for the next thirty years was crushing. After the vivid horrors and joys of the front, how could he go back to that monochrome life?

He got up and left shortly after the conversation ended, his earlier buoyant mood sunk somewhat by his father's words. Sunk but not entirely submerged. He stopped by the kitchen where Mrs Pierson had made up a picnic lunch for him and Harry, which she handed over with a curt nod. Young John was skulking in the outside doorway and Ash remembered what Harry had said about the boy telling stories about his night-time disturbances. The thought made him flush and he looked away from John's sullen gaze.

All in all, he was glad to escape the house. The morning's promise of a fair day looked like it would be fulfilled and there was even a little warmth in the spring sunshine today. The sky was a clear blue, washed clean by yesterday's rain, the air verdant. He let the weight of his father's expectations slip off his shoulders as he walked toward the stables, pushing aside the reality of next Tuesday's meeting when he saw Bella saddled and waiting with Boyd while Harry led Sable out into the yard. What did any of that matter now, when he had the whole day ahead with Harry?

Harry offered a guarded smile when he saw Ash, the spring sunshine picking out the gold in his hair. "Morning, Mr Ashleigh."

"West," he said, allowing the formality for Boyd's sake. "We've a fine day for our ride."

"Yes sir."

"I hear you're heading to Rowbarrow Pond," Boyd said, walking Bella over.

"That's right — at least, that's the objective."

"Well, I know you're familiar with the area, Mr Ashleigh, so forgive me for saying it but make sure you stay on the bridleway today. It'll be marshy out that way after yesterday's rain."

Ash reached out to stroke Bella's nose. "Thank you for the

reminder, but don't worry, I won't let anything happen to the horses. You have my word."

"Thank you, sir. Shall I take your bag?"

With a nod, Ash handed it over and let Boyd stow it in Bella's saddle bag. While he did so, Ash allowed his gaze to wander over to Harry and found Harry's eyes already on him. They exchanged another smile, lingering just a moment too long for innocence. Ash's pulse skipped and he saw a flush touch Harry's tanned cheek as he turned away to check the buckles on Sable's tack. Still smiling, Ash admired the way Harry's coat tightened across his back when he moved, the competent way his broad hands worked on the saddle. Satisfied, Harry mounted with easy grace and Ash had to look away, partly to avoid staring and partly to smother a flash of envy. His own mount and dismount would be clumsy.

Clumsy, but adequate, and with Boyd holding the reins Ash swung up onto Bella's back and even managed to manoeuvre his prosthetic foot into the stirrup without Boyd's assistance. That was a small victory for which he was inordinately grateful. And then they were off, Ash leading the way out toward Rowbarrow Pond. They rode single-file along the road, then two abreast once they reached the broad bridleway that ran through the forest. It had been years since Ash had ridden this way, but even so it felt like every turn in the trail was familiar, the trees unchanged even though he had become an entirely different man.

They didn't talk much, but the quiet between them was easy. It had always been easy. They did look at each other, however. Every time Ash glanced over, it seemed that he caught Harry's eye or saw him just turning his head away. And there were several times when he felt Harry's eyes on him, felt his skin heat beneath his gaze.

"Do you want to try a trot?" Harry suggested after a while. The bridleway ahead was firm and straight, the trees having fallen away to expose the rough heathland of the forest, gorse and heather and grasses on both sides of the path and not a soul in sight.

Ash shifted his weight, testing the angle on his prosthetic. It would probably hurt but what the hell? "Alright," he said. "Let's have a go." He softened the reins and squeezed his legs, hoping he was getting the pressure correct on his left. After a moment Bella responded and Ash's instinct took over as he rose to an awkward posting trot, the stiffness of the prosthetic not making it easy and the angle of his leg uncomfortable. Nevertheless, he was doing it and that was enough to make him smile. He flashed Harry a look and he grinned back, trotting along next to Ash.

"A canter might be easier," Ash decided and sat down, tipping one hip forward as he squeezed his legs to ask for the canter. Bella tossed her head and then they were off, the balance easier now he was sitting and the weight was off his leg. Harry kept pace, the wind blowing the hair back from of his face and adding an interesting flush to his cheeks. Ash's racing heart pounded in time with Bella's hooves, although whether from the exhilaration of the ride or from the sight of Harry at his side he wouldn't have liked to say.

They cantered for a short time, then dropped back into a trot and then a walk. Ash was breathless from the unaccustomed exercise, blood singing and thighs burning, but he couldn't stop grinning. It was the most alive he'd felt in a long time. "That was bloody good fun. Christ, I've missed this."

Harry breathed hard too, face bright as he said, "You look good on a horse, Ash. You ride well."

"Thank you." The compliment made him blush and he looked away, smiling and uncertain. He wanted—He hardly knew how to think about what he wanted. He wanted Harry, his smile and company and the warmth between them, but there was also a deep, dark beat of desire fiercer than any of that. A desire he might never be brave or foolish enough to act on. "You, ah, you've got a good seat yourself."

"Aye, so I've been told." Harry grinned at him and Ash felt himself blush harder. Was that—? Was that flirtation? Harry nodded toward a sparkle of sunlight ahead. "That's our pond, is it?"

Tearing his gaze away, Ash squinted ahead and spotted the edge of the water. "Yes, that's it. We should find a spot near there to stop and eat. Are you hungry?"

"Ravenous. Breakfast was a long time ago."

Ash had hardly eaten in the end, and after all this unusual exercise he was feeling hungry too. "If I remember right, there's rather a nice old tree we can stop at. You have to be careful around here, like Boyd said — there are mires and so forth."

Harry cocked an eyebrow. "Like the one old Pierson drowned in?"

"You heard about that?"

"Aye, Boyd told me."

Ash nodded. "Bad business, that." But his mind's eye saw Jimmy Tilney struggling in the waterlogged shell hole, begging them not to let him drown, and Ash lying to him, promising they'd get him out until Jimmy's face went under, limbs thrashing, and —

"Ash." Harry touched his arm, reaching over from Sable, his face clouded with concern. "Alright?"

He startled back to himself, the greens and blues of the world almost blinding. "Yes, I… Sorry."

Harry didn't let go of his wrist, his warm fingers strong and uncompromising, his expression knowing. But, thank God, he didn't say anything other than, "Is that the tree you were talking about? The oak?"

Ash still felt dislocated, but he blinked a couple of times and focussed on the tree with its sturdy branches covered in the first flush of spring leaves. "Yes. Yes, this is the place." He looked around at the still pond, the heathland and birds skimming over the water, and it looked alien, as if he'd transplanted himself straight from Flanders to this bucolic English scene. He half expected to look down at himself and see his uniform.

"Come on." Harry let go and the loss of his touch disturbed him like the loss of an anchor. Panic rose and he bit it back with a ruthless act of will. *I'm not there, I'm here. I'm here with Harry.* Fixing his attention on Harry's back, he watched him walk Sable onto the grass and swing down from the saddle, hitching her reins to a low branch. Turning, he came forward to take Bella's reins, his fingers brushing Ash's as he handed them over and their eyes meeting for a fluttering second. Christ, but Ash was all over the place today. He felt thin as paper, liable to be swept up and away by his riotous feelings.

Once Bella was tethered, Harry moved around to help Ash dismount. As before, he swung his bad leg over Bella's back and felt Harry's hands on his waist to steady him, to take his weight until he could get his good leg on the ground. And all he could feel was the strength of those hands, the way Harry's fingers flexed against him, the heat of his chest pressing against Ash's back. He leaned into that touch, but only for a moment because Harry stepped back suddenly, clearing his throat and turning away. Ash couldn't move, concentrated on stroking Bella and taking his time to unstrap his cane, giving himself a moment to slow his pounding heart and decide what to do. It was possible, he thought when he'd stood there too long, that he'd never know what to do about Harry West.

"I brought a blanket."

Ash glanced over to see Harry spreading it out in a patch of warm sunlight under the tree. He looked up and their gaze met and held again and — good Lord — Harry bit his bottom lip in a gesture so deliciously uncertain that Ash thought his heart might leap right out of his chest. He'd barely got enough wits about him to remember to pull the picnic from his saddle bag before he made his way over to the blanket.

He manoeuvred himself down onto the ground without help, although he could feel Harry watching him with a heat much fiercer than the warm spring sunshine. They sat a respectable distance apart while they ate, a twelve-inch no man's land stretching between them. It was a gulf he had no idea how or whether to cross.

Cook had packed a veritable feast: pork pies, lemonade, apples and two big slices of pound cake. It was delicious and he tried to focus on that as they watched the water, enjoying the quiet. But he was too aware of Harry, as if each nerve was attuned to the man. When Harry shifted, Ash felt it, when his eyes flicked to Ash, he felt their heat. When Harry lay back on the blanket to stare up through the leaves, Ash watched with such a knot in his chest he could hardly breathe. He wanted to kiss him, that was the thing. He wanted to lean down and press his lips to Harry's mouth just like Harry had once kissed him. But this time he wanted to taste lemonade on his lips, not blood and tears. He wanted to run his fingers into his hair and kiss the delicate skin of his eyelids, the firm line of his jaw, the vulnerable Adam's apple bobbing as he swallowed. But he didn't dare. Instead he lay down too and gazed up at the fluttering leaves, past them to the blue of the sky, until his eyes drifted shut and a lazy sleep overtook him.

***

Harry didn't doze. He lay on the blanket, propped up on one elbow, and watched Ash sleep. His lips were gently parted, dark lashes stark against his too-pale face, with a thick tumble of hair falling over his forehead making Harry's fingers itch to push it back from his face. Gazing at him like this felt like a privilege, although they'd slept side by side often enough in dugouts and support trenches. He'd slept with Ash's head on his shoulder, so close he could have kissed his hair had he dared. He wished he had, wished he'd thought to do it back then when he'd had the chance. Here, it felt impossible. Ash was lord of the manor, Harry his loyal retainer, and the world was set against them in every possible way. If he'd been a gent himself, or Ash a working man, then maybe there would have been a way for them, but as things were....

God, he wished they lived in a different world. In that better world Ash thought they deserved. Then he could lean down, take Ash in his arms, and —

And if wishes were horses, Harry West, beggars would ride.

He wrenched himself away. The worst of it was that he was certain Ash wanted the same as him, but Ash wasn't doing a thing about it. And he was right not to, Harry knew that; it was too bloody dangerous, too big of a risk. If they were caught… He had to think of Kitty and the girls, couldn't bring any shame to them for his own selfish reasons.

With a grunt, he got to his feet and stalked toward the soggy edge of the pond. Behind him, Ash stirred but Harry didn't turn around. He needed a moment to himself, to get his churning feelings under control. The pond wasn't much like the sort of pond he knew. It had no real shape to it, a haphazard marshy type of dip in the ground with the sun glinting on its surface and birds flitting and chirruping all around. A bleak landscape, really, and he wouldn't like to be here on a miserable day like yesterday. With the colour leached out of the boggy heath, it would be a very different place. He pushed the thought aside before it could get its claws in and looked away to his right, where the water's edge curved back on itself. A crop of pretty purple flowers drew his eye, just the colour Kitty would like. He headed over to look—

—and the ground disappeared from beneath his feet. "Fuck!" Shock sucked the air from his lungs as he found himself up to his waist in cold clammy mud.

"Harry!" Ash scrambled awkwardly to his feet, staggering over the uneven grass towards him. "Don't move."

"Jesus fucking Christ it's cold. No wait!" He held up a hand to ward Ash off. "Don't come closer, you'll end up in it as well."

"You won't get out without help." Ash was sheet-white as he looked around frantically. "Damn it," he balanced himself awkwardly and held out his cane. "Here, can you reach the rifle?"

Harry stared at him. "What?"

"The-the-the—" Wild panic twisted his features. "The cane. C-Can you reach it?"

Harry tried, but when he leaned toward it, he started to tip forward, deeper into the mire. "No. Shit. Is there a branch or something longer?"

"No. I c-can get closer."

"Don't!"

"I won't let you drown."

"I'm not going to drown. Ash, *stop*." But Ash had already dropped awkwardly to his knees, edging forward and reaching out with the cane. This time it was almost close enough. He could touch the end of it with his fingertips but couldn't get hold of it.

"Grab it," Ash barked, then flinched, flattening himself against the ground. "Just fucking grab it, man."

And, no, this wasn't Ashleigh Dalton of Highcliffe House. This was someone else entirely, someone Harry remembered well. "Hang on." Harry kept his voice calm as he probed with his feet. He'd found the bottom, he wasn't going to sink deeper, and edged forward half a step. Ash watched him from a haunted face and Harry was dead certain the poor bastard was seeing ghosts. His fingers closed around the cane, but he was afraid to tug too hard for fear of unbalancing Ash. "I've got it, can you pull?" Ash didn't move. "Ash? I've got the cane." Nothing. Ash just stared right past him, glassy eyed. "Dalton?" Bollocks. "Captain. Hey! Captain Dalton."

Ash blinked, twitched, and stared at Harry. "W-West?"

"Pull me out," he snapped. "Come on, pull."

Ash nodded, scrambling backward as he hauled on the cane until Harry could reach solid ground with his hands and started to push and wriggle himself out of the mire. Flopping without any dignity onto his belly, he hauled his legs free of the mud. Then he rolled onto his back and sucked in a breath of air. "Ugh, that was bloody stupid."

"Yes, rather." Ash sounded all wrong and Harry squirmed onto his knees to peer up at him. Ash was on his feet but didn't look well. For a start, he was shivering like he was frozen, his face grey and eyes too wide.

Standing up, Harry forgot the chill of his sodden clothes and took a step closer. "You got me out," he said, treading carefully because he knew full well where Ash's mind had gone. It was an effort to keep the memory at bay himself, but Ash had always felt this worse.

Jimmy had been one of his men, after all. His responsibility.

Ash nodded, blinking rapidly. "Yes. Yes, that's right. I, uh… I —" He pressed a shaking hand to his mouth. "S-s-sorry —" He made a choking noise and it took Harry a moment to realise it was a sob. "Oh G-God."

He hesitated for half a heartbeat, wrestling with what was proper, before deciding to hell with proper and pulling Ash into his arms. "I know," he said, holding him close. "It's alright, I know."

After a slight resistance, Ash sagged against him, his head dropping heavily onto Harry's shoulder. "I c-c-c-couldn't reach him."

"There was no way to." Harry cupped the back of his head, stroking his hair, trying to soothe him. "We were under fire. You did all you could."

"It w-wasn't enough."

"No." He flinched from the memory. "But nobody could've done more."

"I d-dream about him all the time. He st-st-stares at m-me and I c-c-c-can't reach him."

"Ah, Ash, you poor sod." Harry held him tighter and it was so natural in that moment to press his lips against his hair that Harry barely knew he'd kissed him until Ash stilled. Harry's heart thundered into life, pounding hard enough Ash must feel it hammering against his chest. Even so, Ash didn't draw back and Harry didn't let go; he couldn't bear to. He just breathed in the woodsy scent of Ash's hair and, with terrifying tenderness, let his lips brush the shell of his ear. A soft noise escaped Ash's throat, breath shuddering hot against Harry's neck, lips moving tentatively against his skin. Harry's stomach contracted so hard it hurt.

Airless with anticipation, he turned his head to nuzzle Ash's jaw, let their noses bump, breath mingling. Into the vanishing space between them Ash whispered "Harry" and then their lips touched with a soft, generous heat. Harry trembled from head to toe, hair rising on the back of his neck, running in shivers along his arms. In that moment, there was nothing in the world beyond Ash's lips moving against his own, his fingers curling into Harry's lapel, pulling him closer and deepening their kiss into something infinitely tender and utterly overwhelming.

It was the most perfect moment of Harry's life. He wanted to inhabit it forever.

But then one of the horses snorted and Ash jerked around, looking over his shoulder in alarm. There was nobody there but when Ash turned back toward him his tear-streaked face was flushed with concern, eyes dazed beneath his dark lashes. Harry suspected he looked the same. For a while, they just watched each other, the sun skipping in and out from behind the clouds and the birds swooping over the water. Ash gave a nervy laugh and said, "Christ, I've wanted to do that for the longest time."

"Me too." Harry lifted a hand to Ash's hair, sweeping it away from his forehead, just as thick and silken as he'd imagined. He loved how it felt slipping through his fingers. "That too," he said with a smile.

"You did that once before." Ash's gaze darted backward and forward over Harry's face as if he was trying to see beneath his skin. "When I was injured."

"You remember that." He'd hoped Ash had been too far gone to remember anything about those hellish hours.

Ash reached out and touched his face, fingertips brushing his lips. "I remember you kissing me."

"A last kiss, for the dying." Harry's voice caught at the memory, turning husky. "Worst bloody days of my life, those were. I thought I'd lost you."

"You'll never lose — " But he was making promises he couldn't keep and they both knew it. Ash's expression crumpled. "Harry, what are we going to do?"

He had no answer, not one worth a farthing beyond this moment. He didn't want to think about a future without Ash, but he couldn't imagine one where they were together. It was impossible, he knew it was impossible. So he gathered Ash closer, threading his fingers into his hair, and kissed him again. Ash pressed in hungrily, the taut lines of his body softening in Harry's arms, his breath a wash of heat against Harry's lips. It was urgent and desperate and when Ash staggered a little, Harry barely managed to keep them both from toppling over. Ash looked as wild as Harry had ever seen him, his hair dishevelled, chest heaving, cheeks flushed.

Harry set his hands on his shoulders and held him at bay. "What we're going to do," he decided, "is get ourselves home and out of these filthy clothes. This bloody mud stinks worse than a latrine. And then…"

"And then?"

He smiled, squeezing Ash's shoulders. "Then we'll work out how we can do this again. And again. For as long as we bloody well can."

CHAPTER ELEVEN

Ash sank beneath the surface of his hot bath, blinking up at the blurred ceiling through the water. Wavering morning sunlight cast the room pale gold, making patterns on Ash's stomach. Slowly, he surfaced into the steam, leaning back and letting the water lap about his ribs. Outside, the sky was the cool blue of spring and somewhere beneath it was Harry West.

Harry, who'd kissed him yesterday and brought him home shivering from the cold mud and memories, who'd handed him over with a long look into the languid care of his mother. Harry, who meant the world to him, and who the world would deny him. Harry, whom he loved.

He traced a fingertip over his bottom lip, as if that might recapture the sensations of their kiss. But nothing could match the heat and softness of Harry's mouth, the gentle nip of his teeth, the sensuous slide of his tongue. He remembered everything, from the cold, dream-terror clawing out of the mire to snatch at his ankles, to the astonishing comfort of Harry's arms around him, of his lips caressing his ear, of their hot, incendiary kiss that had jolted him back to life. Until that moment, Ash had had no idea his body could ignite in such a way, every inch of skin blazing, desire running through his veins in place of blood. Heart aflame.

He'd loved Harry for a long time — known him to be his closest companion, his dearest friend — but this acute physical desire was new. Or, rather, not new but newly uncovered like coals with the ashes knocked off. Dreaming of kissing Harry in an abstract way was as nothing to the reality, and now he'd tasted it for real it was all he could think about. He wanted more, he wanted to go further. Could they go out riding again today? Would it look strange? He didn't think he could wait any longer.

As if to confirm his pressing need, he had a roaring jack for the first time since he'd been wounded. He gazed down at himself and trailed a finger across the swollen head of his prick, marvelling at the indisputable fact that he could still muster a rise. It had been a long time and he'd wondered whether it had been knocked out of him along with everything else, but one kiss from Harry and… Christ, just the thought of him had Ash twitching. He daren't take himself in hand, however; the bathroom door wasn't locked because, of course, he needed help getting in and out of the bath. He cursed the fact, tried to will himself under control, and, when that didn't work, stared deliberately at the raw, truncated end of his leg. That was enough to sober him.

After Culham had helped him out of the bath and left so that Ash could dress with some modicum of dignity, he sat for a while staring out over the gardens below. There was no possible future for this love he felt for Harry, he knew that. Queerness aside, their difference in social rank made even friendship impossible. He knew it with the same certainty he knew that one day he would die.

But he was familiar with death, had seen it drop out of a blue sky with a thud and turn a smiling face into bully beef. And it occurred to him, sitting in his birthday suit in the bathroom, that he was familiar too with living under death's shadow and taking every moment left, every ounce of time allotted, not giving a damn for the dark wings above. In a similar way, the knowledge that he and Harry must one day part didn't stop him from wanting to pursue what was blossoming between them. Quite the contrary: it made Ash want to savour every illicit moment, not to waste another second. He wanted everything they could have and he wanted it right now because, for them, there could be no tomorrow. There was only today.

The thought made him impatient with the morning. It was Sunday, and the household must be seen in Church. Ash hated church, even more so now than before the war when the ritual had simply bored him. Now he felt restless beneath the cold, silent weight of medieval stone as if he and it couldn't exist in the same place. Now, the martyred saints looking down at him from stained glass windows reminded him of other martyred faces and he thought those long dead saints hadn't suffered half as much as his newly dead men.

Now he wondered what use he was supposed to have for a God who'd witness hell on earth and not lift a finger to end it.

He sat with his parents, arms crossed over his chest, cane resting against the end of the pew. Sensation prickled the back of his neck and he glanced over his shoulder, his gaze unerringly meeting Harry's. He sat near the back, with Boyd and the other servants, but Ash hardly noticed them. He smiled, couldn't help himself, at the sight of Harry, his heart inflating with joy. Harry didn't smile, not with his mouth, just gave a respectful nod. But Ash could see light in his eyes and felt his helpless grin broaden. It was an effort to turn back around when the service began.

He made a point of not listening as Reverend Pratham delivered his serman, bowed his head and let his mind drift during the prayers, lips mouthing 'Amen' when required. He decided he would find Harry in the stables after lunch, persuade him to ride out again this afternoon. Harry wouldn't be working, so there could be no objection on that front, and if his father thought a Sunday ride wasn't quite the thing then too bad. He was sick of his father's antediluvian opinions.

"…our glorious dead," Reverend Pratham said and Ash looked up sharply. Pratham, smug faced, stood with hands clasped piously before him. "In London, a great victory parade is to be held on

Peace Day to mark the signing of the treaty, and here in Hinton we're to have a Peace Pageant on the same day – Saturday the 19th of July – on the village green. I'm sure you'll agree, it will be a fitting way to celebrate our victory."

Celebrate. Ash shifted on the pew, a flash of liquid anger spreading out from behind his breastbone. *Celebrate?* His chest tightened and he had to loosen his tie. It was hot in the Church, the spring sun shining directly onto him through the sorrowing face of St. Stephen. He looked up and for a strange moment it was Harry's face looking back at him, grey with fear as the whistles blew along the line.

Ash jerked his head around, sweat sticking his shirt to his back. A *pageant*? What use was a pageant to the dead, what use to the maimed? Pratham droned on and the air in the church thickened until it was unbreathable, sticking in Ash's throat, clogging his lungs. He coughed, earned a reprimanding glare from his father, and clenched his fingers into fists.

He should say something — object — but the words stuck in his craw, choking him. What could he say that these people would hear?

The organ wheezed into life and the congregation stood. Ash pushed himself upright, swayed beneath a flash of light-headedness and had to catch himself on the pew in front. His stomach cramped and he felt sick, trying not to double over as his mother started warbling *Abide With Me*. His body expressed what his voice could not — the hard pressure in his chest was a scream of fury, pain and frustration buried deep and deadly as a mine.

A hand squeezed his arm. Harry stood in the aisle next to him. "You look like you need some air, Mr Ashleigh," he said quietly. "Let me help you outside."

Ash stared, that trapped scream choking him. When Harry gave him a meaningful look, head cocked, Ash could only nod. They walked up the aisle together, Harry's hand on his elbow, steadying him, and the tap of his cane against the stone floor audible over the organ and the congregation's singing. Eyes followed him but Ash ignored them all — all but John Pierson's smirking gaze. He felt *that* like cold water against fevered skin, a cold fear squirming in the pit of his belly.

Stupid. Pierson was barely more than a boy.

Harry turned them to the left, through the door, and then they were past the vestibule and out into the spring sunshine. Ash gulped in a breath. It felt like the first one he'd taken in minutes, and Harry guided him to the bench beside the doorway. "Sit," he ordered, and Ash sat, leaning forward to rest his head in his hands. "Bloody hell," Harry said softly. "A parade. And a pageant?"

Ash barked out a laugh and it released some of the intolerable pressure in his chest. It was such a relief to be understood without having to explain. "Quite."

"How much is it going to cost, that's what I want to know. This bloody government can't pay a soldier a decent pension, can't find work for half the men back from the war, can't house them — can't even bloody well feed them — but somehow there's money for a victory parade through London?"

Ash lifted his head, startled by the vehemence in Harry's voice. "I hadn't thought of that," he admitted. "I was only thinking of…" He waved a hand, as if that could encompass the bloody ruin of war.

"I know." Harry shoved his hands into his pockets and sighed. "Some people will like it, I suppose."

"The likes of John Pierson and his mother," Ash agreed, sitting up. The pain in his stomach had eased, his breath no longer too tight in his chest.

"They're grieving." Harry said that with more compassion than Ash felt. "It brings them comfort to think of the man they lost as a hero."

Ash worked his jaw around a bitter reply, but if he couldn't say it to Harry then he couldn't say it to anyone. "What right do they have to comfort? Why should they imagine glory when the truth is blood and mud and horror?"

"Because it's kinder."

"Kinder?" Ash snorted. "Easier, you mean. Wrap it all in King and Country and forget what war really is. It betrays them, it betrays everyone who died."

Harry fell silent. "You think they'll forget?" he said after a pause. "You think the people in there will *forget* what they've lost? Giving a grieving mother comfort doesn't betray the dead, Ash. You think Jimmy Tilney would want his mother to know how he died?"

Ash felt himself pale, blood draining. "No," he said softly, gaze fixed on Harry's flushed, upset face. "No, of course not."

"No. And the same goes for all the other poor buggers who bought it out there."

"Except…"

Harry's lips thinned but Ash pressed on regardless. He couldn't seem to stop.

"Except it's a lie, isn't it? How can we respect the dead when we're not even telling the truth about how they died? That's not respect." He shook his head. "A pageant, Harry. A *celebration*."

Harry sighed, shoes scraping against the paving stones. "I don't like it, either. It feels…wrong." A pause. "Everything feels wrong. Has done since I came back, if I'm honest."

He was standing close enough that, when Ash reached out his hand, he could touch the tips of Harry's fingers. "Not everything," he said quietly.

Harry lifted his eyes to Ash's. "No." Turning his hand, he tangled their fingers together, expression softening. "Not everything."

Voices drifted from within the church and Ash dropped his hand. Under his breath he said, "When can we see each other again?"

"I don't know." Harry eyed the church door. "We have to be careful."

"We are."

"John Pierson —"

"Is a little shit. So what? What's he going to do?"

Harry didn't answer, but it was a stupid question anyway; it was obvious what he could do if he knew what they'd done. Ash pushed himself to his feet and took a step forward, close enough that his fingers brushed Harry's again. "Come on," he said. "We'll go riding this afternoon — somewhere secluded."

When Harry swallowed, Ash could see his throat move and he stood so close he could hear the hitch in his breathing. "Yeah, alright. You'll come to the stables?"

"As soon as I can get away. I want — " He almost lost his nerve. "I want to kiss you again."

Harry's lips parted and Ash had a flash of memory — the warmth of his lips, the press of his strong body against Ash's own. "Yeah," Harry said roughly. "Me too. And more."

More. Ash felt a twitch below his belt, a flush of heat across his skin and goosebumps rising on the back of his neck. "Christ, Harry," he said just as the first of the congregation emerged into the sunlight.

Harry took a casual step back and Ash turned away, staring out across the church yard until he was master of himself again. When he eventually heard his father thanking Reverend Pratham, Ash turned around and re-joined his parents.

"Ashleigh, darling," his mother said. "Are you feeling better?"

"Yes, thank you." To the vicar, he added, "I'm so sorry Reverend Pratham, I hope I didn't disturb the service too badly."

"Not at all, Mr Ashleigh. You did look rather green about the gills. But now look, here's Miss Allen come to say good morning. She'll put you right." He offered Ash's mother an unctuous smile. "Just the ticket, eh?"

Good lord, had his mother been dropping hints? Feeling ill for an entirely different reason, Ash turned around to see Olive striding toward them. She gave a perfunctory nod to Pratham, then looked Ash in the eye. "Are you in pain? What happened?"

"I'm fine. Felt a little light-headed is all." Suddenly afraid he'd be stopped from riding, he added, "Nothing that fresh air and exercise won't cure, I'm sure."

"I quite agree. That's what Major Edwards tells all the men at Chewton, Mrs. Allen. Fresh air and exercise is a cure-all."

His mother smiled and Ash tried not to think of the poor bastards in their bath chairs.

After saying good morning to Reverend Pratham, Olive turned to walk with Ash back toward the road. Conscious of his mother's knowing smile, Ash felt like the worst kind of fraud. He was letting them believe what they choose about him and Olive while his heart beat only for Harry West. He couldn't think of anything else but this afternoon's ride. Not even Olive's conversation was enough to distract him from wondering where they could go that would be secluded. How long they could stay away without raising an alarm, how much they'd be able to —

"I say, Ashleigh." Olive looked amused. "You're rather dreamy this morning. I don't think you've heard one word in ten I've said."

He felt himself flush, chagrined. "I'm so sorry. How rude of me."

"Oh, as if I care about that. I'm more interested in what's put that smile on your face." Her expression softened. "It's rather nice to see. You don't smile often enough."

Christ, was he such an open book? Too bloody sensitive, his father had always scolded. But it wasn't just his own secret he was keeping now and he knew he must do better, even with Olive. She may be a friend, but he daren't trust anyone when it came to Harry. Of the two of them, Ash was fully aware who would bear the brunt should their secrets come to light. "I had rather an enjoyable ride yesterday," he said, hoping that would be explanation enough. "You were right, I should have started riding again months ago."

"Yes. Next time, perhaps, you'll listen to me."

"Naturally."

Olive's intent gaze pinned him, however. Bright, like the glint of wet stone in sunlight. "You rode out with West, I take it?"

"Yes." He looked away, past the rowan trees at the churchyard gate toward the road back toward Highcliffe House. He could see Harry walking with Boyd, Pierson and his mother behind them. He'd recognise Harry's broad shoulders and long-legged gait anywhere.

"I like West," Olive said. "He's good for you. Brings you out of your shell." Ash looked at her, startled, but now it was Olive gazing straight ahead. "I hear you're going to London on Tuesday."

Ash swallowed hard. "I — Apparently I am, yes."

She nodded, turned her serious gaze back to him. "I spoke with Major Edwards. If you're willing to stay overnight, you could have your new prosthetic fitted at the Queen Mary hospital while you're there."

"Indeed?" It was difficult to think about that when his mind was full of his last train journey, to Hinton from the hospital in Southampton with his mother clutching his hand and his body flooded with quicksilver panic every time the whistles blew.

"We have a house in town and you'd be most welcome to use it," Olive continued, cutting through his thoughts. "No staff, though, but — Ashleigh, would you like me to go with you? I know you haven't been to town since you were wounded. Some men find it difficult. All the bustle, you know."

"I —" He cleared his throat as they drew to a halt just past the gate. "I can't say I'm looking forward to it, but I'm sure I'll manage. Thank you, though, for the offer of your company. I'm sure you have more important things to be doing at Chewton."

Her expression told him he was right. "Well, perhaps I do." She brightened suddenly. "But suppose your West went with you?"

Your West.

His heart kicked and contracted all at once and he knew a sharp whisper of fear. "West has his duties in the stables. He doesn't have time to babysit me."

"I doubt he'd see it that way. He's your friend, isn't he?"

Ash couldn't — wouldn't — deny that much. "He's the best friend

I ever had." His voice cracked and he had to stop speaking, blinking rapidly as he turned away.

Olive moved to stand between him and the people leaving church, shielding him from their sight, and he felt a sudden sweep of affection for her. "Take your friend with you, Ashleigh," she said. "Let him help you, if he can."

"My father will think I'm —"

"Oh, the devil take him!" Her voice was hot, her sallow skin flushing with feeling. "I'm tired of people's opinions on what a person should and shouldn't do."

"And I imagine you hear a lot of them. You're a good and wise friend, Miss Allen." He took her hand. "Are you sure you don't want to marry me?"

"Quite sure." Her laughing expression looked a trifle alarmed as she pulled her hand free. "But shall I telephone Queen Mary's and tell them to expect you next Wednesday?"

Suddenly his heart started pounding with a strange mix of terror and anticipation. The train journey would be torturous, but with Harry at his side perhaps it would be endurable. And if they were to spend a night in London… He swallowed hard. "Yes. Thank you, Olive."

"Don't be silly. And you're to stay at our town house in Mayfair. I'll ask mother to arrange it."

Well, Ash thought as he watched her go, now he had some news to tell Harry. He only hoped Harry's circumspection would allow him to agree to the plan because, now that the prospect was on offer, the thought of a whole night alone with Harry West sounded like heaven and Ash was determined that nothing would keep it from happening.

Chapter Twelve

Harry had been in a lather since yesterday. He still couldn't believe that glorious, mad moment when they'd kissed was real. And then today, in church, when the bloody vicar had started on about pageants and parades and he'd seen poor Ash vibrating with fury…

Maybe he shouldn't have gone to him, but no other bugger seemed to give a toss and he couldn't just sit there and wait for him to explode. That would have done nobody any good, least of all Ash. But he'd have to let that anger out somehow, that was for sure. It was a poison if you kept it bottled up, rotted you from the inside. Eventually you had to bleed it out.

Boyd nudged his foot. "What's got you so sullen-looking?"

"Nothing," Harry said, and went back to his mutton and potatoes. They were eating their midday meal in the kitchen with the rest of the staff, as usual. "Just thinking."

"About Mr Ashleigh?" Piped up John Pierson, all smiling insolence. "After him feeling queer in church, I mean."

Ignoring the little sod, Harry spoke to Boyd. "What do you make of this pageant, then? To mark the treaty."

Boyd didn't answer right away, but Harry could see him thinking as he chewed a mouthful of food. "The peace ought to be marked. It was hard won."

"Aye marked, but not celebrated." He prodded at a lump of undercooked potato. "Can't say I've got much stomach for making out like Arras was Agincourt and parading around the village green waving a flag."

"Don't suppose you do, lad."

"Still, it's not for us, I suppose. That's what I told — " He stopped himself just in time. "That is, people need a way to remember, don't they? Me, I'd rather do it quietly."

"Ain't nothing wrong with that. Lord knows, you've earned the right."

After they'd eaten, Harry headed down to the stables and made himself busy even though it was his afternoon off. Boyd planned to see his son later, who was motoring up from Southampton. As much as Boyd complained about him working as a chauffeur, Harry could hear the pride in his voice when he spoke of his son and listened with a smile while he checked the tack and waited nervously for Ash to arrive.

He was dying to be alone with him again. Yesterday, with Ash shaken and Harry cold, they hadn't had much chance to talk about what had happened between them. Maybe they were taking a risk riding out again so soon, but he hadn't survived four years at the front without taking risks. Besides, when Ash looked at him with heat in his beautiful brown eyes, Harry would risk anything for the chance to kiss him again.

Alert for the sound of footsteps, Harry was already walking out of the stables to meet him when Ash arrived in the yard.

"Boyd!" he called, lifting a hand to wave as he approached.

Harry glanced at Boyd, who watched Ash with a guarded expression that suggested he was imagining his afternoon off spoiled. For himself, Harry only offered an appropriately deferential nod.

"Any chance I can borrow West this afternoon?" Ash said, coming to lean on the fence. "I'd rather like to ride out again after we had to cut things short yesterday."

Boyd looked between them, eyebrows twitching into a frown. "If you're sure you want him, Mr Ashleigh. I hear you had to pull him out of the mire yesterday."

Even from this distance, Harry saw Ash's expression flicker and knew where his thoughts had gone. "I-I-I'm sure he could have escaped without me," he got out after a moment. "B-but it was my fault, not warning him away from the edge of the p-pond." His smile looked strained. "I'm the local, after all, and you d-did remind me of the d-danger."

Boyd shook his head. "Just grateful the horses didn't stray too close. I'd hate to have lost one."

Harry had seen hundreds of horses floundering and dying in the mud and was half convinced he'd eaten some of them in his Maconochie. All Ash said was, "I'd n-never have forgiven myself if they had." He glanced over, but Harry looked away and tried to appear busy. "I'm conscious of West's duties," Ash carried on, "b-but if you can spare him this afternoon, I'd be grateful."

Boyd lifted a questioning eyebrow. *Want me to make an excuse?* When Harry shook his head, Boyd shrugged. "It's his afternoon off, Mr Ashleigh, so it's no skin off my nose what he does with his time."

"In that case, what do you say, West?" Ash barely reined in his grin. "I p-promise not to lead you into any more mires. In fact, I thought we could head up to my father's old hunting box. I'd like to take a look. Not been used since b-before the war, I should think."

"I should think you're right," Boyd said. "And that's a nice ride, Harry. You'll enjoy it."

Harry had to turn away to hide a flash of excitement. "Reckon I will," he said. Then, to Ash, "I'd appreciate the opportunity to ride Sable again, sir. I'll go and saddle up the horses."

They didn't talk much until they were off the road and onto a broad tree-lined bridleway leading through the forest, the canopy above a lush green and the loamy scent of earth kicked up by the horses' hooves scenting the air with the promise of summer.

Ash let out a sigh, shoulders relaxing as if he were shaking off some great weight, and he turned to Harry with a heart-stopping smile. He didn't smile often, but when he did… Harry's stomach tightened. Ash looked lovely in the dappled sunlight, dark hair gleaming under his cap, and his face flushed with more colour than he'd had for a while. Harry would have liked to tell him he was beautiful, but it sounded silly. Instead, he said, "How far is it to this hunting box?"

"Not far." Ash smiled and, to Harry's delight, flushed. "If we ride fast, we'll have more time to…" He looked down at his hands gripping the reins and didn't finish.

Harry's heart kicked harder than a horse. "What are we waiting for then?" he said, and nudged Sable into a gallop.

Behind him, Ash barked a laugh and they raced until Ash slowed Bella back to a walk and Harry dropped back with him. They were past the trees then, out onto the heath, and Ash lifted a hand to point. "The box is in that stand of trees over there."

As they approached, he saw that the hunting box was more like a small wooden cottage than anything else, its windows shuttered and a good deal of moss on the roof and the stone steps leading up to its door. It didn't look like anyone had been inside for years.

Dismounting, Harry led Sable over to the hitching post and tied her up before turning back to help Ash dismount. "Ready?" he said, squinting up against the blue sky.

With a nod, Ash swung his duff leg over and Harry caught him at the waist to take the weight until he had his good foot out of the stirrup and on the ground. But this time… God, this time he didn't let go. Slipping his arms around Ash's waist he pulled him back against his chest, buried his face in the hair behind Ash's ear and breathed him in.

Ash gave a soft sigh, leaning into Harry's embrace, one hand coming to rest over Harry's. "Hello," he said quietly.

Harry smiled against his neck. "Hello yourself."

Bella huffed and snorted, and Ash laughed. "All right old girl," he said, patting her neck. "Do you want a drink?" To Harry, he said,

"There's a pond behind the box — come on, I'll show you. It's very secluded."

He wasn't wrong. Behind the building was a small pond shaded by tall trees and a small overgrown enclosure for the horses. After they'd let them drink, Harry put them into the paddock so they could start work on four years' worth of undergrowth.

"Father used to come here with his friends when we were children." Ash smiled, a little ruefully as he peered in through the window. Inside, it looked empty and uninviting. "I doubt he ever hunted. Probably just wanted to get away from the noise of two young boys."

It was much nicer outside. With the trees looming over the pond, and the lodge at their backs, it was as private a place as they were ever likely to find. "I like it here," Harry decided, and took Ash's hand in his own.

The colour rising in his cheeks, Ash said, "I brought a blanket. Shall we sit?"

It didn't take long to spread the blanket out on the grassy bank, and Ash had brought a flask of tea and some slabs of cake, too. Not that Harry was hungry. Not for tea and cake, at any rate. Eating was the last thing on his mind as he watched Ash manoeuvre himself down onto the blanket, sighing as he stretched out his bad leg. Harry came to sit next to him, facing him.

For a moment they said nothing, simply gazed at each other in the spring sunshine. Yesterday, their kiss had been born of the moment, of grief and longing and years of pent up feeling. It had been rash and instinctive. But this would be deliberate, and Harry felt all his old uncertainties crowding in until Ash broke the spell.

"Harry," he said, pressing his palm to Harry's face.

He mirrored the gesture, stroking his thumb over Ash's cheek. His face felt smooth, bones refined beneath Harry's fingers. To touch him like this, to gaze into those deep dark eyes with such freedom… "Bloody hell," he murmured and leaned in to kiss him, capturing his soft lips with his own. Ash sighed, fingers winding into Harry's hair, his other hand resting lightly on Harry's thigh. He groaned beneath that touch, his prick filling as the low pulse of desire between them beat with rising urgency. When Ash squirmed closer, Harry slipped an arm around his waist, cradling the back of his head and leaning him backward, pressing their bodies together as he lost himself in that endless heart-pounding possessive kiss. *Mine*, he thought fervently. *Mine*.

Eventually gravity had its way and they sprawled onto the blanket, Ash on his back and Harry gazing down on him. Breathing hard, face flushed, Ash watched him through eyes somehow both darker and brighter than ever. Harry touched his face with shaking fingers, heart hammering against his chest. "You're lovely, you are," he said, feeling himself colour. He'd never said such a thing before.

Ash smiled and, God bless him, looked shy. "Nothing to you, Harry West." He reached up to kiss him again, slow and warm as the spring sunshine. When he pulled back, he studied Harry with an uncertain expression, as if he didn't dare speak the words hovering on his lips.

"What is it?" Harry said, stroking a hand through his hair.

"It's only—" His cheeks pinked. "Have you done this before? With a-a-a man?"

That wasn't as simple a question as it appeared. "Not quite this," Harry said after a moment's thought. "Not with someone I…" He swallowed the word on the tip of his tongue. "But I've had, er, encounters with men." He studied Ash's face, considering. "Have you?"

A shake of his head. "I've never felt— That is, I've not wanted to with someone I d-didn't trust."

Harry's heart, already a sodden mess, melted a little more. "You can trust me, Ash."

"With my life." He pressed a hand to Harry's cheek. "Show me, then. I w-want to make love with you. Show me how."

Jesus. Harry dipped his head, pressing it against Ash's shoulder and breathing in the woodsy scent of him. He'd always thought

Ash had several layers of skin fewer than other men, and now here he was baring himself utterly. So trusting, so vulnerable. Harry wanted to hold him forever, keep him safe, and it broke his heart that he could do neither. But he had this moment, at least. And he could love Ash now, with his heart and his body, and let him feel cherished. He could give him that. Lifting his head, he kissed Ash's forehead, the bridge of his nose, his hot eager lips. When Ash reached for him, arms coming around his neck, Harry slipped one leg between Ash's thighs and began to rock gently against him, the sensation of his own hardening prick rubbing against Ash's — even through several layers of clothing — making him breathless.

Ash got the hang of things quick enough, hips finding the rhythm as they ground against each other, his hands ranging over Harry's back and down to his arse. Harry groaned in delight and slipped a hand under Ash's backside, pulling him closer, squeezing hard.

Ash jolted beneath him. "*Yes!* God. I want — I can't — "

"Hush," Harry soothed him, shifting to lay next to him. "I know what you want." He ran a hand over the sizable bulge in Ash's trousers, smiling as he looked up into Ash's face. His eyes were heavy-lidded and dazed as he gazed back at Harry, lips parted, chest heaving. "Can I touch you, Ash?"

"Yes," he whispered. "God, yes."

Harry smiled and let his fingers drift over Ash's prick once more, enjoying the way he pressed up into his touch. His own desire was so fierce he had to roll his prick against Ash's hip to alleviate some of the tension as he carefully unbuttoned Ash's fly. Ash watched avidly from beneath his lashes, bottom lip caught between his teeth, breaths coming short and sharp. Gooseflesh raced over Harry's skin, his own climax already hovering in the wings. So different from every anonymous fuck he'd ever had. He wouldn't have to work for this at all, he was practically there, and no one had even touched his prick. He swallowed, concentrating on unbuttoning Ash's underwear, and slipped his hand inside. Harry shivered, eyes drifting shut. God, yes, he felt good, hot, hard and silken beneath his fingers.

Ash barked a breathless cry and dropped back onto the blanket, flinging an arm over his face. "Jesus," he hissed. "Harry, God, I'm going to… I'm…God."

"Let me," he said, curling his fingers around Ash's prick and giving it a slow, experimental stroke. "Let me do this for you." Leaning down, he kissed Ash's jaw, nuzzling into his warm neck, stroking him and grinding against his hip.

"*Christ.*" Ash gasped in answer, rocking into Harry's touch, and then his hand joined Harry's, guiding his pace and pressure, their fingers entwining around his prick.

"That's it," Harry breathed, watching avidly. He loved the way their fingers laced together, wanted to feel them on his own prick. "God, Ash, you're bloody beautiful. You're lovely. You're — "

With a wordless cry, Ash climaxed, his release pulsing through their joined fingers, his whole body juddering as he jerked up into their hands. Harry had never seen anything more erotic, his own urgent desire scorching under his skin in response. Fumbling open his fly, he took himself in hand with a groan of relief, fingers still slick with Ash's spend. The thought of that, the sight of Ash gasping and wrecked next to him, sent him over the edge after three swift tugs and he came with his face buried into Ash's neck and Ash's trembling hand stroking his hair.

For a long time after, Harry lay with his head on Ash's shoulder and one arm flung about his waist, holding him close. He didn't want to ever let go. Above them, tiny birds flitted through the trees and the sun moved slowly across the sky, casting lengthening shadows on the water of the pond. Was Ash sleeping? If so, Harry was hesitant to rouse him, knowing how his nights were disturbed. But the afternoon was wearing on and they'd be missed if they stayed out too long.

Just as Harry was about to give him a little shake, like he'd done many a morning, Ash spoke. "I've a favour to ask," he said in a voice quiet and alert, which made Harry suspect he'd been thinking not drowsing all this time.

He tightened his arm around Ash's waist. "I imagine I'll agree."

Ash huffed a laugh and shifted, propping himself up on his elbow. His hair was dishevelled, lips pink and skin flushed — it made Harry's heart dance to know that he'd done that, to remember that wild moment of ecstasy he'd given him. He palmed his cheek, smiling as Ash leaned into him like a cat. "Go on then, what is it?"

Lashes lowered, lips compressed, he said, "I'm to go to London on Tuesday. Father's arranged it — a meeting at the bank, about my p-position."

A low pulse of alarm beat in Harry's chest, like the pounding of distant guns. If Ash returned to his city job, and Harry was left down here at Highcliffe House…?

"I wondered — " Ash looked up. "It would be a comfort to have you on the train, Harry. And… And Olive said I can get my new prosthetic fitted on Wednesday, so if we spend the night, I could kill two birds with one stone."

"Spend the night?" That thought derailed all others.

Ash smiled, a sweet curve of his lips as he glanced up. "Olive said we could stay in her family's town house — there'd be nobody there but us. No staff."

The pounding in his chest transformed into a full-blooded beat of want. A whole night together. In a bed. "That sounds…" A grin tugged at his lips. "Like an opportunity not to be missed."

"Yes. I thought so too."

Harry drew Ash back down with him. "You'll have to ask Boyd if he can spare me."

"I know. And my father. He'll think I'm — " Settling his head against Harry's chest, Ash puffed out a breath. "Well, he'll think I should manage alone."

"He doesn't know what he's talking about, though," Harry pointed out. "You spent three bloody years at war, Ash. You don't have to prove a damn thing to him or to anyone else."

Ash tightened his arm around him. "Whatever would I do without you, Harry? Wouldn't have survived those three years, that's for sure."

"Course you would."

"I can't imagine it. Can't imagine living without you."

Harry's heart gave a hard kick, his stomach cramping. "Me neither," he said roughly, holding him close. But surely Ash knew what this visit to London meant? Their one night notwithstanding, when Ash returned to London permanently, he'd have to assume all the trappings of his life and station.

And there'd be no room in that life for the likes of Harry West.

CHAPTER THIRTEEN

Saying goodbye was painful, the distance between them felt like an ache.

Ash's body still thrummed with the memory of Harry's touch when they parted at the stables with a lingering look and bland, layered words.

"Thank you for your company, West."

"You're welcome, Mr Ashleigh. It was my pleasure."

Afterward, Ash felt too restless to go back to the house. What they'd done together must surely be written on his skin and he needed longer to prepare himself before facing his parents. If his father ever suspected... Well, it didn't bear thinking about. Turning his steps away from the house, Ash followed the path that led around the lawn to the stream and the circular archway that separated the garden from the wilderness beyond.

It was late afternoon by then and the scent of roses was heady as he paused and took a breath, gazing out into the woodland beyond. It was still Dalton land, but left to run wild. As boys, he and Dodge had played there, climbing trees and charging each other in pretend battles. If he looked hard enough, he thought he could see the ghosts of his boyhood playing there still.

Bang, bang. You're dead.

He shook off the memory, fixed his mind on Harry instead and on the soft, impossible delight of his kiss, on the heart-stopping joy they'd found in each other's arms. Strange that something the world considered obscene could feel so unutterably right, as if the earth had been formed for the single object of allowing Ashleigh Dalton to love Harry West, as if they had been made only for that purpose and for each other.

He smiled at his own whimsy, thinking how Harry would laugh to hear it, and aching that this glowing love in his heart must be hidden like a capped candle. Reaching out a hand, he pressed it against the cool stone of the archway. The trees beyond grew tall, bracken tangling beneath their bows, shadowy in the evening light. A narrow path cut through the brush, made by deer, probably, leading into the wild. He took a step toward it. Then another...

"Ashleigh!" His mother's voice floated across the lawn, calling him back. "Where are you going? It's time to dress for dinner."

He turned, placing his foot carefully so as not to stumble. "Yes, I'll be along directly."

She nodded and turned away, disappearing into the house. Ash watched her go, fingers curling around the head of his cane, before following. Behind him, he heard the birds singing in the trees and wished he was as free.

Dinner was stultifying. His mother looked smilingly at him and asked what he and Olive had been discussing so secretly after church. Her hope was unconcealed, and Ash took care to play along — aware that the façade couldn't last forever. They were talking about riding, he told his mother, cheeks heating at the memory of Harry.

His mother squeezed his hand, quite misconstruing his blush. "She's a lovely young woman. And I'm sure she'll settle down once she has a home and a husband to care for."

"Once you've been up to the bank and confirmed your position," his father added, "you'll be able to make her an offer. Don't hang around, boy. Miss Allen's a valuable catch: property as well as a hefty fortune."

"Property?" His mother sounded doubtful. "You mean Milford Cottage? That hardly counts — it's practically derelict. And Ashleigh will want to live in town."

"Land is land, my dear. An Englishman's castle etcetera etcetera." His voice darkened. "And this blasted government is taxing us into extinction, so Ashleigh will have to marry well."

Ash could only nod along. What point was there in arguing? But his chest tightened nonetheless. One day he'd have to decide about his future, but if he didn't marry then what? What escape was there from this suffocating life?

He pushed the thought aside, unable to bear it. Instead he said, "Regarding my trip on Tuesday, Olive received a message from Major Edwards saying that my new — uh — new leg will be ready for fitting on Wednesday." His mother made a pained expression and his father puffed out a breath, moustache fluttering. Neither liked to hear about his injury. "If I extend my visit by a night, I can save myself another trip." He shot his mother a look. "Olive's offered me the use of the Allen's town house." He knew exactly what they'd both think of *that* show of intimacy.

"Indeed!" His mother smiled. "Well, how very kind of her."

"Yes," Ash said, fixing his gaze on his lamb chop. "I took the liberty of accepting." A pause while he steadied himself. "It has the advantage that there'll be somewhere for West to stay."

"West?"

"I'd like to bring him with me. You know we were comrades, and I'd rather not stay alone just in case..." He made a vague gesture toward his leg. "Besides, West has a sister in town he'd like to visit."

His father grunted. "I'm not paying him to be your valet, Ashleigh."

"Oh, my dear, don't be such a misery," his mother protested. "Of course Ashleigh must have a man with him. Lord knows, the Allens won't have any staff in town. Nobody does these days."

"That's true," Ash said, then smiled and added. "West can rustle me up some breakfast. He worked miracles with a can of

Maconochie. I'd like to see what he can do with an egg or two."

And so, reluctantly, his father agreed the plan. Ash had to work hard to keep from grinning.

He retired shortly after dinner, blaming the afternoon's ride for having tired him out. But unlike every other evening, Ash wasn't dreading the night to come. If he couldn't sleep, then so be it — he'd use the time to remember this afternoon, to trace in his mind every sensation. From their first soft kiss to the feel of Harry's hand on his prick, their fingers tangling together and that incandescent moment of ecstasy. And then afterward, being held so tenderly in Harry's arms…

He stripped down to his shirtsleeves, un-strapped his leg with a sigh of relief, and lay on the bed. The curtains stood open to the night breeze — he couldn't bear the dark — and he watched moonlight pattern the ceiling as clouds flitted across the sky. Outside, the rustle of the leaves and the bark of a distant fox were the only sounds. He fell asleep smiling at the memory of Harry's touch.

Much later, the crunch of footsteps on gravel woke him. He started upright in bed, heart pounding. As always, it took a moment to orientate himself, to feel the linen sheets beneath his hands, to catch the scent of the garden in the air. Home. He was home. He turned his head to the window and realised it was already close to dawn. For once he had slept, undisturbed, all night.

His heartbeat slowed and he became aware of a thin, shadowy figure passing close to his window — John Pierson, heading back from the outhouse. Mindful of what Harry had told him about the tales the boy told, Ash kept still so as not to draw attention and watched as John made his way to the servants' quarters behind the kitchen. When he'd gone, Ash swung his legs off the bed and used the windowsill to brace himself as he hopped to the chair by the window. He'd become rather good at that over the months he'd been home. He reached for his cigarettes as he sat down and noticed he was still wearing yesterday's clothes. Not that he cared. Some distant part of his mind raised an eyebrow at his lax standards, but the rest of him simply shrugged. He'd lived like a beggar for weeks at time at the front, why should he give a fig for pyjamas now?

He lit up, sucked in a long breath, and blew smoke out through the window, watching the tip of his gasper glow. The horizon was starting to brighten and he smiled at the thought of what tomorrow night might bring. He wanted more than they'd done yesterday, although he hardly knew what. He wasn't experienced, knew only the insistent tension in his body. Remembering Harry's hand made him stiffen; imagining Harry's mouth had him biting his lip to stifle a moan. Could they do such things? Would Harry want to? Would he want to do *more*?

He took another drag on his cigarette, blood racing.

And then he saw him, emerging from the pre-dawn shadows at the side of the house. Harry walked across the gardens, long legs striding too fast for Ash to catch up even if he'd had his damned leg on. It was too early to shout, so Ash could only watch as Harry made his way across the lawn to the garden wall and though the arch into the wilderness beyond.

Ash sat for a few moments longer, wondering what Harry was up to out there, but it was no good. He couldn't bear this enforced inactivity. Making his way back to the bed, he strapped on his leg, found his other shoe and stood up, glancing at the door. He didn't like the idea of running into one of the maids and, besides, he was feeling reckless. So he pulled the chair back from the window, opened it wide and sat on the ledge to swing his legs over one at a time. He slipped down, landing on his good foot with a wild sense of triumph and reached back in to fetch his cane. Heart pounding with glee, he headed after Harry as fast as he was able to walk.

Dawn was breaking fast now, a clear cloudless morning, and the roses around the arch glowed in the cool light. He paused at the threshold, taking a breath of the earthy woodland air, then stepped through into the wilderness. Above him, the leaves whispered in the soft breeze, the dawn chorus in full voice, and Ash smiled. No, he *grinned* with pure delight.

"Ash?" Harry wasn't far away, leaning on the wall some distance from the arch. It looked like he'd been enjoying a smoke but was regarding Ash with astonishment now.

"I saw you," Ash explained, keeping his voice low as he walked toward him. His duff foot snagged on something and he stumbled, but Harry caught his elbow before he could fall.

"You daft sod," he said, smiling. "Did anyone see you?"

"No, I climbed out of the window."

Harry laughed softly. "Did you now?"

"I wanted to —" Now he was here, with Harry's hand on his elbow, he felt shy. "I wanted to see you."

"I wanted to see you, too." Harry's grip tightened. "Ah, Ash," he said, and pulled him close, wrapping his arms around him.

Ash breathed out. Just...breathed out, felt his body relax as he sank into Harry's embrace. This, he thought, was all he needed. All he wanted. Harry lifted a hand to Ash's hair, threading his fingers through it, and when Ash turned his head, Harry's lips found his cheek, the corner of his mouth. And then they were kissing, slow and smoky, and the upside-down world felt right again.

"You're cold," Harry said after a while, chafing his hand up and down Ash's arm. "Where's your coat?"

"Doesn't matter." Ash pressed closer, their whole bodies touching from chest to toe. "I could stay here forever."

A low laugh. "Boyd would have something to say about that."

"I suppose he would." Ash rested his head on Harry's shoulder. "And I suppose we can't ride again today."

"Not a chance."

Ash looked up, scanning his face. "You sighed. What is it?"

"Nothing. I've work to do, is all, especially if I'm coming up to town with you tomorrow." He cupped Ash's face, ran his calloused thumb over one cheekbone. "But, Ash, we have to be careful. You know that."

"We are being careful."

Harry's eyebrows rose. "Are we?"

"It's barely dawn. Nobody's up."

"The servants are up, you dolt." He softened it with another smile, threading his fingers through Ash's hair again, his expression one of wonder. "Just be careful, Ash. You've a deal more to lose than me."

"A man's allowed an early morning walk, isn't he?"

"Half dressed?" Harry slid a flinger over Ash's Adam's apple, down through the hollow of his throat at the open neck of his shirt. "Not that I'm complaining, mind." Christ, but that simple forbidden touch was enough to raise gooseflesh across Ash's skin, to stir a rise in his prick that Harry must feel. Ash swallowed hungrily, half embarrassed and half thrilled. "But it's not quite right for a gent."

"Don't worry," Ash said. "They all think I'm half mad anyway."

Harry's expression hardened. "Then don't give them more reason to, eh?"

"Are you joking? This is the sanest bloody thing I've done in years." Ash leaned in and kissed him again. "But you're right, I'll be careful." For Harry, if not himself. The last thing he wanted to do was queer the pitch for Harry. Reluctantly, he pulled away. "Shall I come to the stables later?"

"Best not."

His heart sank, even though he understood. "Tomorrow, then."

"Tomorrow." With a squeeze of his hand, Harry let go and started back toward the garden. "Wait a few minutes," he said over his shoulder. "And make sure nobody's looking when you come out of here. Especially John."

Ash nodded. They had no choice about being discreet, but the secrecy was oppressive. It felt like a tight band around his chest, one more strap on the straitjacket the world was so keen for him to wear.

Chapter Fourteen

The day of their trip up to London dawned through a sea mist, the air damp against Harry's face as he made his way up to the house from the stables. He was surprised to see a motor car in the driveway, but then the front door opened and Miss Allen walked out with Ash trailing behind her looking grim and determined. Harry knew that expression well and didn't enjoy seeing it again.

"Ah, there you are, West!" Olive called as she ran down the steps. "I'm giving you and Ashleigh a lift to the station this morning. Put your bag in the back seat, there's a good fellow."

Harry did as required, then moved to help Ash get into the car. Their eyes met, but neither said anything as Harry opened the passenger door and offered Ash his hand for balance. It was more of an excuse to touch him than anything else, and the feel of Ash's cold fingers only confirmed what Harry could already see. Ash was terrified. "You'll be alright, Captain," he said with a nod.

Ash returned a thin smile. "Thank you, West. I appreciate your confidence."

Glancing up, he found Olive watching them from the other side of the car, her gaze slipping away as she climbed into the driver's seat. "Into the back, West," she said and started the engine.

He slid himself in next to their bags, and then they were off.

Before the war, he'd not had much experience with motor cars, but he'd ridden in enough since to remove the novelty. Even so, whizzing along the country lanes with the wind in his face was an exhilarating experience — even with the mist. It only took half an hour to reach the station, and before long he and Ash were standing on the pavement watching Olive drive away.

"Well," Harry said, "here we are."

They bought their tickets — Ash insisted on first class for them both — and waited on the platform for the train. Ash was silent and tense, the dark circles beneath his eyes enough to stir Harry's memories of other damp grey mornings and pale, frightened faces. He shifted closer until their shoulders touched. At the front, all the men had huddled together for warmth and comfort, had slept like a basket of puppies sometimes, all atop the other. But back in England, it wasn't acceptable to stand so close, not even to offer comfort. One of many things that set the world off kilter.

At least the train was on time, great clouds of steam spilling onto the platform as it drew in, and Ash led them to the first class carriage with his fingers locked tight on the head of his cane. Harry took both their bags, and if anyone thought it strange that a servant should sit with his master in first class he didn't give a damn. It was either that or Ash sitting with him in third, because there was no way he'd be anywhere but at Ash's side on this journey.

Harry stowed their bags in the overhead rack and came to sit next to Ash on the bench seat. Luckily, so far, they had the compartment to themselves. Ash was milk-pale as the carriage door slammed, eyes closed and head resting back. When the first whistle blew, he started and Harry gripped his hand.

"Open your eyes," he said firmly.

Ash didn't move, but another whistle shrilled and his lips parted as if letting out a slow breath.

"Ash," Harry said over the constant bloody blasting of the whistle — how many times did the bugger have to blow it? "Look at me."

The train lurched forward and Ash opened his eyes. "I c-c-can't st-stop it."

"I know." Harry squeezed his hand. "Train's moving now, look." He nodded to the window, saw Ash's attention shift toward it. "We're here, see? Not there. No one's there anymore."

"N-no one's there." Ash nodded. "Yes. Last time, c-coming down, you w-were still out there."

Harry swallowed. For all the misery of those hellish days when he'd thought Ash had bought it, the idea of sitting at home with Ash still at the front was appalling. "Well I'm back now," he said firmly. "We both are. And those whistles are just for the trains."

Ash nodded, his death-grip on Harry's hand easing. "Thank you," he said. "This helps."

"Good." Harry kept hold of his hand.

Later, his gaze still fixed out of the window, Ash said, "Do you ever w-wonder what's happened to the b-battle fields?"

"Not really." Unlike Ash, who couldn't seem to stop thinking about it, Harry considered himself the sort who looked forward not backward.

"So m-many men lost there. Their b-bodies, I mean."

"I hope the trees grow," Harry said, giving it some thought. "All those blasted stumps… I hope the trees grow back."

Ash gave a faint smile. "Yes, that w-would be fitting." After a pause, "Would you ever go b-back? To p-pay your respects."

Swallowing, Harry squeezed his hand tighter. "Not for a while, Ash. Not for a good long while."

By the time they reached Waterloo, Ash looked drawn and sallow. Harry had to pry their hands apart as the train pulled into the station. Luckily, Ash's appointment at the bank wasn't for another hour, so, once they'd reached Charing Cross, Harry marched them both to the Strand Corner House and sat Ash down with a pot of tea and a fruit bun.

The city was as loud and chaotic as always, but less sombre than when he'd left. Spring had arrived in London, too. Ash regained some colour as he ate, although he didn't entirely lose his haunted expression. Under the table, Harry pressed their knees together and when Ash looked up, he smiled. "Better?"

Ash nodded. "Can't say I'm looking forward to the next bit, either."

"You don't want your old position back?" It wasn't something they'd talked about, but nothing Harry had seen made him think Ash missed his role at the bank.

"Would you want to sit in an office all day?"

"No fear." He gave an exaggerated shudder.

"Not unless horses start working as clerks, eh?"

Harry laughed and turned to watch the traffic, a raucous mix of horse drawn vehicles and motor cars. The world was changing, that was for sure, and who knew where his place in it would be.

"Imagine," Ash said suddenly, leaning forward across the table and speaking in a low voice. "Imagine if we could live in the country together, you and I."

Harry glanced around cautiously, but nobody was listening. "And do what? Or are we to be gentlemen of leisure in this dream?"

"God no." Ash wrinkled his nose. "I've had enough of idleness to last a lifetime. No, we'd work. You'd do something with horses and I'd — "

"I'd own a stud farm," Harry said. "If we're talking of dreams, then I'd breed Thoroughbreds fit for a king. Make a bloody fortune."

"Yes!" Ash's eyes lit up. "And I could help you. I'd run the business while you concentrated on, uh, horse things."

"Horse things?" Harry laughed and gave Ash's knee an affectionate nudge. "That's what it's called, is it?"

"We could have a house right there at the stable and…" His voice cracked and he flashed a bright, deflecting smile. "And I'd never have to get on another bloody train."

"We'd buy a motor car," Harry suggested, heart twanging with a sweet pain. Longing, he supposed, was the word. "Then we could go wherever we liked."

"We could take a holiday. To Devonshire, perhaps. Have you ever been?"

Harry shook his head. "Never taken a holiday anywhere."

"No." Ash bit his lip, looking away. "I suppose not. But I'd like to take you there one day, Harry. It's so beautiful — so peaceful. And there are wild ponies on Exmoor. I think you'd love it."

"I'm sure I would."

Their eyes met and held, full of impossible dreams. "We've got today," Harry said softly. *We've got tonight.*

With a decisive nod, Ash pushed to his feet. "And I've got an appointment to keep. Knowing Pollock, probably a luncheon to endure as well." He cocked his head. "Will you visit your sister today?"

"If that's alright."

"You don't need my permission, Harry. You're not my —" He bit that off, but it didn't change the fact that Harry *was* his servant. More quietly Ash said, "I'd like to be introduced, but…"

"But that would raise too many questions." Harry stood up, too. "Kitty's a canny woman, Ash. No one pulls the wool over her eyes." And the sons of baronets didn't pay social calls on their stableman's family. He looked at the clock on the wall by the door. "I'll be back by three. Shall we meet on the corner here?"

"At three." Ash straightened his shoulders and put on a brave face; it didn't fool Harry. "Wish me luck."

"Always." Only he wasn't certain what manner of luck Ash wanted — to be given his old position back, or not. But what other choice was there for a man like Ashleigh Dalton? Fantastical dreams aside, they were both trapped in a world they didn't fit and would have to snatch joy where they found it — however fleeting it might be.

***

What a strange experience it was, walking back into the offices of London Joint City and Midland after four years away. Everything was at once the same, yet different. Same desks, same scent of wood polish, same sound of scratching pens. But many new faces among the clerks, including several women. Before the war, Pollock would never have sanctioned such a radical step. Desperate times, Ash concluded.

Which made him think of Olive and the way she was battering at the door of a male world. He hoped she'd succeed although, ironically, her class — specifically her father — might hold her further back than these young working girls. One of whom glanced up with a curious tilt of her eyebrows making Ash look hurriedly away, afraid of giving offence. He'd never worked alongside women in the office and wasn't entirely certain how to behave.

Luckily, at that moment, Pollock's door swung open and out came the man himself. The privations of war, such as they'd been for the likes of Mr Albert Pollock, hadn't diminished his round belly or subdued the rosy flush of his nose. "Dalton!" he exclaimed, mutton chops quivering atop his jiggling jowls. "Here you are at last. Began to think you'd never make it."

Ash offered his hand to shake. "Mr Pollock. Thank you for seeing me, sir."

"Stuff and nonsense." Pollock gripped his hand hard. "Told your father we'd hold your position. Least we could do" — his gaze flitted to the cane in Ash's hand — "under the circumstances."

"I hope I earned that kindness on my own merit, sir. I don't expect any special treatment." Or pity, he might have added. "There's plenty of good men in London looking for work."

"Well, well," Pollock blustered. "Come into my office and we'll talk, Dalton. Lots of changes at London Joint City and Midland since you were here. Not least the name, eh?"

For the next hour, Pollock droned on about the recent absorption of the London Joint Stock Bank while Ash nodded and made the occasional comment. But his mind was elsewhere. The air in the office was stultifying, its stuffy, dusty scent so familiar he was instantly transported back to those years before the war. But far from making him nostalgic, it made him realise what a half-life he'd been living in those days. He'd been trapped behind a wall, bricked off from the world. A dead, unfeeling life. For all the hardships of the front, he'd never known such comradeship anywhere else — not at school, not at Cambridge, and certainly not at work. Never had he felt such love for other men, a pure platonic love for those frightened, brave, raucous, fragile men of all rank he'd lived with in the worst of times. And the best of times, too; everything had been heightened. To come back to this desiccated, colourless world of bank mergers made him feel like a great fist were closing around his lungs and squeezing out his breath. Like a snake returning to its shed skin, it would be impossible slip back into this old life.

Yet he had to work somewhere. Unlike his brother, he had no fortune to inherit and God knew he wasn't fit for any other kind of work. Not like Harry. All Ash knew was money and business and —

He was struck by a sudden picture of himself standing in a stable yard with Harry, their hands clasped and the warm summer sun shining down on them. Thoroughbreds. Ash knew nothing about them, but Harry would know. Harry would know everything. And that…that would be a life. That would be a life to make his soul sing.

"…what do you say, Dalton? We can discuss the details over lunch at my club, eh? Toast your return."

"My return." That was why he'd come here, wasn't it? There was no realistic prospect of refusing, of telling his father that he didn't want his old position. That he was going to run away with Harry West instead and breed horses in the depths of the countryside, somewhere they could live and love far away from the censorious gaze of the world. "Of course," he said mechanically. "I'd be delighted."

Pollock's club was filled with old men and Ash garnered a few nods of respect or approval as he limped after him between the dining tables, as if his maimed leg was a badge of honour among these old armchair warriors. Ignoring them, he sat down opposite Pollock and downed the brandy he was offered in one go. Anything to numb the creeping sense of claustrophobic horror.

They agreed — that is Pollock suggested it and Ash nodded mutely — to him starting work on the first of July, and Pollock named a generous salary. "Enough to settle down on, eh?"

Ash made a non-committal noise around his mouthful of food.

"Got a lady in mind, Dalton?"

"No." He spoke before he remembered Pollock was a friend of his father and may well be aware of Olive. "That is, I've not been in a position to make any plans, sir."

Pollock gave a braying laugh that set Ash's teeth on edge. "Plenty of pretty misses in France, I dare say. But you can't beat a good solid English girl for a wife, Dalton."

Ash didn't answer. He loathed these conversations, had always done his best to escape them whenever the port was passed around after dinner. Until now he'd had nothing to contribute, neither love nor desire to confess. But today his heart rebelled. Today he wanted to say, *Yes. Yes, there is someone I love. Yes, there is someone I want to share my life with.*

But love like theirs could only exist on the fringes of the world. They were outlaws, he and Harry; society made them so. Shockingly, a high desperate laugh escaped his lips. He clamped his mouth shut, but the rush of feeling wouldn't be silenced. Outlaws? Well, why not? Why not run away and live in the wildwood together? Surely it was saner than locking themselves into this oubliette of a life.

Pollock raised a bushy eyebrow at the unmanly show of feeling. "Are you quite all right, Dalton?"

"I —" His throat closed around the polite response, refused to let it out. All he could say was, "I can't."

"Can't what?"

"Go back." He set down his cutlery.

Pollock looked around uneasily, afraid of embarrassment.

"Fighting's over, Dalton. Nobody's asking you to go back — "

"No." Sweat prickled his top lip, his breaths shortening. "I mean the b-b-bank. I'm sorry."

Pollock sat back in his chair in astonishment. "What? Why the devil not? You won't get a better position."

"I know that, sir. I w-want..." He cleared his throat. "I n-need a d-different life, that's all."

"A different life?" Pollock stared. "Need I remind you that I've held your position open as a favour to your father? Would you disrespect us both by this…this malingering behaviour?"

Ash shook his head, folding his napkin on his lap with shaking hands. "I mean no d-disrespect, sir. And I a-apologise for w-wasting your time today. But until right n-now I hadn't realised that I… I c-can't go back, Mr Pollock. The w-war changed me and I — "

"Changed you?" he scoffed. "You're damned lucky you came back at all."

"I'm w-well aware of that, sir."

Pollock puffed out a breath, looking suddenly awkward. "Nerves, is it?" he said after a pause, voice dropping. " Sir Arthur mentioned something about it…"

Nerves. Mental weakness. He knew exactly what his father thought of his distress since returning to England. And he didn't have the stomach for denial. His nerves *were* shot — the dreadful journey this morning was evidence of that — but it wasn't all that had changed. If he was damned lucky to be alive then he'd be damned stupid to waste this gift of a life in the offices of London Joint City and Midland. "You're right," he said, feeling steadier. "My nerves aren't up to it. I d-didn't realise until today." He stood, reaching for his cane which he'd propped against the chair. "Thank you, sir, for keeping my p-position open. I don't expect you to d-do so any longer. If — " This was a lie; he would never voluntarily return. " — If I ever feel able to return, I'll t-take my chances with the other m-men looking for a position, sir."

Pollock stood too. "Your father will be disappointed to hear of this, Dalton. But there are doctors… Electric shock therapy and wot-not that can cure this kind of thing."

"I d-don't think so, sir." Pollock couldn't know it, of course, but there were other things doctors used electric shock therapy to 'cure'. As a result, he had little faith in doctors of the mind and would never put himself in their hands. Quacks, the lot of them. Offering his hand, he said, "Goodbye, Mr P-Pollock."

After a disgruntled pause, Pollock shook his hand. "Goodbye, Dalton. And good luck."

"I'll t-take that, sir," Ash said. "And with thanks. I'm quite likely t-to need it."

CHAPTER FIFTEEN

Harry surprised Kitty at the end of her shift at the sorting office, walking home with her and insisting she took the money he'd saved from his wages. "As part payment for what I owe you," he told her. "And something extra for the girls."

They shared a pie at the Cat and Fiddle — his treat — and he told her all about Highcliffe and as little as possible about Ash. He hadn't been exaggerating when he'd called her canny, and the last thing he wanted was Kitty's suspicions roused against them. Traditional as they came, was Mrs Kitty Morgan. She wouldn't understand what had grown between him and Ash. Not at all.

Hell, he wasn't sure he understood it himself. Love, yes. Bright as a rocket blast and just as dangerous. But he wasn't thinking about the danger, not today. How could he when they had the whole night before them? Just the thought of it brought a smile to his lips and he had to fight to keep his attention on Kitty and avoid betraying himself to her sharp eyes.

After they parted with a fond hug, Harry took the tube from White Chapel to Temple and killed time walking along the Embankment to Charing Cross. London looked different in the spring, the trees in leaf and even the sludgy Thames gleaming in the sunlight. For the first time in years, he felt something like optimism. Or perhaps it was just that his heart was lighter than it had ever been, so full of Ashleigh Dalton he could burst. They'd only been apart for a few hours and already he was excited to see him again — giddy with anticipation, foolish as a puppy. As he walked up Villiers Street, he considered taking a stroll around the Embankment Gardens to admire the flowers blooming in neat beds, but he was too impatient for that, too eager to see Ash, even though he was almost an hour early. But thank God he hadn't dilly-dallied because, early as he was, Ash was earlier still. Harry spotted him immediately, looking handsome and elegant in his fine woollen overcoat and rakish Homberg, one shoulder braced against the wall of the Corner House as he cupped his hand around the fag he was lighting.

Ash wasn't much of a smoker, except to calm his nerves. Clearly, his meeting hadn't gone well. Whatever 'well' might mean for Ash.

Still, despite Ash's jittery looks, Harry's heart gave a delighted kick at the sight of him, his grin breaking out with irrepressible force. He picked up his pace, darting across the road in front of a lumbering omnibus. "Mr Ashleigh," he called, when he was close enough to be heard over the traffic. For Ash's part, he smiled like an exhausted sentry watching his relief approach.

"West. You're a sight for sore eyes."

Harry glanced at the clock. Ten past two. "You're early."

"Hmm." Ash agreed and took a long pull on his fag. "How was Kitty?"

"Surprised to see me," he said, and didn't press Ash on the obvious change of subject. There'd be time enough to talk later, when they were alone. God, he couldn't wait. "But she's well, and so are the girls."

"Good." Ash smiled a nervy smile. "Glad to hear it."

If they'd been alone, Harry would have pulled him into his arms. Ash looked like he needed comforting. Instead, he pushed his hands into his trouser pockets and glanced around at the teeming street. "Well," he said and lifted his eyebrows in query. "Nothing else to do this afternoon, then?"

"No." Ash gave another tense smile and Harry began to wonder whether he was nervous about the night to come. If so, he wasn't alone. A casual fumble round the back of the Old Stairs in Wapping was one thing, but tonight…? This would be something different. This, Harry knew full well, would make him fit for nobody else. Yes, Ash wasn't the only one with butterflies in his stomach.

"We should find the Allens' house," Ash said, dropping the rest of his cigarette onto the pavement. Harry crushed it out for him. "Charles Street in Mayfair. I have a key."

They took the tube to Green Park, Harry keeping a careful watch on Ash as he navigated the escalators. Neither of them spoke much, lost in their own thoughts, although they exchanged a couple of glances as they rattled along in the tube and again as they emerged into the afternoon sunlight.

It was a miracle nobody paid them any attention as they made their way through the London crowds, a miracle that their intentions weren't clear. Harry felt as though his anticipation must be shining out of him, that he must be glowing like a hot coal. It felt impossible that nobody could see his feelings written on his face.

Charles Street was a well-to-do road close to Berkley Square. Ranks of black shiny front doors stood to attention in stately terraces along both sides, iron railings fronted the properties and respectable-looking servants, nannies and tradesmen bustled along. No one cast him and Ash a second glance, not even when Ash stopped outside one of the houses and squinted up at the number.

"Thirty-six," he said. "This is it."

Harry set down their bags and flexed his fingers. One set of steps ran up to the front door, another set led down to the basement — the tradesman's entrance. For appearance sake, he wondered whether he should use it. But if the house was empty the door would be locked, and perhaps he was worrying too much. No one was paying them any attention. And so what if they were? What would they see but a gentleman and his servant?

Ash started up the steps without saying anything, and Harry followed with the bags. He couldn't help smiling to see Ash manage the steps so fast, despite his duff leg, eager to get inside. Harry's pulse picked up its pace too.

At the top of the stairs, Ash stopped and glanced over his shoulder, his face bright with excitement. Biting his lip, Ash pulled a brass key out of his coat pocket. His fingers shook so hard he fumbled getting the key into the lock and let out a shaky, laughing curse. Reaching past him, Harry closed his hand over Ash's, and they turned the key together. When Ash looked back at him, heart in his eyes, it was all Harry could do not to kiss him right there in the open.

He wasn't so foolish. Instead, he followed Ash into the silent house and breathed in the scent of fresh beeswax polish while the door closed behind them with a soft click. It was a grand place, though smaller than Highcliffe House. A large square reception hall gave way to stairs on the right and, on either side of the hall, doors opened onto reception rooms. In one of them, the furniture was still covered, but the other — a parlour — had been made ready for use. Fresh flowers stood on the table by the window.

"Well," Ash said, placing the key on a polished table at the foot of the stairs.

Well indeed. Harry set down their bags and went to Ash, who hadn't moved from the table. Putting his hands on Ash's arms, he ran them down the sleeves of his coat until their fingers met and threaded together. Ash sighed, leaning back against him, and Harry let his lips find the curve of his ear and press a soft kiss into his skin. With a shiver, Ash sank more heavily into Harry's embrace and Harry's heart overflowed, affection flooding through him as he wrapped Ash in his arms and held him tight. This. This was what he'd longed to do all day, just to hold his friend close and safe. "You're alright," he said quietly. "You're — "

The quick clack of footsteps on the tiled hall floor had Harry starting like he'd been shot. Heat flooded his face, pulse pounding as he turned to find a startled maid staring at them over an armful of linen.

"Beg pardon, sir," she said, bobbing a hasty curtsey. Christ alive, had she seen? "We didn't think you was coming until later."

Harry looked instinctively to Ash — Captain Dalton — as he'd always done in a crisis. Pale but calm, Ash said, "That's quite all right. I'm sorry to have surprised you. My meeting was shorter than I'd anticipated." He spoke in his most patrician tones, sounding like his own bloody father. After a pause, he added, "And I understood the house was unstaffed."

"Yes sir." The girl was a wiry thing who looked like she knew hard work. No more than fifteen, Harry would have guessed. "Mrs Palmer sent me and Betty over to open the place up for you, sir, and to put some food in the larder."

"How kind. And Mrs Palmer is…?"

"My mistress, sir."

A flicker of a smile touched Ash's lips. "Yes. And a friend of Mrs Allen, perhaps?"

"Aye sir." She bobbed another curtsey. "Betty's just laying a fire in the bedroom, and then we'll be on our way." She glanced at Harry. "There's linens in the servants' rooms upstairs."

"Thanks," he said, the tension in his body loosening. Surely if she'd seen them together, she wouldn't be acting so normally?

"What's your name?" Ash said, fishing in his pocket.

"Sarah, sir."

Ash set two half-crowns on the table. "One each for you and Betty," he said. "With my thanks for making me welcome."

Her eyes lit up. "Thank *you*, sir." She hesitated. "You want me to put the kettle on for tea or — ?"

"No, no," Ash said quickly. "Thank you, but a couple of old soldiers like us can shift for ourselves. I'm sure Mrs Palmer is expecting you back."

Once Sarah had left them alone, hurrying up the stairs, Ash let out a shaky breath and murmured, "Bloody *hell*."

"You think there's any good whisky in this house? I could use a stiff drink."

"Best wait for them to finish," Ash said, setting his cane aside to shrug out of his coat.

It was a fair point. "I'll take the bags upstairs," Harry decided. Better keep as far as possible from Ash; they'd had a narrow escape and he didn't want to push his luck.

When he reached the first-floor landing, he spotted the other maid — Betty, presumably — leaving one of the bedrooms. A gangly girl with light brown skin and a couple of curly dark strands escaping her cap, she stopped in surprise when she saw him. Sarah was on her heels.

"That's Mr Ashleigh's room, is it?" Harry said. "I've got his bag."

"That's right," Betty said. "I've laid the fire, but it's not lit being as it's so warm."

"Alright. I'll see to it later if he wants it."

"Boiler's lit in the kitchen, though," Betty went on with a huff of annoyance. "A right so-and-so it is, an' all, but Mrs P said to light it, so we did. There'll be hot water if his nibs wants a bath."

Harry swallowed a smile. "Much obliged," he said, and tried not to think about Ash taking a bath. Or taking a bath with Ash…

"Back stairs are through the kitchen," Sarah said as she and Betty moved past him. "And you're to make sure the doors are locked at night. There's all sorts round here these days."

'All sorts' being demobbed soldiers, Harry supposed. Down on their luck and looking for work, just as he'd been a few weeks ago. He forced a smile — "Will do, ma'am" — and gave them a mock salute, which made Betty laugh and Sarah roll her eyes.

While they clattered down stairs, whispering together, Harry pushed open the door to the guest room. It smelled of lavender, the sash window lowered to let in the sun-warmed afternoon air, and it was dominated by a large bed made up with crisp white linen.

Harry couldn't take his eyes off that bed as he set Ash's bag on the floor. He was going to take Ash to bed today. He was going to take him to bed in that bed.

It might be the only time they ever had the luxury of a bed and a house to themselves. It was a taste of a life they could never have and, standing there amid the scent of fresh linen and lavender, Harry didn't know whether the feeling that suffused him was delight or despair.

Not that it mattered. Things were what they were and nothing on God's green earth was going to change that. But if they had to live on memories, then he'd make damned sure their memories lasted a lifetime.

For appearance sake he found the cramped servants' rooms at the top of the house and left his own bag there. He'd retrieve it later. Then he went back down — using the back stairs, this time — and found himself in a compact but functional kitchen, from where he navigated his way back to the entrance hall. He paused at the bottom of the main stairs, looking around cautiously, ears pricked for any sound of the maids. All was quiet, save the clink of a bottle on glass from the front parlour. Stepping inside, he saw Ash standing at a sideboard pouring whiskey into two glasses. He turned at the sound of Harry's footsteps and gave a weary smile, weary but warm. "They've gone," he said, before Harry could ask. "And I've locked the bloody door behind them. *All* the doors."

Harry laughed, crossing the room to claim his drink. It was an elegant parlour with dark floral wallpaper, a large fireplace, and an elaborate wooden overmantle. It drew his eye, not least because he could see Ash reflected in the dozen small mirrors it contained, his pensive expression clear when he turned back to the sideboard and topped up his glass.

"You've had a rough day." Harry sipped his whisky slowly. It was a good one, smooth and smoky.

Ash hummed his agreement and knocked back his drink like it wasn't his first. Definitely a rough day. Setting down his glass, Harry put his hand on Ash's shoulder. "Come here," he said when he felt him tense. "Ash, come here."

With a sigh, Ash turned, his duff foot scuffing over the rug, and Harry pulled him into his arms. It felt so good to hold him, so natural to feel Ash leaning into him, his forehead coming to rest heavy on Harry's shoulder. Rubbing a hand over his back, Harry said, "Do you want to tell me what happened?"

Ash shook his head. "Maybe later."

A huff of warm breath caressed Harry's neck as Ash closed his arms around him. Cradling the back of his head, Harry pulled him closer still, until there was no space left between them. They stayed like that for a long time, the silence of the room disturbed by not so much as the ticking of a clock. The one on the mantle hadn't been wound, Harry supposed. This room — this house — was a place outside time. From the street came the noise of passing traffic, chattering voices, and clacking footsteps, but inside was only Ash's steady breathing and the warmth blooming between them.

Eventually, Ash lifted his head, just enough that Harry could see his face. Lovely dark eyes watched him from beneath thick lashes, but they were shadowed with anxiety and weariness. He'd bet good money Ash hadn't slept last night. He looked pale, sallow with exhaustion, his features fine and handsome but too thin. He'd look healthier if he gained a stone. But, even so, to Harry, Ash's face was the dearest in the world. It always would be, whatever the future had in store for them. "Do you want to rest? Catch forty winks?" He smiled, rubbed his thumb over Ash's cheek. "There's plenty of time. It's not even four o'clock."

But Ash shook his head. "I don't want to sleep." And then he smiled too, a flush putting some colour into his face. "But I wouldn't mind going to bed."

"Is that so?" Harry pulled him a little closer, a subtle rocking of his hips making Ash's eyelids flutter. "I wouldn't mind that either."

"Then what are we waiting for?" Ash squeezed his hand. "Take me to bed, Harry West."

Although the house was empty, Harry shut the bedroom door

behind them and drew the curtains against the afternoon sun. Filtered through the drapery, the light became thick and golden, dancing across the bed in shifting patterns made by the breeze-stirred curtains.

All Harry's past encounters with men had been, by necessity, fast and fumbled, so this premeditation was something new — sweet and tender and exposing. His heart pounded high in his chest as he watched Ash watch him. They'd discarded jackets, ties and waistcoats and laid down on the bed together, throwing back sheets and blankets to sprawl half-clothed on the pristine linen. Harry had never slept on sheets so fine.

Ash lay on his back, Harry propped up on one elbow at his side as one by one he undid the buttons on Ash's undershirt. When he slipped his hand onto the warm skin of his chest, Ash caught his breath and bit his lip. Despite his thick dark hair, his chest was smooth under Harry's touch. Bloody gorgeous. Harry bent his head and kissed him there, over his heart, pushing his clothes aside.

"Harry," Ash whispered, running light fingers through Harry's hair, down his neck and over his shoulders. Harry wished he had his own shirt off, he wanted to feel Ash's touch skin-to-skin.

Kissing up his chest, back to his throat and jaw, Harry said, "Let's get undressed. I want to touch you all over."

Sitting up, he pulled his shirt off and was working on the buttons on his trousers when he realised Ash hadn't moved. He was staring at the ceiling, one hand gripping the waistband of his trousers.

"Ash?" Harry said in concern. "What's wrong?"

He was silent, lips moving like he was working on words but hadn't found them yet. With a horrible feeling that he knew what was coming, Harry held his tongue and waited, only putting his hand over Ash's clenched fist. At last, in a reluctant whisper, Ash said, "I don't want you to see it."

Harry's heart cramped like he'd been kicked, a raw emotion filling his throat. Instinctively he tried to deflect the conversation, offering a teasing laugh. "I'm hoping to do more than see it, mate."

Ash turned his head, eyes impossibly wide. "I mean — "

"I know." Harry tightened his hold on Ash's hand, his laughter fading. There was no avoiding it. "I know what you mean."

"It's ugly." Ash stared back at the ceiling, blinking rapidly. "I can't stand to look at it myself, and I'm sure you'll think — "

"No."

Ash looked at him, surprised perhaps by the bark in his voice.

Harry was surprised too. But it had to be said, the truth burned too fierce not to be spoken. "I'll tell you what's ugly," Harry said, more roughly than he'd have liked. "Seeing you with your foot blown half off, your uniform gone black with blood. Your face the colour of…of the dead. That — " His voice caught, but he made himself carry on. "That was ugly."

Under his hand, Ash went still but he didn't speak. And Harry was only half there anyway, the rest of him going back to memories he'd made a point of avoiding. But he'd do anything for Ash. Even this. "Watching them carry you away at the dressing station, that was — " He could see it so clearly in his mind's eye: the stench of the place, the cries of the wounded, the silence of the dead. "That was worse. Your arm, it — It flopped over the edge of the stretcher like a corpse, just hanging there. And I wanted to run after them and lift it up and tell them to take better care of you. I wanted to tell them that you were… were precious to me. But I couldn't. I *couldn't*. All I could do was watch them take you away, and I thought you were already gone, Ash. I thought you'd bought it. I thought I'd never see you again and I — I wanted to die."

"Harry…" Ash clutched Harry's hand, strong fingers gripping his.

"That first night, I was going to stand on the sodding fire step, light a fag, and let the Bosh do the rest." He choked, throat too tight to swallow. "So don't you tell me anything about you is ugly, because you're *here*." A sob escaped, hard and painful in his chest and throat. "You're here and that's the fucking miracle I prayed for. And I don't care about your leg, or any other bloody thing, Ash, because I love you." He shocked himself into silence, saying those words out loud, and sucked in a shaking breath. Swiping at his eyes with his free hand he ploughed on, "I love you, Ashleigh Dalton, every single beautiful, damaged, precious bloody piece of you."

"Harry… Oh my dear Harry, come here." And then Ash was kneeling up, his strong arms around Harry's shoulders, sweeping him into a fierce embrace. "I'm a selfish bastard. I hardly even *thought* how it was for you. At the time, I didn't know you felt like this or — "

"Well I did," Harry said fiercely. "I *do*." It was an awkward embrace, Ash half kneeling on the bed in front of Harry. But it meant Harry could touch his injured leg, feel the firm muscle of his thigh and, past his knee, the hard straps that held the prosthetic in place. "I love you, Ash, and if you think I give a damn what your leg looks like then you don't know anything."

Ash released him enough that he could look him in the eye. "I love you, too," he said. "You know that, of course. You know I love you."

"I do," Harry said with an unsteady smile, struggling free of his bleak memories. "I do now."

Leaning in, Ash found his mouth with a soft, ardent kiss that tasted of smoke and salt tears, and slowly they sank back onto the bed together. They kissed on, hands finding ways beneath clothes, a gradual disrobing as the heat rose between them and burned away the sadness. The past could not hold out against the urgent, pressing need of the present.

Harry touched his lips to the hollow of Ash's throat. "I love the way you smell," he murmured, tongue flickering against Ash's collarbone as if he could taste the fragrance on his skin.

Ash gave a breathy laugh and wound his fingers tighter into Harry's hair. "Sandlewood soap," he said, and groaned as Harry pressed another kiss to the bolt of his jaw. "My mother's."

They both laughed and, laughing, Harry rolled Ash onto his back, looking down at his flushed face and kiss-swollen lips as he deliberately ground their hips together. Even through layers of clothing, the feel of Ash's hard prick against his own made him groan, and when Ash started to move his hips in slow, sinuous rolls, rocking them together, Harry thought he might explode there and then.

"Bloody hell," he said softly. "I want to feel you. All over."

"Yes. God yes. I want to feel you, too, I just — " Ash swallowed. "I just hate — "

Harry kissed the words from his lips, then pulled back and said, "How about we pull the sheet up over it?"

Ash said nothing, looking uncertain.

"Come on, I won't look. Get yourself undressed, take off your leg — can't be comfy — and pull the sheet up over it." He put a hand on Ash's chest, feeling the racing beat of his heart beneath his palm. "I swear it won't bother me, Ash, but you have to feel comfortable too, eh?"

He nodded, pushing himself up on his elbows. "Yes. Yes, alright."

Harry smiled and kissed him, sliding a hand to the tempting bulge in his trousers. "Don't take all day about it, either," he said, giving his prick a gentle squeeze. "I have plans for this."

"Fuck," Ash said, eyes fluttering shut. Somehow, in his refined accent, the obscenity sounded deliciously erotic.

Harry busied himself with stripping out of his trousers and underwear, listening to the sounds behind him. The thud of Ash's prosthetic hitting the floor, the rustle of fabric and the creak of the bed. It broke his heart that Ash thought the way he did about his injury, but he reckoned he'd be able to change his mind. He'd give him something else to think about at any rate.

Eventually, Ash said, "Alright" and Harry turned around.

He lay on his back, propped up on his elbows, the knee of his good leg bent up and the other leg lost beneath the white sheets. In the rich afternoon sunshine filtering through the curtains his bare skin was all ivory and shadow. Strong shoulders over a trim, sparely muscled chest. Ribs a little too prominent, his belly flat with a scattering of dark hair which arrowed down to a sizable, half-hard prick and long, lean thighs. Harry's mouth went dry at the sight of him. "Blimey, Ashleigh Dalton, you're a sight and a half, you are."

Ash was drinking his fill, too, and Harry glowed with pleasure to see him bite his lip hungrily as Harry approached the bed.

"Stunning," Ash breathed. "A Barberini Faun."

"You what?" Harry climbed back onto the bed, pausing at the last moment. "A fawn?"

"A statue. Roman. You look — " Ash sank back onto the pillows. "It doesn't matter. God, Harry, just touch me before I go mad."

"I hardly know where to start."

"Everywhere," Ash said, opening his arms. "Everywhere, Harry."

They came together reverently, and Harry almost wept at the feel of all that warm bare skin against his own. He'd never felt anything like it, not in his whole life. Chest to chest, prick to prick, kissing and rubbing together, touching intimately. Harry slid an arm under Ash's back, a hand into his hair, tipping his head back so he could kiss him deeply, their tongues tangling as Ash threw one leg around Harry's hips, urging him closer as they rocked together, pricks sparring in the hot, slick space between them. So good. So bloody good.

Timeless minutes passed as Harry lost himself in the feel of Ash's body, in the taste of his skin, and the overflowing of his own heart. No words between them, just breaths, no thoughts to trouble them, just touch and taste and feel. Only delight, only joy. Only love.

Harry shifted them until the angle was better, his prick sliding over Ash's again and again, his hands sinking into the warm flesh of his arse. Ash kissed his jaw, then his shoulder — sharp, bity kisses that made Harry groan with pleasurable pain. Bloody hell, he'd never felt so aroused. His blood was red fire, blinding behind his eyes.

Ash breathed in short sharp breaths. "Yes," he gasped. "Oh yes, oh God."

And suddenly everything was tensing up, from thighs to balls to belly. Too soon, but unstoppable. "Ash I'm — "

"Oh, Christ *yes!*" Ash arched back as he climaxed, fingers biting into Harry's shoulders, the cords in his neck straining.

And it was enough to trigger Harry's own release, sweeping through him like rolling thunder. "Ash," he gasped, burying his face against his shoulder. "Oh God, *Ashleigh.*"

A heavy flood of emotion followed, rising like a river after a storm to sweep everything before it. All Harry could do was hold on, sweaty and breathless, helplessly in love. He kissed Ash's shoulder, the side of his neck, his jaw, his lips. Everywhere he could reach. "I'm yours," he breathed into the silent space between them. "I'm yours, Ash, heart and bloody soul."

"And I'm yours," Ash whispered back, watching him with those dark soulful eyes. "Always, Harry. I'll love you forever. Whatever happens."

Harry drew him closer, pressing a kiss to his sweat-damp hair, a spike of unease snagging his heart like barbed wire. Because Harry knew there was no forever. Not for them. Such things were impossible.

There was only today, there was only tonight. And he'd do well not to forget it.

Chapter Sixteen

A sh slept deeper than he had in months. Years, possibly. When he finally surfaced it was to fading daylight and a chill on his back. But still he didn't want to move.

They'd curled together in sleep, his cheek against Harry's shoulder and Harry's arms holding him close, one large hand settled on his shoulder and the other stroking over his hip to his thigh and back in slow, careful caresses. Their legs were entwined, and — He froze. That was his left leg Harry was touching, his left leg that he'd curled over Harry's while he slept.

He felt a sinking disgust in the pit of his stomach, allowed the feeling for a moment, then opened his eyes to look. Harry's hand moved over his hip, stroking down his thigh, and beyond his knee the raw truncated end of his leg nestled between Harry's shins. His stomach clenched, but he made himself look — made himself remember Harry's heartrending account of his grief when he'd thought Ash had died. Christ, what if Harry had really done it? What if he'd stood on the firestep and let a German sniper end it for him? What if Ash had received *that* letter in the Calais Field Hospital: Private Harry West, killed in action. Even the thought of it stopped his heart. Surely the reality would have finished him off. And if it hadn't, what an empty, colourless life he'd be living now. Half a life with half his soul missing, and the better half of his soul too.

So he owed it to Harry to look down at the stump of his leg, to not flinch away, to allow Harry to see all of him. "Major Edwards said they did a good job at the Field Hospital. I was lucky."

Harry's hand paused on his thigh. "Does it still hurt?"

"No, not all the time. The prosthetic… It chafes the wound sometimes and putting too much pressure on it hurts. Olive said that will get better though, over time."

Harry moved his hand further down his leg, to his knee. "I can see where the straps rub," he said. "Looks a bit sore."

"You know what's strange?" Ash uncurled his leg from around Harry's and straightened it out on the bed. "My foot hurts, sometimes. The missing one."

Harry shifted so he could look him in the eye. "It never does."

"It's true," Ash said. "It's the way the nerve endings were severed, apparently. Some men have it much worse than me, though. Constant pain, poor buggers. And no pills can touch it because the limb isn't there anymore. They call it phantom pain — like a ghost."

"Huh." Harry sat up to get a closer look, running his hand down Ash's leg but not touching the scar. "Looks pretty healthy to me. I mean, the skin's a good colour and it seems to have healed up well." He touched one of the red patches where the straps of the prosthetic attached above his knee. "This looks painful, though."

"Olive said the new prosthetic will fit better. It's lighter, too, apparently, so I hope to get around a bit better."

Harry studied him. "You admire your Miss Olive, don't you?"

"Yes, of course." Ash felt a swell of pride in his friend. "She does wonderful work at Chewton Lodge, Harry. And she wants to be a doctor. She'd make an excellent doctor, I've no doubt."

Harry lifted an eyebrow. "A lady doctor? It *is* a new world, after all."

"There are already female doctors — so Olive tells me. And a medical school to train them, too. But, of course, Olive's father wouldn't hear of it and she won't have her fortune until she marries — and then her husband would have a say." He sighed, thinking of Olive's frustrations and thwarted ambitions. "We're not the only ones trapped by society's prejudices."

Harry opened his mouth, as if to say something, but apparently changed his mind. Instead, he reached out and ran a finger down from Ash's bellybutton through the thatch of dark hair below. One corner of his mouth curled up into a smile. "We made a right mess of each other."

True enough. Ash had fallen asleep directly, their — uh — emissions now drying on his belly. His cheeks flamed. "There's a flannel in my bag, I can —"

"Never mind your flannel. One of the girls told me there's hot water for a bath." His eyebrows wiggled. "Shall I see if the tub's big enough for two?"

"A bath… Heavens, I'd love a bath."

Harry kissed him on the lips, sweet and swift, leaped out of bed and padded stark naked out of the room. He was back before Ash had swung both legs over the edge of the bed.

"The bathroom's bloody enormous!" he declared. "Never seen anything like it. Come on. I've got the water running."

Ash laughed at his enthusiasm and reached down to retrieve his prosthetic from where he'd discarded it next to the bed. Normally, when bathing, he used crutches to reach the bathroom, but since he didn't have them with him —

Harry loomed in front of him and Ash looked up. "Don't bother with that," he said. "It's only around the corner."

"Well I can hardly hop," Ash said, indignant at the idea.

"I'll help you." Harry held out his hand and, after considering for a moment, Ash took it. If it really wasn't far, he supposed they could manage. He hated feeling so dependent, though. He was starting to tell Harry to go around to his left side when Harry gave him a wink, ducked, and without warning hoisted Ash over his shoulder like a sack of potatoes.

Ash yelped. There was no other word for it: he yelped. "Put me down!"

"Stop wriggling or I'll drop you," Harry warned cheerfully, turning for the door.

"Harry, put me—" But his outrage couldn't last and, somehow, he found himself laughing. "Oh my God, Harry, you lunatic. Put me down."

"Nah," Harry said. "I'm enjoying the view too much." And with that, he gave Ash's backside a playful swat.

Ash gasped but swallowed his objection when he realised his own view wasn't half bad either. Reaching down, he gave Harry's fine, firm arse a squeeze. And then it was Harry's turn to yelp.

"Oi, cut it out!"

"Don't think I shall," he said, and found himself laughing—giggling!—as Harry wobbled his way around the corner into the bathroom while Ash helped himself to a nice handful of his backside.

Steam was already filling the room as they entered, and Harry shifted his arms to lower Ash with infinite care to the floor. Harry looked flushed with the exertion, but he was smiling, and Ash couldn't stop laughing. Really laughing. It was all so ridiculous: the war, the nightmare things they'd seen and done, Ash with half his leg missing, and them here alone in this house together, making love, standing in the steamy bathroom without a stitch on, and Ash feeling like champagne was flowing through his veins.

He was happy, he realised. Deliriously, impossibly happy.

"Lord," he said, when his giggles subsided, "I can't remember the last time I laughed like that."

"I can." Harry's grin faded, his expression softening. "That night we spent in Rouen." And he was right, Ash remembered it well—them walking the town together, laughing and happy, arms around each other's shoulders like any other Tommies with forty-eight hours leave. "I wanted to kiss you so badly. You looked so bloody lovely."

"Then kiss me now," Ash said, and Harry did, taking him in his arms and making Ash's champagne blood fizz in delight.

Too soon, Harry pulled away. "Park yourself here," he said, helping Ash to a chair, "while I sort out the bath before it overflows."

The tub was a grand claw-footed thing with a modern shower contraption over the top. Steam rose from inside, fragranced with floral-scented bath salts. Harry helped Ash over to the bath and he sat on the edge to swing his legs over, lowering himself in with his hands braced on the sides of the tub. God, it felt good, and he sank back with a happy sigh, looking up at Harry watching him.

"Want me to scrub your back?" Harry said with a comical twitch of his eyebrows.

Ash scooted forward, making room behind him. "Come on. There's room for two."

Barely, as it turned out, and they had to stifle their laughter for fear of causing a flood as Harry manoeuvred himself into the tub behind Ash. But eventually, they got themselves situated, Harry leaning back against the bath and Ash leaning back against Harry's chest. It was more intimate than practical, but Ash didn't care. Who knew if they'd ever get a chance like this again?

Eat, drink and be merry for tomorrow we die.

"Blimey," Harry said as they settled together beneath the warm water. "I'm used to a tin bath in front of the fire. Never seen a bathroom like this before."

It wasn't much larger than their bathroom at Highcliffe, Ash thought with a guilty pang. "I'd rather a tin bath in front of the fire, with you in it, than all the grand bathrooms in London." And that was the truth. What did any of this matter, if he wasn't with Harry?

"You might think different, freezing your arse off in two inches of water," Harry said, without any reproach. "But it's not like we'll have a choice either way. Believe me, my Kitty would be no better friend to us than your mother and father. The world ain't made for the likes of us, Ash. We'll have to live in the shadows."

Ash twisted his head around to see him better. "But you have to wonder how long it can all last."

"How long all what can last?"

"This." He waved at the huge bathroom. "In Russia, they're tearing everything down and starting afresh. And they almost managed it in Glasgow, too."

"Are you a Bolshevik now, Mr Ashleigh of Highcliffe House?"

He snorted. "Hardly. But surely there's something between Bolshevism and this? Christ, Harry, there's men home from the war begging on the streets, there's women like Olive wasting their God-given talents, and there's men like us…" He ran a hand over Harry's chest, a lump rising in his throat at the thought. "There's men like us doing two years hard labour for falling in love."

Falling in love. Such sweet, painful, dangerous words.

"The world is what it is." Harry closed his hand over Ash's fingers, pressing them flat against his heart. "And it ain't all bad."

"But it could be *better*. It has to be, Harry. The war… If nothing changes, then what the hell was it all *for*?"

"King and country?" Harry said, a wry tilt to his lips.

"No. It can't be. Things *will* change, I know it. We'll live to see a kinder world. One where Olive won't need her father's permission to study medicine, and you and I…" He trailed off, his imagination failing.

Harry considered him thoughtfully. "I'd marry you, in that world, Ash. If you'd have me."

Startled tears pricked his eyes. It was a fantastical notion, yet it infused him with such longing he could hardly breathe. "In a heartbeat," he whispered when he'd recovered his voice. "I'd have you in a bloody heartbeat, Harry. You know I would."

"Well" Harry's smile wobbled, failing to hide the emotion shaking his voice. "I'll consider that a promise, then. For when the day comes."

The wave of water that landed on the bathroom floor when Ash pulled Harry into a ferocious hug made them both laugh.

But who cared about bathroom floors? All that mattered in the world was Harry West. The rest could go to hell.

∗∗∗

Harry had their tea cooking — a saucepan of fragrant stew heating on the stove and a loaf of fresh bread — by the time Ash found his way to the kitchen. The tell-tale tap of his cane and the heavy tread of his prosthetic foot meant he'd never be stealthy, and Harry was already turning to the kitchen door when Ash stepped inside.

He'd changed into casual clothes, slacks and a soft-looking pull-over sweater in blue and cream stripes. His hair was still damp and fell across his forehead in a way that did silly things to Harry's sentimental soul. "Hungry?" he said, turning back to give the pot a stir before it started catching. "The girls left us a nice-looking tea, I'll say that for them."

"Starving, actually," Ash admitted. "I didn't eat much lunch in the end."

And he still hadn't told Harry what had happened. Perhaps he'd get it out of him over tea.

He heard Ash come up behind him and didn't realise he was anticipating his touch until Ash slipped one arm around his waist and leaned against his back. At least he wasn't alone in this constant need to touch. An embarrassingly soft noise escaped his throat as Ash kissed the back of his neck.

"I wonder if there's a decent bottle of wine to be had," Ash said, and moved away to explore the kitchen.

"Won't they mind us pinching it?" He watched Ash poking around in the larder.

"The Allens? No. I doubt they'll notice. Rich as Croesus. Ah-hah!" He retrieved a dusty bottle and examined the label. "This should do nicely."

Harry had never tasted wine before he'd been in France, and there he'd only drunk the plonk they served in the local dives open to soldiers. If he was honest, he was more of a beer man. But he knew Ash liked his wine, so what the hell? He was living in a fantasy world tonight, he might as well go all in. "This is warmed through," he said, lifting the pot off the heat. "Beef stew," he added. Meat was still rationed, so that was generous of whoever had provided the meal.

While Ash went in search of a corkscrew and glasses, Harry

found plates and cutlery and set places on the kitchen table. It felt warm and domestic, a little glimpse into Ash's imagined future that was as sweet as it was impossible. What a dream, though, to live together like this. Although he supposed some men managed something like it, those 'confirmed bachelors' who shared rooms and wore velvet dressing gowns and smoked cigarettes in long holders. Everyone knew what they were up to, but blind eyes were turned. They were all respectable middle-class blokes, though, friends from Oxford and the like. Theatre types. Not the son of a baronet and a nagman from Bethnal Green. Now *that* would never be acceptable to anyone. Truth was, it would be almost as scandalous for a man like Ash to marry Kitty as it would be to set up house with her brother. There was more than one way the world divided them, even if Ash didn't always seem to notice.

Harry set the pot on the table between them and Ash brought wine and a couple of glasses with proper stems and all. He smiled as he set them down. "We could be at Toc H."

"Only it's quieter." Toc H had always been rowdy as hell, but comfortable too. One of his favourite places in Flanders. Ash poured the wine and lifted his glass in salute. "Absent friends," he said, and Harry clinked their glasses together.

The stew was plain English grub: beef, carrots, parsnips. Harry tucked in with gusto, and even Ash ate a good portion. They didn't speak much, but their gaze held across the table, full of warm, loving looks. Harry felt utterly in love and allowed himself to bask in the sensation.

But he could tell Ash was distracted, lost in his thoughts and with Ash that was never a good idea. So, when he'd eaten his fill and topped up their glasses, Harry leaned back in his chair and said, "Well then, you haven't told me how your meeting went today."

Ash looked up through those dark lashes of his and gave a familiar nervy smile. "No," he agreed, and reached for his glass.

"I'd say it looks like things didn't go to plan, only I don't know what the plan was in the first place."

"Neither did I. I hadn't really thought it through until I got there and realised…" He took a sip of his wine. "You should have seen it, Harry. Dusty old place, hardly changed since before the war." He gave half a shrug. "A few women employed, that's the only difference. Going back felt like…like putting on a dead man's suit. I suppose I'm just not the man I was before the war."

"It's changed us all," Harry agreed, but maybe men like Ash, who'd never known a day's hardship, were shaken up more by seeing the suffering of their men — and sharing it too.

"You've changed me." Ash looked down at his plate, pushing a piece of carrot around with his fork. "What I feel for you has changed me. How can I live that life now? Wife, children, good job at the bank? Christ alive, I think I should go quite mad trying to cram myself into it."

Carefully, Harry lowered his glass to the table. "Did you turn the position down, then?"

Ash nodded. "Couldn't do anything else."

"You'll have to do *something* else. Unless… I mean, you *do* have to earn money, don't you?"

"Yes." Ash's nervy smile was back. "Dodge will inherit Highcliffe House and I'll have to shift for myself. Besides, I *want* an occupation. Only not in that bloody office." A pause, then, "I'd like to do what we talked about before."

Harry raised his eyebrows. "What we talked about…?"

"Breeding horses." There was a feverish light in his eyes when he spoke. "Why not? You and I could go into business together."

"With what money?" It was nonsense and Harry didn't like talking about something so impossible. "I've barely tuppence to my name, and unless you've a fortune stashed under your mattress…"

"I'll have a small inheritance, when the time comes. Perhaps I could ask Father for it early…" His voice trailed off, face creasing into a frown.

Yes, Harry thought, that's about as likely as snow in June. "Maybe there's another profession you could try? A man like you with an education — must be lots of things you could do. School teaching?"

Ash made a face. "I want to be with you, Harry. That's the point. I want us to be together. Like this."

"Like this?" He laughed, although he wasn't the slightest bit amused. "Ash… You can't really think we can set up house together."

"Why not?"

"You know why not."

Ash leaned forward, reached for Harry's hand. "But if we had stables, out in the country, nobody would know how we lived. We could live as we chose, just you and I, and — "

"You're dreaming," Harry said harshly. It hurt to think about this, he didn't know why Ash was torturing them both with the fantasy.

But Ash only gripped his hand tighter. "It's not impossible. We… we need to get away from everything, don't you see? From all these people telling us how to live. Then we could have this, Harry. We could have *this* every single day. Imagine it! We could have a stable and a — "

"No, we couldn't!" Harry snatched his hand away and stood up, taking his plate to the sink. "There's no point talking about this."

"Don't you want — ?"

"Of course I do." His voice broke on the last word. He set his plate down and braced his hands on the edge of the sink, regaining control. "But if wishes were horses, Ash…"

Silence. Then, "Maybe we could go away together. Somewhere nobody knows us."

Harry closed his eyes. "And do what?"

Another silence. "In France it's not a crime for men to — "

"France?" He turned around, incredulous. "I ain't going back to France, Ash."

"No." He turned his head away. "It's just…"

Anger draining, or at least finding the right direction, Harry went back to the table and sat down. "I know," he said quietly. "God knows, I do, Ash, but we have to be realistic." Reaching out, he took Ash's hand in his and gave it a squeeze. "We've the whole night ahead of us, eh? Tomorrow can take care of itself."

With a reluctant nod, Ash turned back to look at him. "This is too perfect to only be for one night."

Somehow, Harry's heart was singing and breaking at the same time, a sweet sad pain that stole his breath. Lifting Ash's fingers to his lips he kissed his knuckles, then turned his hand over and kissed his palm, his wrist. "But it's more than we dreamed of not so long ago. Don't think about what's to come, Ash. Just think about what's right now."

And, right now, Ash was abruptly in his arms again, his hard body beneath the soft wool of his pullover delicious under Harry's hands, the urgent ferocity of his mouth against Harry's enough to drive all other thoughts from his mind. They made their way back to the bedroom and came together hungrily, touching and tasting, tenderly exploring each other until ecstasy overtook them again. Then they slept naked beneath the sheets and blankets, crowded into each other's arms and boneless with joyful fatigue.

Harry woke later to pitch dark night and an anguished shout.

Disorientated, he lurched upright, heart hammering, waiting for the sounds of bombardment. But all was silent save his own ragged breathing — and Ash, thrashing around beside him, muttering unintelligible dream-words. Then, with a gasp, he sat up, one hand stretching out, staring unseeing into the dark. Or maybe seeing something else. "Grab it," Ash shouted, startlingly loud.

Shit. Harry touched his shoulder. It was clammy with sweat. "Ash," he said, softly. "Ash — "

"Just fucking grab the rifle."

Harry rubbed his back. "It's alright."

"I can't reach!"

"You're dreaming." Christ, it was awful.

"I can't — " Ash sucked in a breath that seemed to catch in his chest and become a sob, and then he crumpled forward over his knees. "Oh *God*."

Pushing aside his own painful memories, Harry curled himself around Ash's back, offering what comfort he could. There were no words to be said that would make it right. A nightmare it might be, but that didn't mean it wasn't real. Ash cried for a few minutes, deep shaking silent sobs, and then he shifted himself enough to put his arms around Harry and bury his face into the space between his shoulder and his neck. His breath was hot, his skin damp with cooling sweat. "It was Jimmy."

"I know." Harry kissed his hair.

"I can't forget."

"No. We shouldn't, neither."

Ash nodded, sagging into Harry's arms. Tired. Well, it was the middle of the bloody night. "Come on, let's lie down."

The sheets where Ash had been sleeping were a little sweat-damp, so Harry pulled him onto his side of the bed, his back to Harry's chest and wrapped his arms tight about him, as if he could shield him from his nightmares with his body.

They lay like that for a while, Harry drifting guiltily toward sleep — he doubted Ash would close his eyes any time soon, poor bugger.

"I'm glad you're here," Ash said after a while, murmuring the words into the darkness.

Harry kissed his shoulder, tightened his arms. "Me too."

He didn't promise to always be there. Whatever Ash might think, Harry knew it was impossible.

And there was no point in wishing for impossible things.

Chapter Seventeen

Contrary to his expectations, Ash did sleep again after his nightmare. Cradled in Harry's arms his body relaxed, his thoughts drifted... And the next thing he knew he was blinking out from beneath the covers at a bright morning and Harry, fully dressed, was perching on the side of the bed next to him.

"Morning," Harry said with a sunny smile.

"Christ, what time is it?"

"Half eight."

"What?" He struggled to sit up. "My appointment's at ten."

Harry ruffled his hair. "Plenty of time." He nodded toward the bedside table where he'd set a plate of toast and a steaming cup of tea. "And you needed the extra sleep."

He was a kind, thoughtful man. "Thank you," was all Ash said, shoving the pillow behind him and reaching for the tea. Harry looked very fine that morning, the sunlight suiting his tanned face and bright eyes. "Will you come to the hospital with me, or do you have other plans?"

"No other plans." He rested a hand on Ash's knee and squeezed gently. It was his bad leg, but Harry didn't seem to notice so Ash decided not to care.

He smiled. "Good, I could use the company. I imagine there'll be something of a wait. You know how these things are."

"Not really, I've never been to a hospital." He knocked on the table for luck. "Expensive business."

That was true enough, and Ash wasn't oblivious to his own luck in being able to afford the best possible care. God knew, there were plenty of men who couldn't.

After he'd eaten his breakfast, Ash dressed while Harry set about packing up their things and they were ready to leave in good time. He paused as they left the bedroom, gaze lingering on the bed they'd shared. A slice of paradise, he'd found in this room, and he sighed with the knowledge that they'd never return.

"Come on," Harry said quietly, taking his free hand. "Time to go."

He was right not to dawdle. But that didn't mean Ash planned to just accept their situation as hopeless. Harry might not think his dreams were realistic, but Ash refused to give up. Or to give in. To hell with his father and the old world he clung to. What the devil did any of them think they could do to stop him from living the life he chose? He'd fought three bloody years for a better world and he was damn well going to have it for himself.

They took the tube to East Putney and then a bus to the Queen Mary Hospital in Roehampton. It was an impressive building, a grand eighteenth century stately pile that had been turned over at the start of the war for use as an auxiliary convalescence hospital, and now had become a specialised hospital for amputees.

"Blimey," Harry said under his breath, watching the numbers of men coming and going with prosthetic limbs. "Who knew there were so many?"

It was startling, certainly. Not that they hadn't seen their fair share of wounded men, but this great building seemed to hold hundreds of men missing arms and legs in various combinations. Ash, not for the first time, felt grateful his own injury had been relatively minor.

And what kind of a world was it, he reflected, where losing your leg from the knee down could be considered minor?

They were directed to a waiting room and took a seat until Ash's name was eventually called. And only fifteen minutes after his appointment time, too. Impressively efficient. Harry stayed put while Ash followed the young nurse into a room which looked as much like a workshop or gymnasium as anything else. It might even have been amusing to see the rows of legs stacked up against the wall had the reason for them being there not been so dreadful.

Still, the doctor who stood to greet him had a friendly face and smiled as they shook hands. He was older than Ash, but not as old as Sir Arthur, his short mousy hair tending to salt-and-pepper and his light blue eyes intelligent. "Dalton," he said, "a pleasure to meet you. I'm Dr Bentley." He sat back down at his desk, shuffled some papers. "We were sent your measurements by Major Edwards at Chewton Lodge. So let's hope we've made a good fist of it, eh?"

This time, when Ash rolled up his trouser leg to remove his prosthetic, he found he didn't feel the overwhelming sense of disgust and humiliation that usually dogged him on such occasions. Distaste lingered, yes, but it felt more muted. Distant, somehow. He could stand to look, for a start, when the doctor lifted his leg onto his lap to examine it.

"Yes," Bentley said briskly. "Some chafing, I can see, from the strapping. No surprise there." He released Ash's leg and bent to retrieve his old prosthetic. "This?" He hefted it in his hands. "Very heavy, yes?"

"Yes, rather."

On Bentley's desk sat what Ash assumed must be his new limb. It gleamed startlingly silver, although the foot was a more natural colour. "Aluminium copper alloy," Bentley said when he saw Ash looking, and picked up the new leg. "Much lighter than the wood, you see? And just as strong." He handed it over and Ash was surprised — it must have been less than half the weight of his old wooden leg. "Shall we try it, then?" the doctor said.

It took some getting used to the new weight, but Olive had been right: the fit was much more comfortable. And he felt the benefit of its lighter weight immediately in his hip and knee when the doctor had him walk backward and forward across the room. No longer having to lift such a weight made his gait feel more natural, too.

"Excellent," Bentley said, crouching down to check the fit around his knee. "Yes, very good." He looked up. "I should think you could dispense with the cane from time-to-time, especially indoors, once you're used to it. Give you an extra hand to use, eh?"

Ash found himself smiling as he sat to roll his trouser leg down and reached for his cane. "Thank you," he said sincerely and offered his hand.

Dr Bentley shook it with a quick smile. "You're an easy case, Dalton. Any problems with the fit, come back to us, yes?"

Ash promised he would and, thus dismissed, returned to the waiting room where he found Harry standing to greet him, head cocked as he watched him approach. "Well?"

"Better," Ash said. "Closer fit, and much lighter." He bent his knee and swung his new leg to demonstrate. "Not sure I'll be dancing a jig any time soon, but it feels much more comfortable."

Harry's delighted smile was all for him. It was a wonder that everyone in the waiting room didn't see the affection in Harry's eyes. And in Ash's heart.

They took the walk back to the bus stop slowly. Partly, Ash needed to become accustomed to the new weight of his leg, but mostly he wanted to prolong their time together — and dwell a little on the warming memories of last night.

"What's got you smiling?" Harry asked as they made their way along the pavement together, stopping to let a group of young ladies pass by.

Ash touched the brim of his hat and watched the ladies cast admiring looks at Harry, amused that his friend didn't notice. "Just thinking how lucky I am to have met you," he said when they walked on.

Harry smiled. "I think about that too. Of all the men at the front, that I should be assigned to you? Seems impossible."

"Fate, then. Perhaps we were always destined to meet. Even if there'd been no war."

"Not sure I believe in fate," Harry said thoughtfully. "But talk about a silver bloody lining."

More than a silver lining. It had to be. Meeting Harry had to be more than blind bloody luck. Christ, he had to believe there'd been *some* method in the madness.

They took the tube back to Waterloo, sitting side by side, shoulders jostling together as they clattered along. And then they made their way into the station proper: a crowded, chaotic place, bustling with irritable people struggling to find the right platform — no wonder they were rebuilding the dreadful old place — full of noise and infused with the acrid, greasy stench of locomotive engines.

Ash could already hear the whistles screeching on the platforms.

Harry braced a hand on his elbow. "Alright then," he said, shepherding him along. "Let's get it over with."

Once more, they sat in the first-class carriage, only this time they were joined in their compartment by a gentleman with his nose buried in a newspaper. It meant Ash couldn't grip Harry's hand. Panic started to rise, his fingers clenching into fists by his side as the memories swept in with each blast of the whistle. But then Harry reached into his coat pocket and, to Ash's astonishment, pulled out his old copy of *The Hound of the Baskervilles*. "Remember this?" he said with a tight smile.

Ash didn't trust his voice enough to answer, he just ran his fingers over the battered cover in wonder. Like them, this book had survived that bloody day at Passchendaele. It felt like a talisman.

"I'll read for a while," Harry said, settling back on the seat so that their shoulders pressed companionably together. And, as he'd done so many nights at the front, Harry read aloud to transport them into a different place and time. Ash did his best to concentrate on the familiar comfort of the story, and Harry's beloved voice, although he still flinched when the platform guard blew his whistle right outside their carriage window.

Harry barely muffled his curse at that bad luck, which earned him a disapproving rattle of the newspaper from the gent on the other side of the compartment. Ash didn't give a hoot. The man looked like a banker, the clubbable sort who'd probably pronounced his opinions on the war from the safety of a chair by the fire — the sort who would condemn Ash's love for Harry out of hand. Ignoring him, Ash fixed his attention on the book as they finally jolted into motion, listening to Harry read until the tension and the rocking of the train conspired to send him into the kind of somnolent trance he'd known so well at the front.

Harry's hand on his knee roused him. "Nearly there."

Blinking awake, he realised they were now alone and that his head had come to rest on Harry's shoulder. "I fell asleep," he said, rather stupidly.

"Yes." Harry squeezed his leg and stood to retrieve their bags from the overhead rack. "Best thing for you."

When he sat back down, tugging the sleeves of his jacket into place, Ash glanced out at the corridor beyond their compartment and, seeing it empty, leaned over and placed a reckless kiss on the corner of Harry's mouth. "Thank you," he said, delighted by the way Harry flushed. "I don't think I could have done this without you."

Harry lifted a hand to the place where Ash had kissed him, watching him with a careful expression. "I reckon you could. But I was glad to be with you."

Their shared look confessed everything else about the time they'd spent together, and about how it would be over with the journey's end. Ash was suddenly furious he'd dozed for so long. The train was already slowing, brakes squealing and great clouds of smoke and smuts puffing past the window, obscuring the trees and embankment. Ash reached over and clutched Harry's hand, squeezing tight as the train drew to a halt on the platform.

As they emerged from the station building, Olive waved from

where she sat on the bonnet of her motor. "Well," she said, jumping down as they approached. "How is it, Ash?"

"Very good, thank you." But it felt strange to be talking to Olive about his leg while Harry busied himself putting their bags into the back seat of her motor car. He *did* want to talk to Olive, of course, but half his attention remained with Harry, aware of the painful jarring of realities.

Here, Harry was a servant. *His* servant. That's how Olive saw him, how everyone saw him. The most important person in his life — even more so, after their precious night together — and now he must treat him like a piece of furniture. It felt wrong. Profoundly, painfully wrong.

"Hop in then," Olive said briskly, striding around to the driver's seat while Harry opened the passenger door for Ash. And for the first time, Ash saw his own angry frustration mirrored in Harry's pinched expression.

He felt it too, then, this hurtful wrongness.

Flushing with shame and vexation, Ash climbed into the motor — it was noticeably easier to lift his duff leg this time — and Harry squashed into the back seat with the luggage. With the bloody luggage. And then they were off, back home to Father and Mother and, really, although he felt profoundly altered, nothing at all had changed. The world was just as it had been, and Ash felt even less suited to it than before.

Especially when he saw his father waiting for him on the steps of Highcliffe House. "My study," was all Sir Arthur said by way of greeting, and Ash understood that Pollock must have written.

"Uh-oh," Olive said quietly, giving him a searching look as she opened the door and helped him out. "What's that about?"

"My bid for freedom, I expect."

She squeezed his arm. "Tell me all about it later." Her gaze flicked up to the open door before she got back into the motor.

Behind him, Ash heard Harry lifting their bags from the back seat and setting them on the ground. He turned around, surprised to see Harry's wary gaze directed toward Olive rather than the gaping front door. "Thank you, West," he said, to get his attention.

Harry's gaze shot to him, then past him toward the house. "Very good, sir." He stepped back with a tense nod that Ash felt in the pit of his stomach.

Then Culham said, "I'll take your luggage, Mr Ashleigh" and moved around him to pick up his bag.

As Culham trotted up the stairs, Ash had no choice but to follow. Keeping his father waiting would only stoke his anger. He glanced once over his shoulder, catching Harry's eye briefly. Harry gave another unhappy nod then turned to walk away and Ash returned his attention to climbing the steps into the house. They were more manageable with his lighter leg. Too bad his heart was heavy with trepidation as he made his way along the poorly lit hallway to his father's study.

He knocked and at his father's curt "Come" entered the lion's den.

It looked no different to last time he'd been there, although his father, bristling behind his desk, drew whatever lingering warmth the room might have possessed and turned it to ice. Before him sat a letter.

"I take it you've heard from Mr Pollock," Ash said, pre-empting the start of the conversation.

Sir Arthur lifted his whiskered chin. "And what have you to say for yourself?"

"Nothing." He watched his father's face darken. "Nothing, other than that I c-can't spend the rest of my life w-w-working in a bank, Father. I… I need more."

"More *what*? Do you know how hard I worked to get Pollock to keep your position open after" — he waved his hand — "you came back? I gave him my *word* you'd be up for the challenge, and by God you will be!"

Ash held his ground. "I appreciate your efforts, sir, but it's not the life I want for myself."

"Good heavens!" his father spluttered. "What self-indulgent nonsense is this, boy? Whoever said anything about what you *want*? An Englishman does his duty, not his pleasure. No, don't look at me like that — you have a duty here. To your father and to your family."

"Are you — ?" Ash's whole body stiffened in outrage. "Are you lecturing *me* on d-d-duty, sir?"

Sir Arthur at least had the grace to flush, the tops of his cheeks reddening over his whiskers. "I gave Pollock my *word*, my word as a gentleman, and you've made a liar of me, Ashleigh."

"I n-n-never asked you to speak to Pollock on m-my behalf."

"You didn't need to," Sir Arthur bristled. "I'm your father. It's *my* duty." His voice softened. "You must earn a living in a respectable profession, Ashleigh. You'll need to provide for your wife and family, and there's no more respectable an institution than the London Joint City and Midland Bank."

"But I d-don't want a wife and family!" he blurted before he could think better of it. "I don't w-want any of the-the-the things you think are important."

His father's flush darkened. "I won't hear such nonsense. You'll do as you're damn well told."

"N-no. You have to l-listen to me. I c-c-can't — "

"I know what this is." Sir Arthur's eyes narrowed as he leaned across the desk. "It's that man, West, you've been spending so much time with."

Cold, slick terror seized him. "W-what?"

"Fraternizing with the lower classes, Ashleigh. Getting *ideas*. I warned you about it."

"Ideas…" He barely squeaked the word past the fist closing around his throat. "Wh-what ideas?"

Sir Arthur's whiskers fluttered as he huffed. "Bolshie ideas. Radical notions."

Ash sucked in a breath, a prickle of sweat cooling on his skin. *Radical notions?* His father didn't know. Thank God. Ash swallowed, trying to work moisture back into his throat. "It's not

W-West, sir." His voice sounded thready. "If anything has g-given me ideas it w-was the w-w-war."

"The war's over. Put it behind you. Time to get back to your real responsibilities." Sir Arthur smoothed his hand across the desk. "I shall write to Pollock and apologise for your erratic behaviour." An expression of distaste crossed his face. "He's aware you've suffered with...nervous exhaustion. I'll tell him — "

"No." Ash forced the word out, feeling his face heat. "Sir, I *w-w-won't* go back there. I'm sorry. I c-can't."

Sir Arthur looked up, his jaw set. "Then what will you do? Sponge off the estate for your whole life? Impoverish your brother? Steal the inheritance from his children?"

Ash stumbled back a step, horrified by the suggestion. "No, of c-course not. I'll find another profession. Just n-not in London. And n-not in an office."

"What profession?" His gaze dipped to Ash's leg. "What can you do but sit behind a desk, Ashleigh?"

It felt like a slap, that casual dismissal. And not least because it spoke to his secret fear. What *could* he do? He knew nothing but banking and soldiering and was unfit for either. "I n-need to consider w-what — "

His father slammed his hand flat on the table, making him jump. "Enough," he snarled. "Enough of this. I've been patient, but it's time to pick up your life again. I shall write to Pollock directly, and if you're damned lucky he'll give you another chance. God knows you don't deserve it. Now get out of my sight."

Shaken, Ash turned and left.

He was furious. Furious with his father, but angrier still with himself for not fighting harder, for not giving voice to the outrage simmering inside. But he was frightened, too.

Terrified he'd drown in this suffocating old world that had him by the ankle and wouldn't let go.

Chapter Eighteen

Boyd was mucking out Bella's stall when Harry stepped into the stables, the light bright on this spring afternoon and the air full of horse shit and hay.

But Harry's mind was elsewhere, back with Ash and whatever he was taking from his bastard of an old man. He was uneasy about Ash's decision to turn down the position at the bank, not least because he he'd done it out of some barmy notion that the two of them could run off together. As if this bloody world would ever permit that! But when he'd seen the fury on Sir Arthur's face, he'd felt afraid for the first time.

Christ. Ash had always been a dreamer, but the ideas he'd talked about last night were all kinds of impossible — and liable to end with one or both of them in chokey if Ash breathed a word to anyone else. Would he be mad enough to speak to his father, to ask him for money to start a stud farm with his bloody stable hand?

"Back from the big smoke, then," Boyd said, leaning on the handle of his broom.

"Aye." Harry shook his thoughts away, struggling to appear his usual self. No point in them both raising suspicions. He took the broom from Boyd. "Where's John? Why ain't he mucking out for you?"

"His ma wanted him in the scullery this morning — it's washing day."

Harry grimaced. As much as he didn't care for the lad's sneaky ways, a morning in the steam of the scullery on washing day was nobody's idea of fun. But he couldn't deny he was glad to escape John's sly gaze.

He started to sweep, enjoying the feel of physical labour after two days sitting about on trains and poking around London. Not that he hadn't got some exercise last night. He hid his smile at the memory, his skin heating with a betraying flush as he remembered rolling around naked with Ash. God, but he looked fine in the throes of passion, sensual and loving. And lovable — that was the key. He'd never met a more lovable bloke than Ash, not to his way of thinking. He stirred all sorts of warm feelings, and not just the ones below the belt.

When he thought about it, he realised he'd probably been in love with Ash since that evening in the support trench at Wipers when Harry had found him sitting with Little Bill, the night before they were first rotated into the firing line, helping the lad write a letter home to his mum. Ash had been patient and kind, not patronising like some of the officers, and the distraction had helped settle the boy's nerves for what was to come. Ash had caught Harry's eye over Little Bill's bent head, smiled, and that had been that.

Harry had been beguiled.

Still was,

He spent the rest of that day exercising the horses in the paddock, hoping that Ash might wander past so they could share a few moments and he could find out what Sir Arthur had had to say for himself. But there was no sign of Ash all day, which was wise yet more prudent than Harry had expected. He couldn't decide whether it was a good sign or bad.

By the time he'd caught up with all the jobs he'd missed during his two days away and had settled the horses into their stalls for the night, it was growing dark and Harry had missed his chance to have supper with Boyd and the rest of the staff. That had been deliberate. After last night, he wasn't fit company for anyone but Ash, and he needed time to think — alone. So he walked down to the Oak instead and sat in a corner nursing a pint.

He didn't come to any startling conclusions, nor any way out of his predicament — that being, he was in love with a man who was so far above him they couldn't even pretend to be friends. A man who was idealistic and reckless and, in Harry's opinion, didn't quite have his feet on the ground. Hard as he thought about it, he couldn't see any future for them beyond a few stolen hours and the constant threat of discovery and shame.

Shame.

Bloody hard to accept that something so beautiful should be a matter for shame, but unlike Ash he was a realist. He'd grown up in a hard, unbending world far from the sleepy contentment of Highcliffe House and he'd never had the luxury of dreaming about impossible futures. Truth was, other people would see their love as shameful, would look on them with disgust. Harry couldn't deny it made him want to take the world by its throat and shake some bloody sense into it — after four bitter years of war, hadn't he and Ash earned the damned right to live and love in peace? — but the realist in him knew that rage was dangerous. Safer by far to hide in the shadows, to let the darkness shield them both from the judgmental old bastards determined to keep anything from changing.

And none of that brought him any nearer a solution. Because there was no solution.

When he'd reached the bottom of his glass, he made his way along the lane back to Highcliffe House. His small room above the stables beckoned, but he headed to the outhouse to relieve himself first. It was close to eleven by then and the house was already dark and shut up for the night. Even Ash's room had no light.

Didn't stop Harry lingering, though, watching the curtains in Ash's ground floor window breathe in and out with the breeze. He should go to bed. He'd be up before dawn to start the day. Only he couldn't seem to move his feet. Hands shoved deep in his pockets, he stood there under a cool, clear sky watching wisps of cloud racing across the stars and remembering last night and how it had felt to sleep with Ash in his arms. They'd slept squashed together in dugouts, too, them and a few other men, muttering and dreaming in the frigid winter nights, huddled close for warmth. And on airless summer nights, too, their noses grown numb to the stink of sweaty unwashed men — and the worse stink of the unreachable dead beyond the wire.

But now, back in this civilized world, they were apart. Ash in the big house, Harry in the stables, and the no man's land between them as impassable as ever. With a heavy heart, he made his reluctant feet turn away, back to the stables.

He hadn't taken a single step, however, when he saw a light in Ash's window — the flare of a match, the red glow of a cigarette tip. And, ghostly behind it, Ash's pale figure.

Harry's heart leaped and for a moment indecision froze him in place. To go to Ash was dangerous. It was *stupid*. And yet the tang of cigarette smoke had already reached him from the open window, and he could think of only one reason why Ash would be sitting there smoking in the dark. Quietly, he crossed the gravel path.

Ash sat in the window, shirtless, all pale shadows and unfathomable dark eyes. But he started as if from a dream when he saw Harry. "Christ!"

"Sorry." Harry lifted his hands. "I was passing and saw the light of your fag."

The cigarette shook as Ash lifted it to his lips. "A l-little late f-f-for a walk, W-West."

"A little late for a smoke."

Ash made a poor attempt at a smile — "B-bad night, I'm afraid" — and pushed one hand through his hair. Sweat-damp, it clung to his temples despite the night's chill. "I hope d-d-didn't d-disturb anyone…"

"No one else is up." Which was lucky because it would be hard to explain why Harry was chatting with Ash through his bedroom window in the middle of the night. Especially to the likes of young John Pierson.

"They d-don't come anymore," Ash said. "I t-told them n-not to. I can't bear their p-pity."

"Do you want me to leave you be, then?"

"No." Ash seized his wrist through the window. "You're different; you understand."

And, he did. All too well. He took Ash's icy hand in both his own. "You're freezing. Why don't you go back to bed?"

"No point." Pulling his hand free, he blew out a stream of smoke. "W-won't sleep now."

"Course you will. You did last night."

Ash fixed him with a long look, put the fag back to his lips. "Last night was d-different."

Maybe it was that look, maybe it was the gravel in Ash's voice, but a dangerous yearning kindled in Harry's chest. He knew he should leave, he knew he should be sensible and careful, but what he said was, "Doesn't have to be."

The silence between them altered, shifted from weary to charged. Ash's breathing hitched and Harry's heartbeat accelerated in response. This was reckless, risky. Thrilling. Their eyes locked but neither moved. Ash licked his lips, stubbed out his cigarette, and in a rough voice said, "Come inside."

Madness! But after a swift glance around, Harry hoisted himself onto the windowsill and climbed quickly over. Ash moved out of the way and Harry stepped down onto the chair and from there to the floor. It was a large room, clearly converted from a parlour into a bedroom, and Ash perched on a narrow cot set with its head against the wall, by the window. "You should lock the door," he said softly.

Harry nodded, went to the door and turned the key. It locked with a low click. Then he turned back to Ash, who was watching him from the bed with wide, dark eyes. A sudden breeze caught the curtains, making them billow into the room, so Harry went over and closed the window. The curtains settled over it, plunging them into deeper darkness.

Too dangerous to turn on a light, but not so dark that he couldn't make out Ash's colourless face and the pale shadow of his shoulders. "This is stupid," Harry whispered as he found the bed and sat down.

"No." Ash leaned into him, sliding his arms around his neck and pulling him close. "It's the only thing that makes sense anymore."

Ash kissed him then, open-mouthed and urgent, and Harry was lost. Lost to reason, lost to danger, lost to good sense. All that mattered was sensation: Ash's hands on the buttons of his jacket and shirt, the urgency of his mouth against his jaw, the warmth of hot breath against his lips. And, finally, Ash's bare chest against his own. Gently, Harry pushed him down onto the narrow bed, settling himself on top to kiss him properly, his mouth, his throat, his chest — sucking a nipple into his mouth and feeling Ash gasp and fight to keep quiet. Harry kept moving down, past the cage of his ribs, his soft belly, the hard jut of his hips. He lingered there kissing along the ridge of bone, listening to Ash's panting breaths, and smiled against his skin.

Untying the ribbon of Ash's pyjama bottoms, he slid them down far enough to free his prick, already hard as a fire poker. Harry rubbed his cheek against it, smiled to hear Ash's muttered curses. He'd never sucked a man's prick, but right then, in the soft, secret darkness, Harry wanted it more than anything. He kissed the head, tasted something salty, then licked his way over it, and Ash bucked his hips with a sharp, quickly-stifled cry.

They both stilled, but there were no sounds from inside the house.

Harry's heart fluttered. Then he closed his mouth over Ash's prick and was overwhelmed by pleasure, as if he were giving the gift of love. Worshipping the man he loved. It didn't take long to bring Ash off like that, his fingers knotting in Harry's hair, and

Harry only narrowly avoided getting an eyeful when Ash came with a muffled gasp. That made them both laugh as Harry crawled back up the bed to kiss Ash again, his own need unanswered until Ash closed his hand around him and between that and the deep, passionate kisses, he reached his own climax quickly, smothering his groan against Ash's shoulder.

They lay like that for a few minutes, catching their breath, until Ash made a slight protesting sound of discomfort and Harry realised he was squashing him. He climbed off, knees shaky.

"There's water in the basin," Ash murmured. "And a flannel."

Harry could just about see enough to make his way over to the stand where the basin sat, fumbled around for the flannel and dipped it in. Returning to the bed, he handed it over and listened to Ash's little gasps at the cold as he cleaned himself up and then sucked in a sharp breath of his own as Ash did the same for him.

In silence, they dressed — Ash back into his pyjamas and Harry back into his clothes. He didn't rush; he didn't want to leave.

"You could stay," Ash said. He touched Harry's shoulder, hand warm through his shirt. "Not all night, just for a while."

He didn't take much persuading. They kissed again, loving now instead of urgent, and Ash curled onto his side, Harry crowding in behind. The two of them barely fitted onto Ash's narrow bed and Harry lay with one arm pillowing his head and the other wrapped around Ash's chest. Ash covered Harry's hand with his own, their fingers lacing, and into the darkness he whispered, "I love you."

Harry's heart filled and he kissed the warm skin of Ash's shoulder. "I love you, too."

Enfolded in each other's arms, they slept.

CHAPTER NINETEEN

W hen Ash woke the next morning, he was alone. It came as no surprise. What did surprise him was the fact that it was close to eight o'clock. He never slept so late, certainly not after one of his nightmares. But of course, he'd been with Harry.

He rolled onto his back and gazed at the ceiling, allowing himself a moment to think about last night. Christ alive, even the memory of Harry's hot mouth on him was enough to stir a rise. He'd heard of such things, of course, but always thought the act sounded rather… crude. But that? That had not been crude, it had been sweet and loving and he felt tears prick just remembering.

After he'd dressed, and unable to face his father's silent anger over breakfast, Ash took a stroll to the stables in the hopes of seeing Harry. He found him working in the yard and his heart lifted at the sight of him, even though Boyd was there too. And John Pierson.

Boyd came forward to greet Ash, Harry sparing a brief look before returning to his work. John watched them both with his usual sullen interest and Ash experienced a twist of unease. The atmosphere felt strained.

"Morning, Mr Ashleigh," Boyd said. "Are you looking to ride this morning, sir? I'm afraid I'll need West, but you can — "

"No, no." Ash risked another quick glance at Harry. He'd turned away so that Ash could only see his profile, but there was a tense set to his jaw that Ash didn't like. It distracted him enough that he lost the thread of his thoughts. "Ah, that is, I only came down to-to-to stretch my legs." He felt a tell-tale heat rise in his face and, to cover it, knocked his cane against his new leg. It gave a hollow, metallic clunk. "Testing out the new equipment."

Boyd's eyebrows rose. "Very good, sir. I hope you find it more convenient."

"Yes, so far so good. I'd like to test it riding, but unfortunately not today." He cleared his throat, spared Harry a final — probably unwise — glance, and said, "Well, better be off. Thank you, Boyd."

He left with the uncomfortable sensation of being watched creeping along his spine. What was wrong with Harry? Had they been seen last night? No. Impossible. If they'd been discovered, something would have happened; it wasn't the sort of secret anyone let lie.

Perhaps Harry was simply self-conscious in front of Boyd — and John, the sly little sod. Afraid of Ash giving something away, probably. He knew Harry thought he was indiscreet, but even *he* wasn't so reckless as to say something blatant when they were in company. Harry was something of a conservative, he thought fondly, and then blushed thinking again of last night — not *too* conservative.

He was still smiling when he reached the house and found that the Allens had arrived. Ready to offer his thanks for the use of their town house, the words died on his lips as he entered the parlour and saw Olive's pinched expression. For a dreadful moment he thought something had happened — a bereavement, perhaps — but Mrs Allen was her bustling, busybody self and bestowed Ash with an indulgent smile.

"Ah, here he is," she said. "I hope you were comfortable in town?"

The obligatory thanks and demurs were exchanged, but all the while Ash's attention was drawn back again and again to Olive, sitting silently next to her mother. What the devil had happened? It seemed to be the morning for unexplained tensions.

Once his mother and Mrs Allen fell into conversation, Ash took the opportunity to say, "Olive, would you care to take a stroll in the garden? I'm trying to get used to my" — he considered blunting it for his mother's benefit; decided against it — "new leg, and sitting down doesn't do much good."

His mother looked his way, her flicker of irritation quickly dissolving when Olive jumped to her feet.

"Rather," she said, with more force than he supposed *her* mother would endorse.

They fetched their coats — it was a chilly morning, without yesterday's sun — and as soon as they were outside, and far enough away from the house to talk, he said, "Now tell me what's happened."

She gave him a startled look. "Is it that obvious?"

"Clear as day. Is it — Did you lose one of the men at Chewton or…?"

"No. That would be — Well, it sounds wretched to say that would be 'better' but…" Her voice wobbled, which was alarming. He'd never seen Olive distressed. But perhaps the expression on her face wasn't distress at all. Perhaps it was fury. Pent up, impotent fury. Yes, he recognised it very well now that he understood. "Father has forbidden me to continue volunteering at Chewton. He said it's… It's putting off my suitors."

Ash grimaced. "And by suitors, I suppose he means me?"

"Yes. Not only you, Ashleigh, but now you're back at the bank they hope — "

"I'm not." They'd reached the end of the house and turned along the path toward the archway into the wilderness. "I turned the position down."

Olive was silent, their footsteps crunching over gravel while she thought. "Good," she said at last. "I'm pleased for you. I know you hated the idea."

"You're about the only one who is pleased," he said sourly. "Father's written to Mr Pollock to demand he gives me a second chance. He's going to tell him I'm some kind of nervous case — hardly going to recommend me, I should think. But Sir Arthur is influential…"

"And you'll still say no?"

"Of course." He saw something flit across her face, envy perhaps. "I have that luxury. Not that my father will make it easy — he's already accused me of sponging off Dodge — but at least I have some independence." He touched her arm. "It's easier for me to defy my father than for you."

Olive gave a tight nod. "Major Edwards spoke to me yesterday. He was very kind. He — " Her voice broke. "He said he can't afford to anger my father by continuing my employment there. And besides, it's only a few months until Chewton closes. It's one of the last auxiliary hospitals, you see, and there will soon be room for all the men to transfer to Queen Mary's." She took a bracing breath, wiped a finger under both eyes. "So, you see, it would all be coming to an end anyway."

An end to the war and with it an end to Olive's freedom.

"I suppose…" It was a stupid question, but Ash didn't know what else to say. "I suppose you've spoken to your father about training to — "

"Oh, don't be ridiculous. If he's refusing to let me volunteer at Chewton because of the damage to my 'marriage prospects' he's hardly going to pay for me to train as a doctor."

"No, quite. Sorry."

She stopped walking, shook her head. Poor thing, he could tell she was clinging to the edge of civility. "I don't mean to snap."

"That's alright. I know — I know exactly how frustrating it is when…when what you want is out of reach. And for bloody stupid reasons, too." He winced. "Pardon my French."

Olive snorted. "Bloody stupid indeed."

"What will you do?"

"What *can* I do? I have nothing but pin money and if I defied him, I'd have nothing to live on at all. Father would cut me off."

They carried on walking and, tentatively, Ash said, "If you married, you'd be a wealthy woman…"

"Oh certainly. I'd have money settled on me. And Milford Cottage — which, by the way, is a dreadful crumbling pile slap-bang in the middle of nowhere! — and a husband who'd trap me there like a brood mare." She looked wretched, horrified. "No, it's impossible. I couldn't do it. I'd rather die."

That was putting it rather strongly, but her stricken expression convinced him of every word. "Could you —?" He cleared his throat. "Could you find paid work as a nurse?"

She shook her head, though he didn't miss the flash of longing in her eyes. "For that, I'd need qualifications and training. And for *that* I need money." She kicked at a stone. "I've considered looking for other work in London — secretarial work, even waitressing. But the pay is so low and with rent on top I'd never be able to save enough to train…" She sighed. "And perhaps I'm a coward, Ashleigh, but I'm afraid to leave all this behind. I don't know if I could cope on my own, without any friends in the world."

Her words struck home. "I've had the same thoughts — of leaving all this behind and striking out somewhere new with nothing. I have the advantage of an education, but… Like you, very little experience of any useful trade. I-I don't know how I'd manage."

"Besides, why should we? Why should we let them drive us out? The world is changing and it's not our fault our fathers don't see it."

"But they still hold all the cards." At the entrance to the wilderness, Ash paused, leaning up against the brickwork arch and looking through it into the forest beyond. He'd kissed Harry out there in the wildwood, hidden from the world.

"What would you do?" Olive said, joining him. "If you had your way."

"I'd have a place in the country." He smiled, letting his mind drift. "Deep in the country. And I'd breed horses."

She gave him a quizzical look. "I didn't know you had any interest in horse breeding."

He looked down, tapped his cane against the gravel. "No. I'd need" — a twist in his heart — "someone to help me."

"I see." After a pause, Olive said, "That sounds rather idyllic, I suppose."

"But not for you?"

"Lord, no. I've spent my life in the country. I want to be in London, or another great city. I want people and ideas and…oh, everything modern."

"Perhaps you could persuade your father to take you to London?" He hated seeing her so downcast. "Don't give up, Olive. Who knows what the next few years will bring?"

Fixing him with a hard look she said, "Nothing. They'll *bring* nothing, Ashleigh. The men who run the world want to keep it for themselves, so the only way to get what we want is to take it. Bugger the rules and bugger the men who make them."

She was right, of course, but it was easier said than done — at least, for him and Harry. Even Olive would baulk at the life they wanted, and he could hardly stand up and fight for it when just breaking cover could land him in gaol. And not only him, but the man he loved. It would be like fighting with both hands tied behind his back, and Ash didn't know whether he dared try.

***

Harry kept his head down all day, saying nothing to nobody. Keeping his nose clean.

Boyd had taken him aside first thing that morning, his walnut-brown face creased with awkwardness. "Nod to the wise," he'd said, "but Sir Arthur come by last night, with words for me about you. Seems he thinks you're a mite too friendly with Mr Ashleigh."

As long as he lived, Harry would never forget the punch of dread he'd felt at those words. He'd barely been able to scrape out an answer. "Meaning what?"

"Giving him revolutionary ideas, apparently. He don't want Mr Ashleigh fraternizing with the staff — told me to keep an eye on you. And not only me, I reckon." He'd sighed. "Look, I know you and Mr Ashleigh was friends at the front, Harry, but you're here now. It's different. And folks like Sir Arthur, they like the old ways preserved — everyone in their place."

Harry agreed with that, only he felt that his place was with Ash and Ash's place was with him. But he hadn't protested to Boyd, just agreed that there was nothing to it but an old man's oddities and got down to his work. Inside, though, he was reeling.

Sir Arthur might have the details wrong, but he was right about the essentials — he and Ash *were* changing each other. Radical ideas? Who they were was a radical idea, how they loved was a radical idea. And the more time he spent with Ash, the more strongly he embraced those ideas.

Creeping out of Ash's bedroom that morning had caused him physical pain, a rending in his chest that lasted all day. Leaving Ash sleeping, warm and tousle-haired, had been a sheer act of will and only terror of being caught had prodded him out of bed. If he'd had any excuse to stay, he would have. And to be told that Sir Arthur had put spies on them, that he had his staff watching Harry for evidence of sedition, turned him dead cold.

He needed to find a way to warn Ash, although unless they went out riding again — and who knew whether Sir Arthur would permit it — the chance of speaking to him alone was slim. When he'd come down to the stables that morning, Harry hadn't even been able to meet his eye for fear of what he, or, more likely, Ash, would give away. And that had hurt, seeing the confusion on Ash's face and being afraid some other bastard saw it, too.

He felt sick at the thought that they might never be alone together again, that he might never hold him or be held. That Ash might wake from bad dreams without Harry to comfort him — without anyone to comfort him.

They were unbearable thoughts and they tormented him all day.

So did John fucking Pierson, watching Harry with his insolent smirk as if he *knew*. Perhaps he did. Maybe Sir Arthur had long ago set John Pierson to watch them. He'd *always* been watching.

He ate all his meals in the kitchen that day, so as not to be seen acting in any way seditious. Bloody stupid idea, but far too close to a more dangerous truth. Retiring early, he took himself to bed with his lending library copy of *Max Carrados* and tried to read himself into oblivion. But not even the adventures of Bramah's blind detective could distract him from his circling thoughts. Perhaps tomorrow they'd be able to speak. Maybe Ash would want to ride and nobody would stop them. They could go to the hunting box again…

Thoughts chased through his head as he tried to sleep. Funny how he'd never had much trouble sleeping at the front while here, in the comfort of his own bed, with nothing but the snorting of the horses nearby to disturb him, he tossed and turned. But there, he'd had Ash with him and now he didn't. He might never have him close again and that —

That was enough to get him sitting up in bed, raking hands through his hair in frustration. Unable to sleep, he went out for a smoke and a piss. And maybe, though he tried to deny it to himself, to walk past Ash's window and check he was sleeping.

Bloody fool he was, but he couldn't keep away.

That's why he was leaning against the wall of the house, finishing his fag, when he heard Ash's shout. He'd been waiting for it, he supposed, this excuse to see him, to touch him and save him from the demons of his own mind. And he didn't hesitate longer than it took to check that all was dark and silent in the house, that nobody was around as he crept up to Harry's window and, like last night, slipped inside.

This time, Ash was still in bed but sitting bolt upright and staring into the past. "I can't get out," he cried hoarsely. "I can't get out! I can't get *out*!"

"It's all right," Harry whispered, settling next to him on the bed. "I'm here."

But Ash's mouth opened in a low wordless cry of fury as he relived his haunted memories.

And it broke Harry's heart to see it, brought tears to his eyes. "Just a dream, Ash." He touched his warm, clammy face. "You're all right, it's over now."

Gradually, his cry faded into ragged breaths and eventually silence. After some time, Ash blinked and then shuddered awake. "Harry?"

"Right here." He stroked his thumb over Ash's cheek.

"*Harry.*" Ash gripped his wrist, fisted fingers into Harry's shirt. "Oh God, Harry." He buried his face against Harry's shoulder, strong wiry arms clinging to him as he shook, pressing wet, stifled noises of distress into Harry's neck. "I w-was him. I w-w-was Jimmy. I c-c-couldn't g-get out."

Harry held him, stroked one hand over his back — his shirt was damp, the bony ridge of his spine stark beneath his palm — and murmured what comfort he could offer. In truth, there was none. At length the shaking stopped and Ash pulled out of Harry's arms, sitting back on the bed. He didn't drop his grip on Harry's hands, though, or lift his gaze from the rumpled bedspread. "I was t-t-trapped. Trapped and-and-and…"

Poor bugger. Harry squeezed his hands. "Just a dream, Ash."

"And I wanted to scream. I was s-s-so b-bloody *angry.*" He lifted his gaze to Harry's, eyes like bruises. "I still am."

"I know." Harry lifted Ash's hand to his lips, kissed his fingers. "None of it's fair." A breeze drifted past the curtains and Ash shivered, chilled. "Come on, get that damp shirt off before you catch cold." Carefully he unbuttoned Ash's pyjama top and peeled it off his arms, throwing it onto the chair by the window. "Now lay down under the covers." He encouraged him backward onto the pillows with a gentle hand on his shoulder. "Try to get some sleep."

"C-can't."

Harry brushed the damp hair back from Ash's forehead. "Just rest then."

"W-will you stay?"

After Boyd's warning he knew it wasn't safe. He stroked Ash's forehead again, rested his other hand on his bare shoulder and felt the low tremors racking his body. Cold, or anger, or grief. Some combination. "I can't — "

"Please." Ash gripped his wrist, fingers biting. "Harry, please. I n-need — Just for a little while. Please."

Helpless to refuse, Harry leaned down and pressed his lips to Ash's mouth, kissing him tenderly, then more deeply as Ash's arms snaked around his neck and drew him closer. Urgent, emotional, tender kisses, it felt as if Ash were seeking out life after his deathly dreams. Harry couldn't walk away, not when Ash needed him like this.

They kissed for a long time, nothing but the sound of their breathing filling the room. Eventually, Harry pulled away far enough to speak, bumping their noses together. "I can't stay long," he whispered, unwilling to tell Ash about his father's spies when he was so shaken. "But I'll stay for a few minutes. Until you're sleeping."

"Thank you," Ash breathed, reaching up to kiss him again. "I love you, Harry. So much."

Like last night, Harry lay down behind him on the narrow bed. He propped himself up on one elbow, threading his fingers through Ash's hair until he felt his body soften and relax, his breathing slow and deepen. From outside, a breeze stirred the curtains and Harry watched them shift, billowing into the room before they stilled.

He'd leave soon, once Ash was deeply asleep.

While he waited, he let his head sink onto the pillow next to Ash's — just for a moment. He allowed his arm to curl around Ash's waist, splaying his hand over the warm bare skin of his stomach, and breathed in the redolent scent of his hair. He smiled, heart full of the knowledge that in his arms Ash could find peace.

And he let his eyes close. Just for a moment.

Chapter Twenty

Ash drifted in a warm safe place between sleep and wakefulness. Around his waist lay the comforting weight of Harry's arm, his slow sleepy breaths tickling the back of Ash's neck. Outside, the occasional chirrup of birdsong presaged the dawn chorus, but the night was still thick and Ash let himself drowse in the comfort of Harry's embrace for a little —

Noise blasted him awake.

He jolted upright into the heart-hammering horror of bright light and bellowing.

"Out!" Sir Arthur roared from the doorway, absurd in his silk dressing gown. "Get this...this...this filthy pervert out of my house."

Culham, who stood at Sir Arthur's shoulder, lurched forward, white-faced in the stark electric light. John Pierson smirked in the hallway beyond, flanked by a grim looking Boyd.

"He was having a nightmare." Harry scrambled off the bed, hands raised in surrender. He looked grey as a bitter dawn, more frightened than Ash had ever seen him. "I was just — "

"Culham!" Sir Arthur roared. "Get him out." The footman, only half dressed himself, grabbed Harry's arm, hauling him barefoot toward the door. "And you, *Ashleigh.*" Sir Arthur spat his name. "On your feet."

He didn't have his prosthetic on and was shaking too much to move. His heart pounded like it might rupture. "I c-c-can't — "

"Up! Stand up like a bloody man."

"For God's sake!" Harry wrenched free of Culham and put himself between Ash and his father. "He doesn't have his leg on, he can't — "

With a guttural roar, Sir Arthur punched him. The wild, enraged swing of his fist sent Harry staggering backward onto the bed.

"Harry!" Ash grabbed him, but Harry pushed him off and surged back to his feet with a murderous cry.

"You bastard!" He shoved Sir Arthur hard in the chest, sending him reeling. "Don't you dare fucking touch me."

Harry lurched forward, fist raised, but Ash caught his shirt and dragged him back. "Stop! Harry, don't!"

Splayed in an undignified sprawl against a chest of drawers, Sir Arthur glared with ferocious loathing. "Get. Him. *Out.*"

Culham leaped to obey, Boyd not far behind. "Come on," he growled, a gnarled hand on Harry's arm. "Come on, boy. Don't make this worse for yourself."

Harry shook his head, twisting around. "Ash..." A world of anguish in that single syllable, a world of despair in his eyes.

"Go," he said roughly, vision blurring. "You have to go." *Run*, he wanted to say. *Run from this place. Run from me.*

Harry's agonised gaze held his for several racing beats of Ash's heart, then fell away and he nodded in understanding. His body slumped as Culham and Boyd dragged him out of the room, but he looked over his shoulder at the last moment, finding Ash's eyes for a final desperate instant before Sir Arthur slammed the door shut between them.

The look of contempt he turned on Ash was excoriating. "Stand up."

Shaking with fury and grief, Ash struggled upright. He didn't reach for his prosthetic but balanced himself with one hand on the bedpost. Shame burned his cheeks. Not for the love he felt for Harry, but for the indignity of standing shivering before his father, half-naked and struggling to balance on his one remaining foot while he listened to Sir Arthur's disgust and contempt spill from his spittle-flecked lips.

His father was apoplectic with rage, disgorging every venomous thought he'd ever harboured about his weak, unmanly, pansyish excuse for a son until he was reduced to a gasping, gaping silence.

"F-father—"

"*You* will call me Sir Arthur. I claim no relationship between us."

That pierced like cold steal. "Y-y-you're disowning—"

"You've brought shame to my house. Venal, disgusting perversion!"

Ash closed his eyes, but his balance faultered and he had to open them again. "Wh-what w-will happen t-to Harry?"

"The police—"

"No." Lightheaded, breathless he clutched the bedpost. "You c-can't. He—"

"He committed unnatural acts—"

"We were just sleeping! That's n-n-not a crime." He sucked in a breath, forced his leg not to wobble. "If you call the p-police it will c-cause a scandal. It w-would damage D-D-Dodge's career."

"Do you think I don't know that?" Sir Arthur took a threatening step closer. "Little you cared about your brother's career when you were buggering the stable hand!"

Ash felt sick but he refused to look away. He couldn't. For Harry's sake, he couldn't. "D-don't call the police. Let W-West leave and—and I'll do w-w-whatever you want. T-Take the job at the bank. M-marry the right w-woman." What was left of his heart shrivelled with every word, but he'd do it all and more to save Harry from his father's vengeance. He'd give his life in any way necessary. "I swear to you, Fa—S-Sir Arthur."

His father breathed hard, whiskers twitching. "I will consider it," he said at length. "But only for the sake of your brother. You will remain here until summoned."

With that, he turned, pulled open the door and stalked out.

Shivering, Ash sank down on the bed and rolled into the fading warmth of Harry's presence. Everything was lost, everything was broken. Better if he'd bought it at Passchendaele, if that ruddy shell had blown off more than his leg, than this misery. Better for Harry too.

God, *Harry*.

His heart cramped and he curled around the pain, struggling for air. His father was so angry. Would he see reason, or would he seek blind vengeance? Sir Arthur knew the magistrate; he could demand Harry be prosecuted. For assault, if nothing else. Panic gripping him he turned his head, screaming his fear and sorrow into his pillow until his throat was raw and dry.

Harry had saved his life in every possible way and Ash had repaid him by ruining him. He'd been weak and reckless. He'd *asked* Harry to stay tonight. He'd begged him. And now Harry would lose everything and Ash—

Ash couldn't save him.

***

Harry paced the stable, his tension making the horses stamp and snort. All he could think about was the door slamming in his face and Ash sitting white-faced on the bed before that bastard who called himself a father. He put a hand to his cheek, felt the swelling where the old man had hit him and regretted not pounding him back.

His own father—

He stopped walking, gut clenching at the thought of his dad finding him in bed with another man. No doubt he'd have reacted the same. And that thought made him sick, but not half as sick as the thought of Sir Arthur raising his hand to Ash.

Outside the stable door, Culham stood on guard duty. He kept his back to Harry, avoiding looking at him as he waited for Boyd to return from the house. Or maybe for the arrival of the police. Harry felt faint with fear. Not of prison, not of hard labour, but of the shame he would bring to Kitty. And of her disgust. He couldn't bear that from her or the girls.

His only consolation, the only easing of the sick knot in his belly, was the hope that Ash would be spared. Surely Sir Arthur wouldn't see his family name dragged through the courts or in the newspapers? Not with Ash's brother in parliament.

No, Ash would be safe. Well, safe from the law at least. What other punishment his father might mete out, Harry didn't know. But if that bastard put a finger on him, Harry would —

What? What could he do from a fucking gaol cell?

A voice drifted in from outside — Boyd dismissing Culham. Harry's stomach cramped, his guts turning watery and his heart suddenly less brave at the prospect of gaol. He found himself frozen in front of Sable's stall. *Ash's horse*, he thought with a sudden clench of emotion. Oh God, would he ever see Ash again? He reached out a shaking hand to stroke Sable's neck, trying to swallow his rising terror. "It's alright, girl." The words rasped in his throat. "He'll be back for you."

But not for me. Fuck, his eyes were burning.

"West?"

He turned at the sound of Boyd's voice, heart thundering and knees weak. Boyd stood just inside the doorway, hands sunk in his pockets. There were no police with him, not yet at least. For a long moment they regarded each other, then Boyd shook his head and slowly started to walk toward him. "You're dismissed, of course. With immediate effect."

Harry nodded; he'd assumed as much. But he had to work moisture into his mouth before he asked, "The police?"

"Not if you leave without a fuss."

Harry sagged back against the stall door, Sable's nose butting at his shoulder. "All right," he said unsteadily.

Boyd nodded, expecting no less. "Ah, Harry, what the devil were you thinking? Didn't I tell you there were eyes on you?"

"I didn't think you meant — Did you *know*?"

"Suspected. And obviously not only me. Bugger it, I should have said it to your face. Warned you better."

"You aren't…disgusted?"

He shrugged. "Can't say I think it's right and I wouldn't want it for my son. But you and Mr Ashleigh done your duty to the country, and the rest's between you and the Lord." He took another step closer, peering up at Harry, brow drawn. "I'm sorry for you, son. I'm sorry for you both."

"Will you — ?" His voice caught, he cleared his throat. "Will you make sure he keeps riding? He needs to."

"I'll do what I can."

"And —" Christ, he wanted to leave a message, say goodbye somehow, but that would be stupid. Dangerous. "If I leave you my sister's address in London, will you write to me if — if there's any trouble for him over this?"

Boyd hesitated, but then nodded. "Aye, alright. If there's trouble, I'll let you know."

"Thank you." His throat tightened, an unmanly rising of loss that broke out in a stifled sob. He turned away, embarrassed, and buried his face against Sable's neck. "Ah, fuck it, I'm going to miss this place." *And Ash, my beautiful Ash.* Another sob, barely repressed.

Boyd's bony fingers closed on his shoulder, a single hard squeeze. "Get your bag packed, son. I'm to see you to the road."

He nodded, unable to find his voice, and pressed his face against Sable's neck again as though through her he could touch Ash one last time. Then, with a ragged inhale of breath, he straightened, wiped his face, and forced himself to keep going. What else could he do?

It didn't take long to pack. He didn't have much except for Ash, who was everything to him and who he was leaving behind. Numb with loss, he shoved his clothes into his bag and met Boyd outside the stables. He could feel eyes on him and saw John Pierson skulking by the paddock fence. That little shit, this was all his doing. Fist clenched, Harry stalked towards him and John startled, looking like he might run. He was a skinny lad, not nearly a man. And grieving,

Harry knew. Christ, this war and the damage it left behind.

"I ain't going to hurt you," he growled, though he loomed over the boy, forced him to tilt his head to look up. There was that angry jut in his jaw, the hardness that might never leave. Maybe it had always been there. Harry didn't know and he didn't care. "I'm sorry you lost your brother," he said, and saw surprise register in the boy's face. "I'm sorry I spoke badly of him. And I'm sorry for you."

"Yeah?" The insolent smirk on John's lips looked forced. "I ain't the one with his marching orders."

"I'm sorry for you," Harry went on, "because this won't make it better. Causing grief to others won't take your own away. Might even make it worse, when you come to think of the harm you've done."

John shifted, looking away. "I only done what Sir Arthur told me."

"No matter the reason, you've done harm here, John Pierson. You've hurt a good man. And if you carry on hurting people just because *you're* hurting then you'll come to a dark place, and there won't be nobody willing to help you out of it. You'll be all on your own."

"I already am," he spat, and it was the first thing Harry had heard from the boy's mouth that felt like truth. His lips came down tight around the words, a thin angry mouth that made him look younger still. He glared down into the dirt at his feet as if willing back tears. "I'm already alone."

Harry's battered heart gave a twist of regret. Maybe, if he'd been kinder to the boy, tried to understand… He sighed. It was too late now. "Look to Boyd as a friend, John. He's a good man. Be more like him and you'll do alright."

There was no more he could say, and he had little enough inclination to be generous. Maybe he'd had his reasons, but John Pierson had devastated his life. And, more importantly, he'd harmed Ash. Turning away, Harry trudged back toward Boyd who waited at the stable yard gate.

"Get to work," Boyd called to John. "We're short-handed now so you'd better pull your weight."

Watching over his shoulder, Harry saw John disappear into the stable. He could neither tell nor really care whether he'd got through to the lad.

"Apple didn't fall far enough from the tree with that one," Boyd muttered as they left the yard together. "A bad lot, the Piersons."

Harry didn't have the strength to reply. He barely had the strength to walk, aware of the house behind him and of who was inside. Looking back, his gaze fixed on Ash's bedroom window — the window he'd climbed through last night and condemned them both to this unbearable parting. And suddenly he couldn't move, couldn't take another step away. All he wanted was to run back. Without thought, he took a step forward.

"Don't." Boyd's hand landed on his arm. "Leave it now, son."

But the pain was agonising. "I have to say goodbye."

"You'll only make it worse for him. And for yourself." Boyd's fingers tightened on his arm. "Come on. Don't give Sir Arthur an excuse to change his mind."

A toot from behind startled them both, and Harry turned to see the Allen's car turn into the driveway. Miss Allen was at the wheel, her matronly mother perched, frowning, in the passenger seat.

Harry touched his cap as they drove past. Olive Allen would be Ash's future, he realised. Her, or someone like her. That had been inevitable from the start and he'd been a fool to forget it, whatever wild dreams Ash might have harboured.

Boyd was right, he had to leave. Walk away. Their parting had been fated from the moment their lips met and they'd both known it, even if they'd chosen to pretend otherwise.

He pulled his arm out of Boyd's grip and slung his bag over his shoulder. "Alright," he said, turning his back on the man he loved and facing the long road leading him away. "I'm going."

CHAPTER TWENTY-ONE

How long Ash lay on his bed, mired in misery, he didn't know. But that was how Olive found him later that morning.

Her brusque knock, followed immediately by the opening of his bedroom door, didn't even give him time to sit up, let alone make himself respectable for a lady's company. He just stared at her and Olive stared back, closing the door behind her with a soft click and leaning against it as if barricading them both inside.

"Well," she said, after a moment of close scrutiny. "Sir Arthur said you were indisposed, but... Whatever's wrong, Ashleigh? You look awful."

He sat up, acutely aware of his bare chest. Olive seemed indifferent to his state of undress and he supposed she'd seen worse. "I — " But what could he say? *I've lost the man I love. I'll never see him again. I'm heartbroken.* His throat thickened around the unutterable words, unmanly tears choking him. "I c-c-can't..."

Olive crossed the room in two swift steps, snatched his pyjama top from the chair by the window and draped it around his shoulders. "Put that on," she said briskly, and he obeyed the order like a good soldier. Her hand went to his forehead. Then she sat next to him on the bed and took his arm, turning it over to press two fingers to his wrist. "No fever, but your pulse is racing. Do you feel ill?"

He shook his head. "It's n-n-not that."

"Have you eaten today?" She glanced around the room, looking for evidence. "Not even a cup of tea?"

"Olive —" He stopped, unable to continue. His truth was literally unspeakable. "You sh-sh-shouldn't be in here. M-M-My father w-wouldn't —"

"Oh, hang your father," Olive said with a belligerent tilt of her chin. "And mine too, while you're at it. What have they to do with the price of fish?" Her expression narrowed. "I passed West on my way in. It looked like Boyd was turning him off…"

Oh God, Harry was *gone*. He buried his face in his hands, breath hitching loudly in the silent room, and struggled to control his overwhelming emotions.

Eventually, after an uncomfortable silence, Olive said, "What happened? Was he stealing or —?"

"No." Ash jerked up, scrubbing at his blurry eyes. Is that what everyone would think? That West had been turned off for larceny? "Of course not."

"But he…hurt you?"

He shook his head.

"You're upset."

"Olive —" Hiding the truth was agony, it burned like betrayal. "I c-c-can't explain."

"He looked like he'd been in a scrap. Did you fight? I know you were friends, but if he struck you —"

"We were lovers."

His rasping confession expanded to fill the room. Silence fell, hushing the world outside until all Ash could hear was the rush of blood in his ears. He fixed his gaze on the bedspread, afraid of seeing revulsion in Olive's eyes. But whatever she thought of him, it was a relief to speak those words aloud. Sir Arthur might force them apart, might keep them apart forever, but he couldn't force Ash to deny Harry West. "My f-f-father discovered us together. That's why Harry's g-gone."

After a long silence, Olive said, "I see."

Ash didn't look up, so he felt rather than saw her rise and walk to the door. Well, it was no surprise. Any young lady would be shocked by such an admission, even one as forthright as Olive. But he risked a hesitant glance when he heard her open the door and request a tray of tea from the maid. She returned his look with a strained smile. "Do up your buttons," she said, nodding at his pyjama top, and proceeded to open the curtains properly and pile his pillows behind his back as if he were one of her Chewton invalids. Too drained and miserable to protest, Ash succumbed to her care and watched when she took the tea tray from the maid and dismissed the girl with a nod.

Once the bedroom door was closed again, Olive poured two cups of tea and gave one to Ash before she sat down in the chair by the window with her own.

Ash took a sip and grimaced; the tea was far too sweet.

"The sugar is for the shock," Olive told him. "It'll revive you."

"Sh-shock?"

"I think we both need it." Her cheeks reddened and she set her tea down on the windowsill. "We had a patient at Chewton last year, Ashleigh. He refused to speak. There was talk of sending him to Craiglockhart — you know, the hospital for shell shock cases? But Major Edwards had another idea." She folded her hands nervously in her lap, unfolded them again. "Turned out the poor chap had seen his pal killed right beside him and he couldn't talk about it because" — her gaze briefly touched his before skittering away — "because they'd been like you and West. And he was afraid people would find out." She cleared her throat and continued more forcefully. "Major Edwards loaned me a book about it — *The Intermediate Sex* by Edward Carpenter. You probably know it?"

Bewildered, rendered almost mute by this speech, Ash shook his head. "I'm afraid not, no."

"Really? Well, I *am* surprised. But you should certainly read it, Ashleigh. It explains all about homogenic love, you see, and about the nervous strain it puts on a man when he feels afraid to express his…his tender feelings." She gave an embarrassed smile, cheeks pinking again. "So, you see, I'm not quite so unworldly as you might imagine."

"I —" He cleared his throat, firming his voice. "No, I see that."

"I do feel rather foolish not to have realised about you and West, but our patient was more of an Oscar Wilde type and I suppose I assumed all men who… Well." She flapped her hand self-consciously. "The thing is, I do understand what it is to feel as if one doesn't quite fit into the world." This time, when she met his gaze, she held it for longer. "Perhaps that's why we've become friends? Neither of us really fits, do we?"

Ash couldn't answer. He hardly knew how to understand that this was possible. Olive's embarrassed sympathy, her kindness, overwhelmed him, unlocked the howling grief in his soul. An ugly, wracking sob forced its way out of his throat. He tried to stifle it with his hand, but it was no good; the floodgates had opened, his grief couldn't be contained.

Harry was gone. Ash would never see him again.

After a moment, he felt the bed dip and the teacup being taken from his hand. "There-there," Olive said softly. "You poor thing."

Wretchedly, he dropped his forehead onto her shoulder, breathing in rose-scented perfume. She stiffened but didn't pull away. "I'm s-s-sorry f-for making such a fuss," he rasped.

"Why should *you* be sorry? It's *them* who should be sorry. Blinkered old fossils keeping us all in chains and letting us go mad for want of the freedom to live our lives. They're the ones who should be sorry, Ashleigh. Not you. Not West." A shaky breath. "And not me."

The first rush of release over, Ash lifted his head and wiped self-consciously at his face. Olive handed him her handkerchief and he smiled at her preparedness for every occasion. "I sh-should have been more discreet. Harry warned me. If I'd only listened."

Olive's lips pursed. "You shouldn't have to be discreet, but of course..." She spread her hands, regarding him with sympathy. "How did Sir Arthur find out?"

He told her the sorry tale, her outrage on his behalf taking some of the sting from his humiliation.

"Will Sir Arthur go to the police, do you think?" she said, when he'd finished.

"I — No, I d-don't think so. Not if he's allowed Harry to l-leave." That was a mercy, at least. "He's t-too concerned about protecting Dodge's career, you see. B-But Harry — " His voice shook. "He'll have been d-d-dismissed without a reference, obviously."

"And there's precious little work for returning servicemen as it is."

"He has a widowed s-sister and t-two nieces..."

Olive puffed out a breath and said nothing, gazing out through the window at the summer garden. Ash supposed it must be mid-morning by now, that Olive had come calling with her mother who was no doubt wondering when and if he was going to make an honest woman of her daughter. And then a darker thought swamped him: when he married, as he'd promised he would, he'd be obliged to do his duty in the bedroom against all his inclinations. After the few precious hours of lovemaking he'd shared with Harry, the thought of intimacy with anyone else appalled him. And no doubt it would appal the poor soul he'd duped into marriage. "I can't do it," he blurted, tight-chested with panic. "I can't m-marry and-and-and — "

"*You* won't have to." He caught the bitterness in Olive's voice, not aimed at him but there nonetheless. "Men have other options."

"No, you don't understand. I p-p-promised Father I'd marry."

She looked aghast. "Whatever for?"

"For Harry. T-To keep him safe. I p-promised I'd be respectable."

Olive snorted. "As if marrying some chit against your will — and probably against hers — is respectable!"

"W-what else can I do?" he said miserably. "They got into a fight. Harry s-struck my father. He could have him p-prosecuted for assault."

"And he's blackmailing you with the threat. Very respectable, I'm sure." She slumped next to him. "They hold all the cards, don't they? We don't stand a chance."

Not a single chance. He turned his gaze to Olive's strong, capable profile. She should be so much more than some gentleman's wife, she had so much to offer the world, so much talent and compassion — it was obvious to anyone who could see. And how many Olive Allens were out there, living squandered lives in servitude to their husbands? How many men like him and Harry, unable to express their love without fear? Olive had once said she'd rather die than marry and he understood now how trapped she felt. Rich or poor, it made no difference. A gilded cage was still a cage. "It can't last," he said, grinding the words like gravel between his teeth.

"What can't?"

"This. All of it. In Russia — "

Olive snorted. "We've never been much of a country for revolution, Ashleigh."

That was a depressing truth. He studied Olive's pensive expression, the firm set of her jaw and the bright intelligence of her eyes. A question occurred. "Do you — ?" He floundered, unsure whether he dared ask. In response to his silence, Olive turned her head, regarding him with a quizzical lift of her eyebrows. "D-Do you, perhaps, have a...an intimate friend? S-someone who means to you w-what West means to me?"

Her expression altered, neither wistful nor offended. "I have friends," she said after some thought. "I count you as one of them, Ashleigh. But I find the idea of bedroom matters repellent. Affection, yes, for a dear friend, but I want nothing...intimate. With anyone."

Ash didn't quite know what to make of that, but Olive plainly knew her own mind and she was a clear-sighted rational woman. "So any marriage would be a punishment for you. Even if you were fond of your husband?"

"If he wished to exercise his marital rights in the bedroom, certainly."

They stared at each other, each blinking as if in a sudden bright light.

"Good God," Olive said.

Ash's heart began to pound. "You told me you'd rather die than marry."

"But that was before I knew about you and West…" Her eyes were wide as saucers. "Dear Lord, Ashleigh. What if we do *exactly* as our fathers want?"

CHAPTER TWENTY-TWO

I t was Peace Day when Harry got the news. Or, rather, stumbled across it.

He'd been in London almost a month, and today the city was heaving, the streets and parks teeming with crowds eager to catch a glimpse of the victory parade. Harry couldn't deny it was a spectacle: thousands of marching men from all over the Empire, tanks and horses, even pieces of captured German aircraft paraded on floats. At the front, General Haig himself rode with some other brass hats Harry didn't recognise.

Although his feelings about the victory parade were mixed, it felt right to mark the signing of the treaty that had ended the bloody business — even if the cost of the parade might have been better spent on the pensions of those maimed in the fighting. Besides, it gave him something to think about beyond his futile search for work and the endless thrum of yearning for Ash.

He found a place to watch the parade near Westminster Bridge. Couldn't get anywhere near the front of the huge crowd, though; some of the silly buggers must have slept the night on the street to secure the prime positions near the curb. More fool them. Harry had had enough of soldiering for a lifetime and the sight of the khaki uniforms and rifles with bayonets fixed brought back visceral memories he'd sooner forget.

Thank God Ash wasn't there to see it, not that there was any chance of that. He'd avoid it like the influenza. Harry couldn't help wondering how the pageant at Hinton was fairing, and whether Ash had been forced to attend. That thought brought a new stab of regret and longing and he pushed it aside with a determined effort, fixing his attention on the spectacle at hand and the cheering crowds watching.

After the parade had passed and the people began to disperse, Harry bought a ham sandwich and ginger beer from a street stall and walked into St. James' park. He found a spot on the grass under a tree and picked up the discarded copy of yesterday's *Times* he found there, the front page full of Mr Woodrow Wilson's campaign to persuade America to join his League of Nations. Harry was no politician, but the idea seemed like a good one to him. It was the twentieth century, after all. People should be able to solve their problems by getting together and talking instead of lobbing shells at each other for years on end. If the war had done nothing else, it had made another such conflict unthinkable. Surely there'd be no appetite for war. Not in his lifetime, anyway.

Chewing a bite of sandwich, Harry turned the page in search of lighter news and froze dead. His eyes, as if magnetised, were drawn to two familiar names: *Allen—Dalton*. Gut twisting, he read on, knowing what he'd find beneath the headline yet helpless to stop even though his heart sank deeper with every word.

Miss Olive Grace Allen, daughter of Mr and Mrs Frank Allen of Hampshire, and Mr Ashleigh Arthur Dalton, son of Sir Arthur Dalton Bt CBE and Lady Dalton, were married at 10 o'clock yesterday morning at Lymington Register Office. The room was decorated with white roses and the bride wore an ivory silk gown. After the ceremony, a dinner was served to relatives at the bride's home. Mr and Mrs Dalton left immediately for London where the couple will now reside, and their many friends and relatives wish them every happiness in their new home.

Harry felt sick, the sandwich turning claggy in his mouth. He'd known in his reasoning mind that this was Ash's future, but he hadn't thought it would happen so fast. Only twenty-eight days since they'd parted! How had Ash had the stomach for it so soon after — Well. Perhaps he'd had no choice. And Harry couldn't bring himself to wish Ash as miserable as himself. He hoped he was happy with Miss Allen. They'd been friends, after all. He hoped Ash was happy even if that hope slid deep into his heart and opened all his scarcely scabbed wounds.

Ash was married.

Only now that it was entirely beyond reach did Harry realise that he'd harboured a secret hope of a future reunion — of holding him again, of loving him. But Ash wasn't the sort of man to betray his vows, no more than Harry was the sort of man to cuckold anyone's wife. No, all hope was gone and only memories remained.

Sinuses burning, a sudden sting in his eyes, he turned the page and scrubbed a hand over his face. But after a moment's pause, in which the pain refused to subside, Harry turned the page back and carefully tore the notice out of the newspaper, slipping it into his breast pocket. He'd keep it with his precious letters from Ash. Stupid, probably, to treasure silly mementoes, but he wanted everything he could have of Ash. He wasn't proud. Perhaps he'd learn pride later, but for now he was a beggar scavenging scraps.

God, he missed him. Ached for him. Longed for a glimpse of his face, to see him smiling and happy. And now Ash was in London, most likely living in the Allen's house in Mayfair, and Harry could go there. Just to look, just to see him and be sure he was well and —

"Stop it." He pushed himself to his feet and shoved the rest of his sandwich into his pocket for later. He'd no appetite now. "Leave him be, Harry. Let him go."

With the parade over and London emptying of its visitors, he'd lost any purpose for the day. But he'd no desire to go home and brood, not under Kitty's scrutiny. Obviously, he hadn't told her why he'd left Highcliffe, beyond a disagreement with Sir Arthur, but he'd been unable to hide the blue devils from his sharp-eyed sister and found it best to stay away from her and the girls. Kitty only worried and he had no way to tell her that his fool heart was broken with no hope of repair. So he kept his melancholy self to himself.

Instead of going home, he bent his steps toward Whitehall and the memorial unveiled yesterday. A cenotaph, they called it — Greek for 'empty tomb', it said in the papers — a memorial to those whose remains rested elsewhere. Like Jimmy Tilney, lost in the mire of Passchendaele.

It was a half hour walk along the Mall, past stands erected to seat the widows and children watching the parade, and when he reached Whitehall there were still plenty of people milling around. The cenotaph itself had been erected on an island in the centre of the street, a white blocky slab designed to look like stonework, even though it was only made of wood and plaster. A union flag lay draped over its top, as if over a coffin, and carved wreathes painted green and red decorated either side of the monument above the inscription: *The Glorious Dead*.

Ash would have something to say about that. And there he went again, thinking about Ash.

But what really drew Harry's eye wasn't the cenotaph itself, but the mountain of flowers and wreaths piled around its base and reaching far up the monument. Even now, with the parade past, there were people arriving to lay flowers — young widows holding children's hands, older mothers grieving their sons, men of all ages with heads bowed in prayer or remembrance. That sight, more than anything else he'd seen today, touched Harry's aching heart and he felt a great swell of sorrow for all those who'd never returned, and for those who'd returned changed forever. What a wretched waste. To him, this silent mourning seemed a more fitting tribute to their sacrifice than any victory parade. Because how could this be called victory? Too much had been lost to call it anything other than *over*. And thank God for that.

He spent thruppence on a small posy and joined the queue filing past the cenotaph to lay his flowers with the rest. *For Jimmy*, he thought as he set the posy down. *God rest your soul.* And then, on impulse, he took Ash's wedding notice from the *Times* and tucked it into the flowers too. Another loss, a deeper grief.

God grant you happiness, my love. God grant you peace.

Stepping back, he looked up at the faux stonework and the flags catching the rising breeze and yearned for Ash with such violence it cramped his heart enough to stop it beating. Perhaps he made a sound of distress because the woman next to him laid a hand on his arm and squeezed gently, though her own face was drawn and she didn't look at him but down at the tributes at their feet.

Her grief mixed with his, though she couldn't know how or who he grieved. But loss was loss, and he covered her cold hand with his for a moment before they parted silently and went their separate ways.

After that, he had nowhere to go but home. Unless he went to the pub and drank away the last of the money he'd saved from his Highcliffe wages. God knew he hadn't found more than a few days casual labour since he'd been back in town, and every penny of that had gone to Kitty for his board.

Avoiding the crowds and the cost of a bus ticket, he walked home to Bethnal Green. As he walked, he reminded himself that Ash was well and happy, and away from his bastard father. Those were all good things and in time Harry would miss him less. Hell, if he could endure four years of war, he could overcome the loss of Ashleigh Dalton.

Only, somehow the war hadn't seemed so awful when he'd had Ash at his side. But without him… He remembered the gaping hole in his life after he'd first been demobbed, the cold despair of those foggy winter nights in London with no work or hope for the future, and felt that terrible blackness hover around him again, waiting to descend.

All too soon he was walking up Bethnal Road toward the house he shared with Kitty and the girls. Even here, people were celebrating, the Cat and Fiddle on the corner overflowing with patriotic pride. Or a facsimile of pride, at least. A kind of hysteria papering over grief. And beneath grief, anger. He saw it in the faces of young men skulking in the shadows, men who'd fought a bitter war and come home to a world too keen to forget.

Instinctively, he swerved toward the pub's gaping door, but stopped himself at the last moment. Money aside, he'd be a sour drunk tonight. A dangerous one, too, liable to spill his heartache and endanger more than himself. No, he couldn't risk that. With heavy steps, he passed the pub and made his way up the street to number six, the door to which, as usual, stood ajar. What wasn't usual were the sounds coming from inside: Kitty's laughter and the high excited giggle of little May. Most summer evenings the girls would be playing in the street and Kitty would be on the doorstep gossiping with her neighbours — especially this evening, he'd have thought, with the feel of occasion in the air. Nevertheless, it lifted his spirits to hear them laughing. Curious as to the cause of the hilarity, he pushed open the door. Kitty sat in her usual chair by the stove, the girls on the floor at her feet, and all of them gazing adoringly at the man sitting at the kitchen table.

Harry stopped dead.

"Hello, West," Ash said as he stood up, beautiful and impossible in their shabby kitchen.

Harry tried to react like any other man would on finding his former commanding officer sitting in his kitchen, but he couldn't help devouring the sight of him, cataloguing every tiny change. His hair was a little longer, falling forward over his forehead, his face thinner, shadows gathering under his eyes. He looked tired. And he was watching Harry with such unreasonable hope that it provoked him. Why the hell had he come?

"Mr Ashleigh's been waiting over an hour," Kitty scolded. "Where've you been?"

"That's really quite all right." Ash spoke with the air of a man repeating himself. "I've been quite well entertained by Miss May and Miss Dot and their marvellous singing." The girls giggled. "And, besides, it's my own fault for turning up uninvited." He offered Harry a cautious smile and it slid like a blade between his ribs. But, oh, what a sweet pain to see that smile again. "My apologies, West. Perhaps I should have written first, but I had your address from Boyd and couldn't — " He cut himself off, smile fading into concern. "How are you?"

And what kind of question was that? How the bloody hell could he answer? *I'm heartsick, lonely, living a life in ashes.* "I, uh," Harry said stiffly, "I should offer my congratulations." He saw a flash of shock cross Ash's face and felt an unworthy prickle of satisfaction. "I hope you and Mrs Dalton will be very happy, sir."

"Thank you." Colour fled from his cheeks, the fingers gripping his cane turning white. "H-How did you know?"

"Saw it in the paper."

"Ah." He cleared his throat. "It c-came as a… a surprise, I imagine."

Harry couldn't reply, and into the screaming silence Kitty said, "Were you recently married, sir?"

"This Thursday last, in Lymington."

"Thursday? Why, you're still honeymooning." She turned a penetrating gaze on Harry. "And to think, he's come all this way to see you when he's got a new bride waiting at home."

"As I t-told you, Mrs Morgan, I owe your b-b-brother my life. There's nothing I wouldn't do for him."

But you're married, Harry wanted to yell. *It's not been a month since we parted, and you're married.* "Thank you, sir," were the words he forced out instead. "That's very kind of you, I'm sure. But, like Kitty says, you should probably be getting back to your wife."

"No." That was revealingly emphatic. Ash looked self-conscious but ploughed on regardless. "That is, I'd like to buy you a pint, West. In honour of the d-day."

"The day?"

"Peace Day. The end of the war."

Harry lifted a sceptical eyebrow; he well knew Ash's opinion of all this triumphalist tosh. A flush touched Ash's cheeks but he met Harry's sceptical look with a silent plea. *Let me explain.* And Harry found he couldn't deny the man anything, no matter the cost. "Aye, alright," he said, though he knew Ash's explanation would hurt like the devil. "If you like, sir."

"I do like," Ash said shortly. "And you can forget the 'sir.'"

Harry met his gaze with a firm eye. "As you prefer, Mr Ashleigh."

For a few pounding heartbeats, they watched each other, then Ash turned to Kitty with a tense smile. "My apologies, again, f-for intruding, Mrs Morgan. And thank you for the tea."

"No apologies needed, Mr Ashleigh. Any friend of our Harry is welcome here."

Ash only smiled in answer to that. He must know, as Harry did, that Kitty would think very differently if she knew the truth of their friendship.

"Come on then," Harry said, keen to get it over with. Ash picked up his hat from the kitchen table and followed him outside, cane tapping on the flagstones, Kitty and the girls trailing them to the door.

Outside, the long summer evening was turning cool beneath crouching clouds, the air sullen with the scent of coming rain. But Ash's smile was sunny as he tipped his hat to Kitty and the girls in farewell. It only made Harry's heart race harder, like a rabbit fleeing a fox. Because he knew he and Ash shouldn't be alone together. Truth was, Harry ached for him down to his bones and, married or not, he wasn't sure he could keep from reaching for him if given the opportunity. In desperation, he started toward the end of the street at a sharp clip. "Cat and Fiddle's this way." There'd be safety in a crowd.

From behind him, he heard Ash's uneven gait as he struggled to keep up, but Harry didn't slow. "Hold on," Ash called. "I need to — Wait." He grabbed Harry's arm and even that simple touch jolted like an electric shock, jerking Harry to a halt. "Wait," Ash said again, sounding breathless and bemused. "I don't really want to go to the pub. I need to talk to you."

Ash was standing too close and Harry could see a sparkle in his eyes. It was excitement, he realised. Christ. He retreated a step. "What's to talk about? Hell, why are you even here, Ash? What good will come of this?"

"You'll find out if you listen." He pulled his hat off and scraped a hand through his hair. "Lord, I've missed you. Is there somewhere we can go? Somewhere private?"

Harry wanted nothing more — and it was the last thing he should do. It would be both dangerous and wrong. Backing up, he shook his head. "No. We ain't like that."

Ash frowned. "Like what?"

"Your *wife* will be expecting you."

"Harry listen — "

"We *can't*. It ain't right. I — "

Without another word, Ash grabbed Harry's lapel and hustled him into one of the narrow alleys that ran between the houses. It was dark and dank and smelled of boiled cabbage. "Harry, let me explain — "

"No!" Wrenching himself free, Harry turned to leave. But found himself standing still, both hands fisted. Paralysed. He *should* go. It was the right thing to do. But he couldn't.

"Harry?" Ash laid a tentative hand on his shoulder. "Please, listen."

It was too much. That soft touch broke his flimsy resolve and with a wordless sound he spun back around. "God forgive me," he rasped and gathered Ash into his arms, crushing their mouths together.

Ash's cane clattered to the floor, his hat tumbling after as they wrestled to get closer, hands knotting in each other's clothes and hair, lips clashing and chasing. With a grunt, Ash pressed Harry hard against the wall, kissing him hungrily, one palm cupping his face. His touch was a balm to Harry's shattered soul, wonderful but wrong. Very wrong. Ash had a wife, he'd made vows. With a soft, broken cry, Harry tore away from the kiss, buried his face into the crook of Ash's neck, and held him tight because he couldn't bear to let him go.

And then a door slammed at the far end of the alley and they sprang apart.

Harry's heart rattled, breaths rasping in the silence, tears damp on his cheeks. He scrubbed them away with the heel of one hand and stared at Ash. In the gloom, his face was all shadow save the gleam of his dark eyes. "You alright?" Harry said shakily. "Did your father — ? Did he hurt you?"

Ash shook his head. "You?"

"No. Other than making me leave you." He swallowed the thickness in his throat and resisted the urge to reach out again. "You shouldn't have come here, Ash. It ain't safe. And it ain't right, what we did just now. You're a married man."

"Harry, listen to me." Ash glanced along the passageway. It was quiet save the distant drone of a woman singing but he lowered his voice anyway. "My marriage to Olive… It isn't real."

Harry stared, chest squeezing with shameful hope. "What do you mean?"

"I mean — That is, we *are* married, but only because it's convenient to us both. There's nothing but friendship between us. Olive doesn't want more, and God knows I don't. Look, I can't explain everything here, but — " He took a step closer, reaching out to squeeze Harry's arm. "Olive knows about us."

"Knows?" He felt sick. "How?"

"I told her. And she's…" He shook his head, the soft smile on his lips twisting Harry up with envy. "She understands. She supports us, Harry. She supports us being together."

What the hell was he talking about? "We can't *be* together." A pulse of fear tightened his jaw. "You shouldn't even be here. For God's sake, Ash, *think*."

"I have thought," he said indignantly. "I've done nothing *but* think. Harry, Olive has a property in the New Forrest. Milford Cottage. It's not in good shape, but I've seen it and it would be perfect. It already has stables, although they're in need of repair, but there's room for a good-sized paddock and it's far from anywhere and—"

"Stop." He couldn't listen to this. "Ash, for God's sake, what are you talking about?"

"Our future. Breeding horses. Olive wants to invest the capital, you'll be the expert and I'll run the business end of things. I'm good with money." He smiled as if he wasn't building castles in the air. "Don't you see? This is how we can be together."

Harry rubbed both hands over his face. "You're dreaming, Ash."

"No."

"We talked about this." He let his hands drop to hang miserably at his side. "I don't know what you and Miss Allen have cooked up in your ivory tower, but I live in the real world. What you're talking about, it's a fantasy."

"It's not." Ash took an urgent step closer, a wild light in his eyes. "It's real. I've seen it, Harry. Milford Cottage is real. We could go there tomorrow."

Harry didn't know whether to scream or sob, because having this impossible dream dangled in front of him was bloody agonising—as if parting last time hadn't hurt enough. "Your father *saw* us, Ash. Boyd saw us. Culham and John sodding Pierson saw us. People *know*. We can't—" He fisted a hand in his hair. "When your father finds out I'm there, what do you think he'll do?"

"My f-father won't know." Ash pursed his lips. "He d-doesn't give a damn what I do, as long I never go near him or my b-brother again. I'm not welcome in m-my family."

Ah, God. Harry ached to offer comfort, but there was none to give and Ash needed to know that. "He'll give a damn if he thinks you're going to cause a scandal."

"That's a risk I'm willing to t-take. I c-can't live a lie, Harry. I won't. I *want* to live with you, b-but if you—" His voice broke and he looked sharply away. "I thought you wanted this, too."

"I *do*. God knows, I do." Harry's throat ached, his eyes burned. "But I can't live a lie, either. And I'd be lying to Kitty. My whole *life* would be a bloody dangerous lie and she'd pay a price if we were discovered. And — Hell, Ash, you're *married*." That hurt, it really sodding well hurt whatever Ash said. "What would I do? Sleep above the stables and pop in for a fuck when your wife's away?"

"Jesus, no." Ash sounded horrified. "I told you, Olive supports us. We're only man and wife in the eyes of the law. Between ourselves we're simply friends and we intend to live our own separate lives. Olive's going to stay in town, for starters, and train to be a doctor, while I live in the cottage — with you, I hope." He took half a step closer. "Harry, it would be our house. Our *home*."

Harry gritted his teeth. "That's bloody ridiculous."

"Why? People do it. Edward Carpenter lives with his male lover, and he — "

"Who the hell's Edward Carpenter?"

"He's a poet and philosoph — "

"Well, I'm a nag-man!" Harry said harshly. "I'm a nag-man from Bethnal Green, and you're the son of a bloody baronet. We can't set up house together without people noticing. It's a fantasy, it's dangerous, and it's — "

"The best I can do!" The words echoed between them and they stared at each other in the ringing silence. "It's the best I can do," Ash said again, quietly. "I *love* you, Harry. I'd risk anything to be with you. But if you don't feel the same..." He backed up, bumping into the wall behind him.

"It's not that I don't feel the same, What you're talking about? I want it so bloody much it's killing me. But it's a dream, Ash. It was always a dream."

"Not to me. To me it was always a hope."

Harry clenched a hand in his hair, as if that tiny sting could mask the stabbing in his chest. "I'm sorry, but I have to think about Kitty and the girls. I can't risk hurting them or — "

"Don't." Ash lifted a hand to cut him off. "Don't make Kitty your excuse."

"My *excuse*?"

"God knows, I understand, Harry. When my f-father burst in on us, it w-was terrifying. Humiliating. I c-can't stand to think about it. I understand why you're so afraid."

Harry stiffened. "I'm not afraid. Not for me, at any rate."

"But things are different now. My marriage protects us —"

"Jesus Christ!" Rage boiled over, a resentment that had been simmering for years. For Harry's whole life, perhaps. "It's so bloody easy for you, isn't it? Sitting there in your country house with your old man a friend of the magistrate. You think you'd do two years hard if we were found out? You think your family would be spat at in the street, would lose their home and livelihood? Would end up fucking destitute? No, of course they wouldn't. Because they have rank and *money* to protect them. And so do you. But I don't, and neither does Kitty, and I won't bring ruin down on her. I bloody well *won't*."

Ash stared, his face ghostly. "I-I-I see."

And just like that, Harry's anger drained away, leaving him scoured raw. "Ash…"

"No. I a-a-apologise. I d-didn't understand." He bent awkwardly to retrieve his cane and hat from the ground, bracing one shaking hand on the wall for balance. Heartsick, Harry longed to go to him, to help him. Yet something held him back. "I'd b-b-better go."

"No, wait…"

"For what?"

But Harry had no answer, his throat aching with sorrow.

"I don't want to m-make trouble for you. I d-don't want to hurt you or your f-family. I —" Ash sucked in a ragged breath, keeping his face averted. "I'll b-be in town until Monday should you —" His voice cracked. "Should you ch-change your mind." And then he was moving, stumbling out of the alley as fast as his bad leg would permit, dashing a hand over his eyes.

"Ash!" Harry called brokenly, but Ash didn't turn around and Harry didn't follow.

He tried to believe it was for the best.

Chapter Twenty-three

A sh woke before dawn on Monday morning. More accurately, he opened his eyes because he'd barely slept a wink. He'd spent all of Sunday knotted with anxiety, jumping at every sound outside and praying it was Harry. Even now, he struggled to accept that he hadn't come. All his hopes lay dashed in that dank London alley and he found it impossible to believe that they'd stay there forever.

But Harry hadn't come, he hadn't changed his mind. Today, Ash would leave London after a scandalously short honeymoon to start work on restoring Milford Cottage, while Olive set about following her dream at the Royal Free Hospital School of Medicine for Women.

Perching on the edge of the bed he'd shared with Harry, he stared at the dark curtains and considered whether to stay another night. Give Harry more time. Perhaps visit him again and —

"No."

His voice sounded loud and rough in the silent room. Harry had made his position clear and Ash would respect it no matter how unbearable. Christ, but he'd had so much hope. When he and Olive had finally made it to London, he'd hardly been able to wait a day before tracking Harry down to tell him the news. What he'd thought to be *good* news.

We can be together.

Stupid of him not to consider Harry's concern for his sister, how the risk they ran could affect her and Harry's ability to provide for her. Easy for Ash to think it was a risk worth taking, especially now he was protected by his marriage and no longer subject to his father's whims. But Harry's position was more precarious, and Ash had been a bloody fool not to recognise that.

Knowing that Harry thought him a privileged, cavalier bastard hurt like the devil. Knowing that he was right hurt worse. Ash had asked too much. *Wanted* too much. And thought too little. His eyes filled and he pressed the heels of his hands into them, sick of tears. He'd spent the night weeping, curled up around the desolate hole in his chest, and he felt as wrung out as mangled laundry.

Today he would leave and spare himself the agony of hoping that at any moment Harry might knock on the door and walk back into his arms. Although how he'd live in Milford Cottage, his bricks and mortar castle in the air, without Harry at his side he didn't know. But he'd endure. God knew, he'd learned how.

At some point, the sun must have risen because grey light started bleeding into the room. Twitchy with lack of sleep, heavy with distress, Ash reached for his crutches and made his way into the bathroom. He washed and shaved at the basin, the bath looming in the corner of his eye, full of memories so tender they hurt.

I'd marry you, in that world, Ash. If you'd have me.

But that world would never exist, not for them. Ash had to set down his razor and suck in a breath against the crushing pain in his chest.

I'll love you forever, he'd once told Harry. *Whatever happens.*

Then, he'd thought it a romantic promise. Now, he knew it to be a curse. Because he *would* love Harry forever, and he'd never see him again.

Grabbing his towel, he dried his face — and his eyes, again — and made his way back to the bedroom to dress. His case sat in the corner, mostly packed. He'd only bought a few things with him, unlike

Olive who was planning a residence of some years in London. Ash pulled on his travelling clothes, combed his hair, and regarded himself in the mirror. Wan cheeks, red sleepless eyes, grim expression: hardly the picture of newly wedded bliss, but he and Olive had decided from the outset not to play those roles. Let the world think what it would about their marriage, they'd never explain nor apologise.

When he reached the parlour where they took their breakfast, Olive was already eating. She was so excited about her new life that she'd spent all of Saturday buying medical text books and all of Sunday flicking through them with a mixture of hope and awe. He had to admit that the subject matter looked intimidating, but if Olive couldn't manage it then he didn't know who could.

This morning, she looked up from her breakfast with a smile that instantly faded. "Ashleigh," she said, lowering her toast to her plate. "You do look miserable." Not having the voice to answer, he just shrugged and came to sit opposite her at the table, watching while she poured him a cup of tea. "And you're still determined to leave today?" she said, sliding the cup toward him.

"I —" He cleared his throat and more firmly said, "Yes, it's for the best."

"Are you certain? What if I went to see West? Perhaps if I explained —"

"No. Olive, you must promise me you won't. It would look very peculiar, you going to see him. And the last thing he wants is his sister to know" — his voice broke on the pain of it — "about me."

With a sigh, she sat back in her chair. "I hate to see you like this."

"It will pass." He tried for a smile. "I expect."

"At least eat some breakfast," she said, setting a piece of toast on his plate and pushing the butter across the table.

"I will if you'll tell me your plans for the day." This time his smile felt less forced. "Remind me who it is you're meeting?"

Olive glowed. "Dr Mary Harding at the Royal Infirmary. Major Edwards introduced us. She graduated from the Royal Free hospital at the start of the war and she's going to help me with my application. According to Major Edwards, she's terribly influential — she's publishing a book about diphtheria."

"Is she? Heavens."

"She's what's called an epidemiologist." Olive smiled. "My appointment to see her is at eleven. When's your train? I could drive you to the station."

"Half-past ten, but don't bother. I can easily take the tube. I shouldn't risk being late, if I were you."

She equivocated, but he could see she knew he was right. "I wish you'd stay a little longer, Ashleigh. I don't like to think of you down at the cottage on your own."

Neither did he, but he put on a brave face. "I've nothing to do here but mope. I'll be better off down there, working. There's so much to be done."

"I'll come down and see you soon." She reached across the table to take his hand. "And promise me you'll come straight back here if you feel" — a squeeze of her fingers — "too lonely."

He turned his hand over beneath hers and squeezed back. "You don't have to take care of me, Olive. I'm not your responsibility, remember?"

She lifted an eyebrow. "You are my friend, Ashleigh. More than that, you've made my new life possible. So, I beg your pardon, but I'll take care of you if I choose to. Now finish your breakfast before you leave."

"Doctor's orders?"

She grinned. "I very much hope so."

***

In the small hours of Monday morning, when Harry couldn't sleep for the unbearable knowledge that Ash would be leaving London that day, he crept from the bedroom he shared with Kitty and the girls and went down to the kitchen below.

He ached down to his bones, couldn't close his eyes without seeing Ash leaving that bloody alley, dashing away tears Harry had put there. Him who would have given his life for Ash! Still would. He'd gladly give his life for Ash, but how could he risk destroying Kitty's just because he was lonely?

Lonely.

What a pale word. Empty, desolate, hopeless — they were closer, but no words could ever fully capture the agonising gash in his heart or his wretched certainty that it would never heal.

By the light of a dim lamp Harry sat at the kitchen table and began to re-read Ash's precious letters. He knew it was ridiculous, but it was all the comfort he had.

My dearest West…

My dear friend, how I miss you…

I remain your most affectionate friend…

I love you, he'd have written if he could. Harry read it in the formal words anyway, remembered how sweet it sounded on Ash's lips, how he'd breathed it between them with such honest feeling…
I love you.

His chest constricted and he doubled over, struggling to stifle a sob. And that was how Kitty found him, head on the kitchen table, silently crying over a pile of old letters.

"Harry?"

He startled upright, scrabbling to gather the letters before she could read them. "What are you doing up?"

"I heard you." She pulled her shawl tighter around her shoulders. "Bloody cold down here, Harry."

He turned away, out of the lamplight so she couldn't see his face. "Go back to bed. I'm sorry to have woken you, I'm — "

"You're miserable is what you are. No, don't try to deny it. You've been miserable as sin since you came back from Hampshire, and worse since Mr Ashleigh visited." She looked at the letters under his hands, then back to his face. Her expression was difficult to read in the lamplight as she sat down on the other side of the table. "What did he come here for, Harry? Don't lie. I know it weren't just to buy you a drink."

Harry tightened his fingers on the letters, drawing them closer. *I can't live a lie*, he'd told Ash. But here he was, lying to his sister and she knew it. "He —" His throat closed, he cleared it. "He wanted me to — to — work with him. Back down in Hampshire. He wants to start breeding horses."

"Him and his wife?"

"Yes."

"And you said no."

He looked down at his clenched hands, uncomfortable under her direct gaze. "I — I'd miss you and the girls."

"Bollocks. That ain't the reason, Harry West. I told you, don't lie to me. A gent comes all the way to Bethnal bloody Green to offer you a job, breeding horses of all things, and you say no? And then spend days sobbing into your cups like your heart's broken?" She drew her shawl tighter, lips thin as she carefully said, "Look, it ain't none of my business, but was you… was you in love" — Harry's heart stopped dead in his chest — "with that girl Mr Ashleigh married? Is that why you don't want to go down there?"

Relief came so swift and harsh it burst out of him in a soggy laugh. "No, it ain't that." But he instantly regretted his honesty because Kitty had just given him the perfect explanation and he'd thrown it away.

She fell silent, tracing her thumbnail along the grain of the wooden table. "So it's him, then," she said after a while. He opened his mouth to deny it but found his lungs airless. Kitty looked up. "I thought it might be. Hoped it weren't, but..."

Hoarsely, he said, "I don't know what you mean."

"Give over, Harry. I weren't born yesterday. And you ain't never been sweet on a girl." She fixed him with a steady look. "Is he…like you?" Harry swallowed, couldn't speak, but Kitty seemed to read the answer in his face. "That's why you left, then. Because of him. Did someone find you out?"

He tensed at the chill in her voice and the pinched expression on her face. "I'll understand if you tell me to leave. I never wanted to make you ashamed."

"Have I reason to be?" Kitty's gaze was fixed on him intently, her fingers tight where they clutched her shawl around her thin shoulders.

He could lie, he could tell her what she wanted to hear, but he didn't want to make a lie of his life — that's why he hadn't gone with Ash in the first place. And he wouldn't start now. "I loved him. I *love* him. But it's over and I swear I'll do nothing to make you ashamed."

"Of you?" Her lips twisted. "I ain't ashamed of you. Not so sure about this Mr Ashleigh, though."

"What do you mean?"

"Well, marrying some poor lady to hide behind and then coming here and...and trying to pick up with you again." She sniffed her disapproval. "That was what he wanted, wasn't it? And you refused coz you're a good man, Harry West." She shifted as if embarrassed by her outpouring of loyalty, or perhaps by his disbelieving expression. "What? You've always done right by me, Harry, and I'll always do right by you. That shouldn't come as no surprise."

Overwhelmed by relief, he didn't know what to say. "Kitty…"

"I'm sorry for you. You've a hard path to walk and I wish you didn't. And I'm sorry you're so bloody heartbroken over this toff, Harry, but you'll get over it."

He nodded and was surprised by the next words to leave his mouth. "His wife knows. Ash says theirs ain't a real marriage — that it's just convenient for them both — and that if I went down to Hampshire, we could be together. And his wife would support it."

"That's what he told you, is it?" Kitty looked uncomfortable, picking at her shawl. "That she'd just let you and him…'be together'?"

"Ash wouldn't lie." Harry had no doubt about that. "And Miss Allen — Mrs Dalton, I suppose — is a modern young woman. She wants to be a doctor, apparently."

Kitty regarded him in silence for a long moment, then said, "And there'd be honest work for you there, Harry? A good wage?"

"Aye. Both."

She nodded, folding her hands on the table. "Then why is it you're here, getting me up in the middle of the bleeding night with all this nonsense, instead of down there earning good money you could be sending to help with the rent?"

"Because—" He reached for her hand, took her thin fingers in his. "Because it ain't that easy. What if we were caught again? Most people wouldn't think like you, would they?"

"Most people are arses. So?"

"So his father—*Sir* Arthur Dalton—is a baronet. His brother's an MP. If we were found out there'd be a scandal. It would be in the newspapers. And it would touch you and the girls."

Drawing her hand into her lap, Kitty sat back in her chair. "I can fight my own battles, Harry. And the girls' battles too, if I must. That's one thing these past five years have taught me." She sighed, tugging her shawl tighter. "God knows there ain't a lot of joy in the world these days, Harry, and life is bloody short. So why sit around here miserable when you can snatch a bit of happiness for once?"

"I thought—" He rubbed a hand over his face, dizzy with the possibilities unfolding around him. "I never dreamed you'd understand or—"

"You're my brother, Harry. You ain't murdered someone, nor hurt someone. Maybe I don't understand why you're like you are, but *you're my brother*. And I want you happy." Her lips twisted into a smile, cutting through the sweetness of her words. "I want you earning a good wage too, truth be told."

He laughed shakily. "I wish I'd talked to you sooner."

"It ain't too late, though, is it? For you to take Mr Ashleigh up on the job?"

"No, I—" His heart gave a swift, sobering kick. "Shit. He's leaving town today. What time is it?"

"Early enough, unless he's leaving with the larks."

Which, knowing Ash, he wouldn't be. There was still time. But for what? Was he really going to do this? Find Ash, *live* with Ash?

He swallowed, wrestling with his conscience. Kitty supported him, which was an unexpected marvel. She wasn't ashamed of him and she wasn't afraid. Neither was Ash. In fact, there was no good reason not to take what he wanted, so why was he hesitating?

Because, despite denying it to Ash, he *was* afraid. He was terrified — of being discovered, of being shamed and despised. Of gambling everything on a chance of happiness.

And so it came down to one question: was that chance of happiness worth the risk?

He looked down at Ash's precious letters scattered across the table, pressed a hand to his chest, over the great cavernous wound in his heart, and knew his answer.

Scraping back his chair, he came around the table and pulled Kitty up and into his arms. "I love you," he said, squeezing her skinny frame tight. "My God, Kitty Morgan, you've no idea what your words mean to me. No idea at all."

She gave him a swift squeeze and then pushed him back, smiling through a frown. "Alright, alright that's enough. Light the stove for me, will you? You've time for a cuppa before you leave., Casanova"

He made time for two cups. And a wash and shave too — he wanted to look his best for Ash — before he packed his bag, kissed Kitty and the girls goodbye, and headed to Mayfair with a spring in his step and butterflies in his belly. By the time he left the tube at Green Park and made his way up to Charles Street, it was just before ten o'clock.

He paused on the other side of the road, staring at the black iron railings of number thirty-six, the grey sky reflecting off its windows. Stupid to be nervous, but it wasn't every day you walked up to a man's house and begged for a second chance to be his lover. Not that he thought Ash would turn him away, but even so…

Clearing his throat, he wiped his clammy hands on the back of his trousers and crossed the street, not pausing before climbing the steps to the front door. It opened before he reached it to reveal Miss Allen — Mrs Dalton — dressed to go out.

They both stopped and stared at each other for a long, terrible moment. Harry's face flamed. What if Ash had been lying, what if Olive didn't know, or didn't approve, or — ?

"Well," she said, "better late than never, I suppose. But I'm afraid you've missed him."

He stumbled back down a step. "What?"

"Ashleigh's taking the ten thirty to Southampton. He left for the station half an hour ago."

Harry stared at her for half a moment, and then bolted back toward the underground.

***

The people and the bustle, made worse by the endless hammering of the building works next door, made Waterloo Station a challenge at the best of times.

These were not the best of times.

Ash was already miserable and navigating the labyrinthine old station with his heavy case in one hand, cane in the other, made him want to scream. He and Olive had motored into town last week, both excited about what their new lives might bring, and he'd hoped — planned — to make this return trip with Harry. Instead he was facing the enervating journey alone, the distant shrilling of whistles raising the hair on the back of his neck.

Gritting his teeth, he made his way into the shiny new booking hall to buy his ticket. Then he climbed up and over the footbridge to the old Southern Station, with its confusion of platforms and waiting rooms, to board the ten-thirty for Southampton. His leg throbbed like the devil, or perhaps he was simply paying it more attention than usual because the whistles were already sparking flashes of unwanted memory.

Having deliberately loitered outside the station until the final moment, Ash was relieved to see his train sitting at platform three. The less time he spent in the station the better. He showed his ticket at the gate and made his way along to the first class carriage, the great beast of an engine at the front of the train hissing and disgorging clouds of steam as it readied to depart. The platform guard opened the carriage door for him and carried his bag inside while Ash navigated the large step up into his compartment.

"In the overhead rack, sir?"

Ash nodded his thanks and sank down onto the seat with a grunt, grateful for the respite on his sore leg, and the guard closed the carriage door behind him with a soft thud. Through its sooty window, he could just make out the nebulous shapes of other passengers walking along the platform. Some of them, no doubt, would have been in London for Saturday's parade. For himself, he'd taken pains to miss it. And Peace Day only reminded him of the devastating mess he'd made of things with Harry.

Should he write and apologise, or would that be too dangerous? Committing something as criminal as their love to paper might be considered reckless. Not that he gave a damn anymore, but he'd never endanger Harry's safety.

With a sigh, he took off his hat and set it on the empty seat next to him. He hoped he'd have the compartment to himself the whole way; he couldn't bear the idea of making small talk with a stranger while he fought off his damned plaguing memories. To that end, he rose and closed the compartment door, pulling down the blind over the window to discourage anyone walking down the corridor from entering. There wasn't much he could do about the external door, but he hoped for the best at any rate. Not that luck had been much in his favour recently.

Leaning back, he closed his eyes and tried to picture Harry's face. Harry as he'd been riding through the New Forest, or when they'd shared that transcendent night in London: happy, open, smiling. But as the carriage doors slammed up and down the train, and a whistle blew on the platform, the image before him twisted and greyed into Harry's face beneath his tin hat, mud-streaked and grim.

His eyes jolted open, shattering the image, a flash of adrenaline detonating behind his breastbone. Pulse pounding, his fingers knotted into fists in his lap, nails biting into his palms. God damn it. God damn it to hell, would he never be free of this?

Another whistle blast further down the platform tightened the skin over his bones, turned his muscles to iron and strangled his breathing. Old faces flashed in the window, hunkered and cold. He screwed his eyes shut but could feel the metal of the whistle on his lips, could taste its steel tang. *Two minutes, boys.* His heartbeat thundered, breaths short and sharp, and —

"Oi! Oi, you — stop!"

Ash opened his eyes. The engine sounded its low hooting whistles, one long, four short. Steam poured down the platform as the train jolted forward, pistons slowly turning. Through the steam, as if through clouds of gas, he saw a hazy figure running.

Someone blew a whistle. "Stop! Oi stop there! You're too late!" Another hissing blast of steam billowed along the platform and a man ran through it as if for his life.

Ash sat forward in his seat, heart hammering. "I'm not there," he said aloud. "This is Waterloo station." And the man was running through steam, not gas.

"Ash!"

His galloping heart all but vaulted out of his chest. Christ alive, was he delusional or was that Harry's voice?

"Ashleigh!"

Delusion or not, Ash jumped up and pushed down the dirty carriage window, leaning out to see better. "Harry?"

"Ash!" Like a miracle, the steam parted and he saw Harry, not ten paces away, pelting along the platform. He looked like an angel emerging from the clouds, golden hair flying back from his face, hat lost.

"Harry! Harry, come on!"

But the train was picking up speed and Harry would never manage to open the door. No matter, Ash could do it for him. Bracing himself with one hand on the frame, he reached through the window and turned the handle, letting the door swing wide.

"Close that door!" the platform guard shouted, blowing his whistle again.

Harry just grinned and put on a burst of speed as Ash, good foot braced on the wooden step, stretched out his arm. "Come on!" Harry reached for him and after a desperate moment their hands met and clasped. "Jump," Ash barked and Harry launched himself forward. Ash hauled back and they landed together in an undignified heap on the carriage floor.

Harry scrambled up immediately and yanked the door shut just as the train whooshed out of the station. Then he bent over, hands on his knees, gasping in great lungfuls of air while Ash lay winded on the floor, staring up at him.

At which point, the compartment door opened, and the train guard appeared looking none-too-happy. "What in blazes did you think you were doing, son? You could have got yourself killed."

Ash struggled to his feet, using the seat to push himself up and grabbing onto the luggage rack for balance. He kept himself between Harry and the guard. "M-my fault entirely," he said, channelling his father's most imperious tone. "Sent my m-man back for one of my bags"—a casual wave toward Harry's holdall—"and your blasted train left early."

"I can assure you, sir, it left precisely on time. And I need to see your man's ticket."

Harry started to say something, but Ash cut him off. "No time to b-buy one, I'm afraid." He reached into his wallet and handed the guard a couple of ten bob notes. "That should cover it." And some.

After a moment's consideration and a distrustful glance at Harry, the guard decided to turn a blind eye and pocket the money. "No more funny business," he warned with a wag of his finger.

Ash bared his teeth in a smile and closed the door firmly behind the guard. Pausing there, he pressed his forehead against the blind-covered window. He hoped so badly that Harry had changed his mind that he could hardly bear to ask in case some other wild reason had brought him here.

"Ash?" Harry sounded tentative.

Straightening his shoulders, Ash turned around, leaning on the compartment door to brace himself against the swaying of the train. "If you've n-not changed your mind about us b-b-being together, then tell me at once."

Harry took a step closer, hanging onto the luggage rack as the train swayed. "I haven't slept since Saturday. Couldn't close my eyes without seeing your face and regretting what I —" He swallowed, still breathless from his sprint. "You were right. I *was* afraid, Ash. I didn't know what to do. But this morning Kitty found me reading your letters —"

"My letters?"

"I kept them all. Course I did. And she found me reading them and — and *weeping* like a bloody child. And, Ash, she guessed. She'd already suspected about me and she wasn't disgusted or anything. She — I can't say she understands, exactly, but she said life's short and hard and I should grab happiness where I find it. And I find it with you, Ash. You make me so bloody happy I can hardly stand it. And I'm sorry I was a coward. I'm sorry I hurt you. I never want to hurt you again because I love you. I love you so much and, if you'll have me, I want to be with you for as long as this blasted world will let us be together."

Harry ran out of air at the end, stood there breathing heavily and watching Ash with such anxious hope that Ash had to cover his mouth to muffle his ugly sob of relief. He couldn't find words, could barely believe this was real, just held out a hand to Harry and Harry came, enfolding him in his arms as Ash buried his face into the collar of his jacket with another harsh cry.

"It's alright," Harry said softly, pressing Ash up against the compartment door, their joint weight holding it safely closed as the swaying train rocked them together. "Everything's alright now."

And it was. Ash could feel the darkness lifting, his heart warming as if blessed by the rising sun. He lifted his head, drinking in the sight before him. "Am I dreaming? I'd given up hope."

Harry grimaced, pained. "I'm so sorry. I was afraid and blaming Kitty for —"

"Hush." Ash curled his hand around the back of Harry's neck and brought their lips together in a soft, yearning kiss. "My God I want you, Harry. Every single beautiful part of you. Always."

"Then you've got me." Harry smiled against his lips, Ash could feel the curve of his mouth and smiled himself when Harry's hand slid down over his backside and squeezed gently. "But we'd best behave ourselves, eh? No need to court trouble."

Still grinning, Ash pulled back far enough that his head bumped against the door behind him. "No need to rush. We've got all the time in the world. A lifetime together."

Harry cupped his face with one hand. "God willing."

"God can mind his own damn business. And so can my father and anyone else with an opinion on the matter. We're going to spend our whole lives together, Harry, you'll see. And it's going to change the world."

Harry's smile grew fond. "Is it now?"

"This…?" Ash threaded their fingers together, making a fist of both their hands and raising it between them. "This changes the world. You and I, who we are, *what* we are, changes the world. Olive, too. And a thousand others like us, Harry. Slowly, perhaps, but surely, we'll reshape the world. Love will win."

Harry gazed at him for a long moment, eyes widening as if seeing something wondrous. Then he took Ash's face in both hands and kissed him hard, a powerful possessive kiss. "Love *will* win," he said, fierce and tender and true. "Hell, Ash, it's already bloody won."

Epilogue

One year later –17 July 1920, Milford Cottage, Hampshire

H arry woke with a jolt to find Ash sitting bolt upright in bed, one arm stretched out before him, breathing hard. It was early but the dawn chorus was already in full voice and daylight crept past the curtains of their bedroom.

Pushing up on one elbow Harry set a hand on Ash's back, stroked his fingers over his tense muscles. It had been a while since Ash had suffered a nightmare — a couple of months at least. "Ash," he said softly. "You're dreaming."

"I c-c-can't reach…"

Sitting up, Harry wrapped his arms around him. They'd made love last night and had fallen asleep naked, so he pressed his bare chest against the chill skin of Ash's back, hugging him close. "It's a dream, Ash. Wake up now."

In his head, he started counting slowly and by the time he reached six Ash started to relax. His outstretched arm dropped to his side, his breathing deepened and he began to tremble. Harry gathered him closer, rocking them gently the way he knew helped, and when Ash's head finally sank back against his shoulder Harry kissed his clammy cheek. "Alright, love?"

Ash nodded and turned his head to meet Harry's lips, kissing him with the urgency that often overcame him after one of his nightmares; as if visiting that dark place reminded him anew of the glorious life he'd been gifted. Harry responded readily, all too willing to celebrate life in this most vital of ways.

They sank back together onto the bed, kissing deeply, hands roving across each other's bodies until Ash's shivers faded. As morning light suffused the room, Ash pushed Harry onto his back and slid on top of him, their hardening pricks rubbing along nicely together. But his gaze was still distant, crowded with shadows. Harry didn't mind being a distraction or a comfort — he'd be anything Ash needed — and this was hardly a chore. Ash kissed him hard on the mouth, then moved down to his shoulder and chest, his lips tracing a hot, hungry line towards Harry's belly and all points south.

Harry groaned in anticipation when Ash's cheek bumped the head of his prick and Ash looked up through his lashes. No smile yet, too many clouds in those troubled eyes, but Harry saw heat there too. And need. Christ, so much need. Ash licked his lips. "Can I?" he said.

"Yes. Anything you w — "

Ash didn't wait for more, taking Harry into his mouth with that same dark urgency. Trying to slow him down, Harry cupped his face, but it only provoked Ash to look up at him again through his thick lashes, lips glistening, and that sight — It almost got Harry off there and then. He had to stare at the ceiling to hold himself back, because he knew what Ash was really after and Harry wanted to be able to give him everything he needed.

Sure enough, with one final toe-curling caress of his tongue, Ash released Harry's prick and made his slow way back up his body. When Ash kissed his mouth again, tasting faintly of sex, Harry wrapped him in his arms and rolled them both over so that Ash lay on his back and Harry nestled between his thighs.

Gorgeous and fragile, Ash gazed up at him with a wordless plea and Harry loved him more in that moment than he could express in words. He ran his fingers down Ash's inner thigh to the warm crease of his hip and watched Ash's abdominal muscles contract, goosebumps rising on his skin. "You sure you're alright to go again after last night?" Harry said.

With a nod, Ash lifted his hips in invitation and Harry reached up to grab a pillow, and then the jar of petroleum jelly from the bedside table. Their first fumbling attempts at doing it 'Greek Style', as Ash had coyly put it, hadn't been hugely successful. But with practice, patience, and petroleum jelly they'd got it down to something of an art. Ash especially enjoyed being on the receiving end of things when he was troubled. It helped him let go of dark thoughts, he said. It felt like wiping the slate clean.

Once Harry had the pillow under Ash's backside, he leaned forward to kiss him again. He loved kissing him naked, relishing how their slow tangling tongues mirrored the rutting of their pricks, bare bodies sliding over each other. Bloody beautiful. They often got off just like this, but Ash needed more this morning, his hips rocking up insistently and fingers digging into Harry's shoulders. Harry smiled against his mouth, nipped lightly at his lower lip, and sat back up.

He teased him for a while, first with his fingers and then with the slick head of his prick, until he was certain Ash was ready and not sore from last night. Then he let him have what he craved, sinking in with a powerful thrust and watching Ash tip his head back, exposing the long column of his throat, eyes closing as his rosy lips parted silently. The velvet grip of his body was intense, but this morning Harry wanted to focus on his lover's pleasure before his own. So he slid his hands under Ash's knees, pressing his legs back, and watched Ash shiver. "I love you," Harry said, starting to move inside him, pulling back, thrusting carefully forward. "I love you so much, Ash."

Ash nodded, didn't speak, hips moving in time with Harry's. Christ, Ash wanted this badly, Harry could feel his need as if it were his own, the tension coiling in his thighs and balls and belly. His need was fierce, his fuse short, and Harry didn't try to prolong things, not when Ash so clearly needed release. He pressed a kiss to the inside of his left knee, the wounded leg Ash had once flinched from, and when he looked back at his face Ash was watching him with eyes dark and desperate. "It's alright," Harry said. "I've got you."

One hand braced on the bed next to Ash's shoulder, Harry started to thrust in earnest. Deep, hard jerks of his hips that set the headboard knocking against the wall. Ash cried out, lifting his head to snatch a fiery kiss, all teeth and tongues.

Never mind Ash's urgency, Harry wasn't going to last long either. Not when Ash started stroking himself hard. The sight of his flushed face, reddened prick in his slick flashing hand, would have been enough to get Harry off all on its own. "Jesus," he growled, barely holding his release back. "Fuck, Ash. Do it."

Ash tensed, Harry felt him clench around his prick, saw the rigid cords stand out in his neck, stomach muscles bunching… And then he came across his belly with a hard shout of relief and Harry followed, pressing his face into the hot skin of Ash's shoulder as his body shuddered with the force of his release.

Wobbly-legged, he carefully withdrew and flopped onto his back at Ash's side, bones honey-filled and heavy. For a while, the only sounds in the room were their slowing breathing and the chatter of birdsong. But then Ash rolled into him, his breath catching, and Harry wrapped him in his arms and held him until the squall passed.

"Better?" Harry said after a while, once Ash had quieted again.

He felt the answering nod against his shoulder. "It's been so long," Ash said quietly. "I'd hoped I was f-free of them."

Harry stroked Ash's back, pressed a kiss to his forehead. "You know what I think? I think it's because of today."

"Today?" Ash looked up, frowning. "What does today have t-to do with it?"

"You have those dreams when you're fretting about something."

"I'm not fretting." But his words didn't hold much conviction.

Nudging Ash onto his back, Harry propped himself up on one elbow so he could study his face. Despite the bad dream, Ash looked well. His skin, pale and sickly a year ago, was tanned from all the work they'd put into renovating the cottage and stables. And, while Ash would never be burly, he'd gained muscle in his upper body and arms. Shadows still lurked, and maybe they always would, but Harry could see his bright smile hiding beneath them ready to return. He reached out to stroke the hair back from Ash's forehead. "You sure you're not worrying?"

Today, in just a few hours, Kitty and the girls would be arriving for a week's holiday — their first time in the countryside, and their first time seeing Ash since Harry had moved back to Hampshire. No matter what Ash said, he'd been fretting about the meeting for weeks.

"It's just…" A nervous smile flitted over his face. "It's silly, I know, but I just hope Kitty will like me now she knows we're… we're lovers."

Lovers. God, how that word made Harry's heart glow. Leaning down he kissed Ash's lips. "I love you," he said, brushing their noses together. "And so will Kitty. I promise."

"I thought we could drive to the seaside tomorrow. Bournemouth, perhaps? Take a picnic. Olive will come too, of course. It'll be quite respectable."

They didn't often stray from their secluded cottage, neither of them enjoying the roles of master and servant required in the outside world. But after a peaceful year together they were growing bolder. And with Olive and Kitty with them, Harry was sure nobody would pay any undue attention. Just another family enjoying a Sunday stroll. "They'll love that," Harry said. "And they'll love you, too. And this place, and the horses. And…and everything. Ash, you've changed their lives as well as my own with the money I send them."

Which was a full half of his wages. The rest went on food and other living expenses, which he and Ash split between them. Harry insisted on paying his way, which Ash perfectly understood. And since neither of them craved luxuries beyond the luxury of loving each other freely, it made for a simple happy life. With enough money left over that the girls could stay in school and Kitty could afford a few finer things for herself.

"I hope they don't think I'm trying to buy their affection," Ash said, still worrying. "I want them to-to-to feel like family." He fixed Harry with a steady look. "I want us to *be* a family. We are, in my eyes."

Harry's throat tightened. "Mine too. Same as if we were married."

"Yes." Ash reached for his hand and threaded their fingers together. "We bloody well *are* married, Harry, in every way that matters."

"Don't you doubt it, Ashleigh Dalton." Bringing their entwined fingers to his lips, Harry kissed his knuckles one by one. "Now come on, shake a leg. We've horses to muck out and feed before breakfast."

It was a rare sunny morning in what had been a dour summer, and Harry took that to be a good omen. After they'd mucked out the stables — they only had two stallions so far, but they were fine animals — and given the boys their breakfast, Harry cooked bacon and eggs while Ash went to wash and brush up. The cottage was large by Harry's idea of a house, with a good-sized kitchen and two parlours downstairs, a bathroom and four bedrooms upstairs — one that he shared with Ash, one for Olive, on her rare visits, and the other two currently set up for Kitty and the girls. Despite having lived here for a year, Harry still couldn't quite believe this place was his home. His and Ash's home, in this dream of a life they were living.

But every day proved it to be true, and sooner or later he

supposed he'd come to take it for granted. Not yet, though, and the sight of Ash coming back downstairs in his Sunday best, dressed to receive Harry's sister and nieces like they were family, made his heart fill.

"Look at you," he said, holding out his hand for Ash. "Like a country squire."

"You should change, too," Ash said, taking Harry's hand. "They'll be here soon. The train gets in at ten and you know how fast Olive drives from the station."

"There's plenty of time." Harry kissed him lightly. "Now relax and eat your breakfast before it gets cold."

But Ash couldn't relax and chased Harry upstairs as soon as he'd finished his tea. Sure enough, Harry had just buttoned up his waistcoat after a quick wash and shave when he heard a motor car turn off the road onto the cottage's long driveway. He hurried downstairs to find Ash hovering in the doorway, tapping his cane anxiously against the step. "Hurry up," he said. "They're here."

"I know." Harry touched his back, a reassuring press of his hand. "Come on then."

Together they stepped out into the yard between the cottage and the stables. One day, when he had time, he intended to plant a kitchen garden there but for now it was a working space. They'd let the horses into the paddock on the other side of the yard, and they trotted over to investigate the noisy motor car as it bumped its way along the tree-lined drive to the cottage.

Kitty sat in the front passenger seat, holding onto her hat, and the girls were waving wildly from the backseat. Olive looked dapper, with dark glasses against the sun and a scarf around her head. They didn't see her as often as either of them would like because she was so busy with her medical studies in London and could only spare rare visits, but she'd wanted to meet Kitty and had volunteered to motor down and collect her and the girls from Southampton. And so they all arrived together in an excited cacophony, piling out of the motor car as soon as Olive pulled up.

"Uncle Harry!" May, the youngest, called out as she ran over to hug him. "There was cows in the road. About a hundred of them!"

Harry laughed and picked her up, squeezing tight. "Was there now? A hundred cows!"

Behind him, he was aware of Ash hanging back so he turned around as he set May on her feet. "You remember my friend, Ash, don't you, May?"

She gave a shy nod. "Hello," she said, and then glanced back at her mother.

Kitty came over, dressed in her best clothes, like Ash, and gave Harry a quick hard hug. She felt more substantial than when last he'd seen her. Better fed. Healthier.

"You look well." Kitty studied him carefully, then turned her scrutiny on Ash. He coloured, shifting his duff foot awkwardly, and Harry fought the urge to take his hand. "Good morning, Mr Ashleigh," Kitty said. "Thank you for inviting us."

"Oh, no-no-no need to thank me," Ash said. "Th-this is Harry's home, too. You'll always b-be welcome. And p-p-please call me Ash."

Kitty glanced back at Harry, something bright and approving in her expression that made his heart swell. To Ash she said, "The girls was wondering, Mr Ash, if they might call you Uncle?"

Ash looked momentarily astonished, and then smiled his heart-melting joyful smile. "Yes," he managed in a voice that shook with emotion. "That would be *w-wonderful.*" And Harry, who still had an arm around his sister's shoulders, squeezed her in silent jubilant thanks.

"Well, girls, in that case I hope you're going to call me Aunty," Olive said with a smile. "I'm sure we're going to be great friends. We had a very jolly drive from the station." She winked at May. "Despite the smelly old cows in the road."

May giggled and nodded and went to re-join her older sister who was standing shyly behind Kitty.

"Well," Kitty said, looking around her at the cottage, the paddock, and the forest that surrounded them. "This is finer than Regent's Park. Are you going to show us around, Harry? We've been imagining this place for months, ain't we girls?"

"Course I am," Harry said, although he cast a quick look at Ash, who was blinking very fast and obviously trying to master unruly feelings. Lacking a few layers of skin, was Ashleigh Dalton, and Harry loved him for it so much his heart hurt.

"I'll lead the way," Olive said, throwing Harry a smiling look; she knew Ash almost as well as he did. Lifting a foot to show off her heavy boots, she said, "See, I've come prepared for the stables. Now, let's go and see the horses. Do you know their names, girls?"

"Blackjack and Champion!" May shouted as she and Dot raced ahead of Olive, Kitty slipping out from under Harry's arm to supervise her excited daughters.

"Alright there?" Harry said as he and Ash followed more slowly behind.

Taking Harry's hand, Ash drew him to a halt in a patch of warm sunshine and gazed at him with glistening eyes, clearly struggling to put his feelings into words. "I'm just so bloody *happy*. I —" He choked off, somewhere between laughter and tears. "Harry, they want to call me Uncle. I feel like the luckiest man on Earth."

"Nah, can't be. Coz he's the bloke standing right next to you."

Ash smiled and squeezed his hand and they lingered together for a moment, fingers tangling as the summer sun warmed Harry's face and gleamed bright in Ash's dark hair. No more words were needed, the love between them was enough — unflinching, unbending, and unbreaking.

"Come on Uncle Harry!" May called from the stable door. "Come on Uncle Ashleigh! Olive says we can play in the hayloft!"

Ash gave an alarmed laugh. "Oh Lord."

"Well," Harry said with a grin. "Sounds like duty calls, Uncle Ashleigh..."

Hand-in-hand they crossed the yard, Ash's cane tapping on the flagstones and the girls' laughter rising into the blue summer sky.

Harry knew that beyond their hidden haven the world still turned, that its hate-fuelled guns still thundered. Perhaps they always would. But here, together, they were building a life in defiance of that cruel old world and with hope for a kinder one to come.

And *that* is victory, Harry thought with a fierce rush of a joy. *This* is peace.

ABOUT THE AUTHOR

Sally Malcolm was bitten by the male/male romance bug in 2016 and hasn't looked back. She writes contemporary and historical romance and her stories are emotional, sweetly angsty and always have happy endings.

She lives in London, England.

To find out more about Sally, find her on Twitter @Sally_Malcolm and Facebook, or sign up to her mailing list at sallymalcolm.com

ACKNOWLEDGEMENTS

As always, I owe enormous thanks to my critique partner, Laura Harper, whose deft touch with the red pen kept me from wondering too far into no man's land — and ensured that Ash and Harry were drinking the right whisky. My thanks also to Joanna Chambers, for her time and the insights which helped shape the second draft of this book. Thank you, also, to Tom Reeve, for going above and beyond in designing many iterations of this cover.

And, finally, I want to thank my school English teachers (Mr. Kempson and Mr. Silvano) who first introduced me to the poetry of the First World War, the fury, tenderness and pity of which has lived with me all these years.

Also By

Check out these other titles by Sally Malcolm!

PERFECT DAY

"A beautifully told second-chance-at-love story that tugs at the heartstrings..." — All About Romance

WHEN JOSH NEWTON, a son of Long Island's elite, fell in love with ambitious young actor, Finn Callaghan, his world finally made sense. With every stolen moment, soft touch and breathless kiss, they fell deeper in love.

Finn was his future…until Josh let his family tear them apart.

Eight years later, Finn has returned to the seaside town where it all began. He's on the brink of stardom, a far cry from the poor mechanic who spent one gorgeous summer falling in love on the beach. The last thing he wants is a second chance with the man who broke his heart. Finn has spent a long time forgetting Josh Newton — he certainly doesn't plan to forgive him.

Drawn together yet kept apart by their history, old feelings soon begin to stir. Back in the place where their romance began, Josh and Finn finally come to realize the truth: love endures. Even when you don't want it to, even when you try to deny it, love endures

Buy now!

LOVE AROUND THE CORNER
(A Christmas novella)

"Wildly romantic, and heartbreaking and ultimately full of love and second chances. It is simply glorious." — Gay Book Review

ALFIE CARTER grew up in New Milton, caring for his sick father and keeping their auto repair shop on its feet. He's touchy about his poor education and doesn't take kindly to snide remarks from the town's prickly bookstore owner — no matter how cute he looks in his skinny jeans. Left to run the family business alone, Alfie spends his lonely evenings indulging his secret passion for classic fiction and chatting online with witty, romantic 'LLB' as they fall in love over literature.

Leo Novak's new life as owner of Bayside Books is floundering. And he could do without the town's gorgeous, moody mechanic holding a grudge against him after an unfortunate — and totally not his fault — encounter last Christmas. Still reeling from a bad breakup and struggling to make friends in New Milton, Leo seeks comfort in his blossoming online romance with thoughtful, bookish 'Camaro89'.

But as the holidays approach, 'LLB' and 'Camaro89' are planning to meet, and realities are about to collide…

Buy now!

BETWEEN THE LINES

"I loved this book... Gentle and lyrical but also engrossing and sexy." — Cat Sebastian, author of *A Soldier's Scoundrel*.

THEO WISHART has given up on finding love. Luca Moretti doesn't want to find it. A handful of summer days may change their lives forever — if they're brave enough to look between the lines.

Eyes might be windows to the soul, but for Theo Wishart they're all shuttered. His dyspraxia makes it hard to read people. He doesn't do relationships and he certainly doesn't do the great outdoors. Two weeks spent "embracing beach life" while he tries to close the deal on a once great, now fading seaside hotel is a special kind of hell.

Until Luca. Gorgeous, unreachable Luca.

Luca Moretti travels light, avoiding all romantic entanglements. Estranged from his parents, he vows this will be his last trip home to New Milton. His family's hotel is on the verge of ruin and there's nothing Luca can do to save it. He's given up on the Majestic, he's given up on his family and he's given up on his future.

Until Theo. Prickly, captivating Theo.

No mushy feelings, no expectations, and no drama — that's the deal. A simple summer fling. And it suits them both just fine. But as the summer wanes and their feelings deepen, it's clear to everyone around them that Theo and Luca are falling in love. What will it take for them to admit it to themselves — and to each other?

Buy now!

TWICE SHY

"A superbly written, beautifully romantic story that is guaranteed to warm the heart" — All About Romance

THE LAST THING Joel Morgan wants is to fall in love again. Scarred by his failed marriage, Joel's determined to keep his life emotionally stable — which means taking a job teaching fourth grade, fixing up his house on weekends, and avoiding absolutely all romantic entanglements. And he's doing great.

Until he meets sweet but struggling single dad, Ollie Snow.

Following the tragic death of his sister and her husband two years earlier, Ollie became the legal guardian of their two young sons — much to the horror of the boys' conservative grandparents. They think Ollie's too young and too unreliable to raise their grandsons. So to prove them wrong, Ollie's determined to parent the boys without anyone's help.

Until he meets reserved but caring teacher, Joel Morgan.

As the only two men in the school's Parent-Teacher Association, Joel and Ollie are thrown together over a series of fundraising events, and somewhere between the Beach Fun Run and the Fall Festival they fall in love. But Ollie has another reason for moving to New Milton — a reason he's keeping close to his chest — and Joel's wounded heart won't trust a man with secrets.

Dare they hope for a future together, or will their pasts keep them apart forever?

Printed in Great Britain
by Amazon

40383012R00156